PRAISE FOR *SIX MONTHS LATER*

"This smart, edgy thriller taps into the college-angst zeitgeist, where the price of high achievement might just be your soul."

—*Kirkus*

"The story is well paced and beautifully written… This romantic thriller will leave readers on the edge of their seats until the very last page."

—*School Library Journal*

"An intense psychological mystery… has the feel of a high-stakes poker game in which every player has something to hide, and the cards are held until the very end."

—*Publisher's Weekly*

"As the plot is slowly uncovered, the suspense rises to a shocking crescendo… With several twists and surprises, this is a well-plotted mystery, sure to keep readers guessing."

—*Booklist*

"The shocking reasons behind Chloe's transformation will keep you guessing until the very end…Pick up this incredible book to find out for yourself."

—*Girl's Life Magazine*

"Confusion and a desperate search for answers drive the action in this captivating thriller… As the mystery builds, so do the stakes and the romantic tension."

—*RT Book Reviews*, 4 Stars

"An intriguing story line… readers will be drawn in to the mystery of what happened to Chloe and will never guess the ending."

—*VOYA*

"Filled with tension and heart-in-your-throat suspense that kept me guessing to the very end. I predict readers will want more and more from her. I know I do!"

—Jennifer Brown, author of *Hate List* and *Thousand Words*

GONE TOO FAR

NATALIE D. RICHARDS

sourcebooks
fire

Copyright © 2015 by Natalie D. Richards
Cover and internal design © 2015 by Sourcebooks, Inc.
Art direction Faceout studios
Cover design by Nicole Komasinski/Sourcebooks, Inc.
Cover photography by Brandon Hill

The characters and events portrayed in this book are fictitious or are used fictitiously. Any similarity to real persons, living or dead, is purely coincidental and not intended by the author.

Published by Sourcebooks Fire, an imprint of Sourcebooks, Inc.
P.O. Box 4410, Naperville, Illinois 60567-4410
(630) 961-3900
Fax: (630) 961-2168
www.teenfire.sourcebooks.com

Library of Congress Cataloging-in-Publication data is on file with the publisher.

Printed and bound in the United States of America.
VP 10 9 8 7 6 5 4 3 2 1

To Ian, Adrienne, and Lydia
To the moon and back times infinity

CHAPTER ONE

. . . .

Late. *So* late. I slam the car door behind me and race across the parking lot. My hair is tangled in the strap of my messenger bag, my shoes are untied, and I have no idea how I'm going to get to my locker without getting caught. I have to try because I *need* those chemistry notes.

Technically I needed them last night when I'd actually had time to study for my midterm, but I didn't think it was a big deal. I know the material, and I figured I could do a little last-minute cramming during first period homeroom. It was a decent plan until my phone battery died, taking my morning alarm down with it. Now I'll be lucky to catch the last ten minutes of first period.

I hop the curb and slow as I slide into the shadow of the ancient brick school. It's probably not classy to barrel through the door like an escaped convict. Of course, it probably wasn't classy flying into the parking lot doing Mach 2 either.

I check my barely charged phone for the time as I climb the first step. My foot slips on something halfway up the stairs. It's like hitting a patch of ice. I lunge for the handrail and jerk myself upright, glaring down at the thing that tripped me—a dropped notebook.

Nothing special. It's a plain, spiral-bound pad, the kind you can get on sale at the drugstore for less than a buck. Pretty much worthless, except I know it's probably chock-full of notes. Notes someone will likely need during midterm week.

Oh, fine.

I snatch the notebook off the steps and shove it into my bag. Lost and Found is going to have to wait though. It's in the student store, which is on the opposite side of the school.

I climb the rest of the stairs and pull the heavy door open. It shuts behind me with a low *whump*, and warm, oil-soap tinged air closes around me. The office waits to my left, and the main hallway, long and dim, leads to classrooms and stairwells. My fingers and cheeks tingle, recovering from the bite of the wind.

When this hallway is empty, the stillness feels like something that lives and breathes. And waits. I shake it off and rush into the front office. Showing up late to class is bad enough. Showing up without a pass will land me in detention.

Mrs. Bluth and Mrs. Pruitt sit behind the high wooden counter, two round-faced mom types who, as far as I can tell, never leave this room. When we were freshmen, Manny and I used to take bets on whether or not they took bathroom breaks.

"Good morning, Piper," Mrs. Bluth says, her smile bright. She pushes the sign-in clipboard toward me. "Yearbook assignment this morning?"

Why didn't I think of that? I spend countless hours here taking pictures of one thing or another for the yearbook. I shake my head though, and wait while she writes my pass.

"Now, straight to class. If you need to visit your locker, you can do so between periods."

"Sure." I force a smile though my shoulders sag. Honestly, I should have given up on the ride here. It's not like I'd have enough time to really look anything over. There are nineteen minutes left in the period, and my locker is twelve thousand miles away from everything else. Seriously, I should get PE credit for the hike. Even if I did sneak up there unnoticed, I'd only have fifteen minutes to study while pretending I'm paying attention.

Not worth it.

I arrive at homeroom where Mr. Stiers is passing out packets to the class. The second I step inside, he swivels on his feet, dark eyes fixing on me.

"Good morning, Piper."

He takes my pass with a smile. My lips twitch in response. Sad effort, but it's all I've got.

"Hey," I say. "Sorry I'm late."

"No problem. I'm glad you're here. I didn't want you to miss the senior project talk."

Ah, Mr. Stiers. Fluent in five languages and a world traveler, he still ended up in Nowhere, Indiana, teaching high schoolers.

I plod to my seat and Manny looks up from the desk behind mine when I set down my bag. He smirks, tapping his bare wrist to note my timing. Still, he offers me an extra packet, and I mouth a "thank you" in return.

Mr. Stiers points at a projected image on the wall that probably

3

matches a page inside my packet. "Now that we're well into November, it's time to get serious about these senior projects."

I tune him out right there and then. I've known what I was going to do since summer—the epidemic of poverty in small-town Indiana. I've got this covered. Chemistry? Not so much.

I unzip my bag, rifling through stuff that's worthless right now: proof sheets from the homecoming dance, my history textbook— might be useful if I hadn't already taken that test—an extra lens cap. My fingers close around a slim, spiral-bound spine. That notebook I found.

I pull it out. Maybe, by some stroke of cosmic luck, it's some-one else's AP chemistry notes. Fat chance, but I'm desperate.

I open the book and frown at the three large words handwrit-ten on the inside of the cover.

Malum Non Vide

Great. Latin notes. I think it's Latin, anyway. Regardless, it's useless to me.

I sigh, running a finger down the cardboard pocket insert that protects the first page. Funny. I've never seen anyone use these stupid things, but I can feel a thick lump in this one. I pull back the cardboard far enough to see what's inside—pictures. A whole stack of them. A photographer not checking out a stack of prints is about as likely as a cat resisting an open can of tuna. It's not exactly snooping, more like creative curiosity.

I slide a couple of photos out by the edges. Poor quality black and white snapshots taken around the school from what I can tell. I straighten the top photo to get a better look. It's Isaac Cooper…but it's *wrong*.

Isaac's eyes are empty. White sockets glare out at me, windows to a place where Isaac's soul used to be.

I feather my thumb over the face, feeling the jagged scrapes and tears in the photo. The eyes weren't just colored over—they were *gouged* out. And someone took their time about it, picking out bits of iris and pupil, leaving nothing but a pale oval framed by his eyelids.

A chill ghosts up my spine, nesting in the hair at the nape of my neck.

Who would do this? I try to picture it; someone hunched over with a needle, scratching away. The image sends my stomach into free fall.

I flip to the next picture. Anna Price. Her eyes are gone too. I keep flipping—Kristen, Ming, that guy who always seems to be dating one of the cheerleaders. Three more pictures. Six more gaping holes where eyes should be. My heart beats faster, pushing ice into my veins.

I put the pictures back with shaking hands.

What the hell kind of book is this?

Halloween prank. Has to be. It was only last month, after all. I check the pages after the divider. No more pictures and no more Latin, but every line is filled with narrow, precise writing.

Tuesday, 9/5

> WhtCrane stole cash from cafeteria register
> Lincoln caught drinking, CCR didn't report
> RTN fwds pictures of penis to freshman girls

The class chuckles and my head snaps up, a counterfeit smile forming on my mouth.

Never mind that I have no idea what's so funny. Never mind that I can't imagine anybody buying this smile anyway, since I'm sure I look like someone's got a gun pressed to my temple.

I shouldn't have this book. I don't know who wrote this, but they could be in this classroom. The thought makes me cold. But no one's looking. And my eyes drag down again.

Wednesday, 9/6

> Magpie threatens to stab WTR in the neck with a pen
> Snakchrm calls Wisguy Homo in Bathroom

Friday, 9/8

> Tricky dealing Happy Pills behind bleachers during lunch
> period

Okay, it's not real. These aren't even real names—they're like gamer handles. For all I know, this is some role-playing thing, or a fantasy football team.

Yes, because nothing says let's-talk-touchdowns quite like photograph mutilation and a sin diary. I flip through the book, determined to find who's behind this—or proof that it's a joke.

The last entry is twenty pages in. It's from yesterday.

Tuesday, 11/16

Gemini hits RJG's car in parking lot—denies incident

Okay, that actually happened. I mean, I didn't see it, but I heard Shane Haywood and some girl I didn't recognize fighting in the parking lot yesterday at lunch. He was pointing at his back fender, claiming something about her paint color. Apparently, no one saw anything.

Except that's not true, is it? Obviously someone *did* see— someone who's keeping a list and checking it twice.

And carving up eyes in his spare time.

I close the notebook, pressing cold, damp hands into the cover. Time to get a grip. I'm not the girl who covers my eyes during scary movies. I'm the one who tells everyone where the special effects suck.

The pictures are creepy, but I can name a handful of kids in this school that I'm pretty sure are future felons. I still sit in class with them every day. So, what's my problem? I'm afraid of scary, white eyes? I'm shocked at the seedy underbelly of Claireville High?

It's not like I live in some rainbows-and-sunshine version of this place. I've personally seen how bad these people can get.

I guess I just didn't know anyone else really noticed.

The book is closed, but I can still see the pictures, the black writing crawling across the pages like veins. I slide the book back into my bag and flip open the senior project packet, but I can't read anything for the chill running up the length of my spine.

Mr. Stiers is almost finished presenting, but I feign fascination. Because I'm not bothered. And I definitely don't feel like anyone's watching me.

• • •

My shoulder blades smack the back of my chair when the bell rings. People tumble from the desks around me, stacking books and tapping pencils, shoving into everything and everyone on their way to the door. Manny knocks on my desk and waves on his way out, but I sit frozen to my chair.

I have an AP chemistry test in seven minutes.

Okay. Not the best morning, but I've dealt with worse. I know the material. I'll probably pull a B, which isn't the A that I wanted, but still.

I grab my bag and apologize to Mr. Stiers again on my way out. The hallway surges in its typical between-periods way, people streaming in every direction. It's like being in a wad of used chewing gum—the walls are a graying pink, and everything I touch is disturbingly sticky.

I put my chin up and try to stay positive. In six months, this place will be a distant memory. A couple of months after that, I'll be on my way to a photography degree at NYU, maybe even Columbia. That's when my *real* life starts and I can't wait.

I focus all my energy into looking like a girl on a mission as I move down the hall, pushing through clusters of conversation and banging locker doors, taking the steps to the second floor two at a time. Kristen Green's just outside the restroom. She's ripping another price tag off another pair of jeans that I'd bet a million dollars she didn't actually buy. She catches my eye and immediately checks her hair.

Hazard of being a school photographer, I guess—the pretty ones always check their hair. Even before they check to see if I have my camera.

They also suck in their nonexistent guts and try to present me with their best side. If I ever manage to get a picture of a group of these girls without one of them over-posing, I'll nominate myself for a Pulitzer.

I check the clock above the gymnasium hallway. Six minutes. I'm making good time.

I find my locker, putting English books away and pulling out a couple of fresh pencils. Just need to grab my notes. I'll look them over on the way.

Beside me, a slim hand with bright red nails reaches for the locker next to mine.

Stella DuBois.

Stella never checks her hair. But then, she doesn't need

to, because she always looks like she just stepped out of a Pantene commercial.

"Have any Hollywood directors called yet?"

The question is loud, but Stella stays silent, twirling her combination lock with her crimson-tipped fingers. She tucks some long red strands behind her ear and pretends she can't sense the person who's standing right behind her. The one who's obviously talking *to* her.

"No? I'll bet someone will be calling. Maybe a 1-900 number," the same someone says. I'm pretty sure it's Jackson Pierce. I really don't have time for an in-crowd peacock session, so I search a little more frantically through a couple of folders, finding nothing. What is *with* this day?

"I can't decide which performance I like better," he goes on. "What about you, Tate?"

"Good question," someone, probably Tate, answers. He's quieter. Sounds pissed off.

I risk a glance over my shoulder to be sure. Dark hair and a linebacker's shoulders—yeah, it's Jackson. He's flanked by Tate Donovan and Nick Patterson. Tate and Nick are both taller and blond, but Tate's got a model's face, all sharp lines and cool eyes, the complete opposite of Nick's dimpled smile and perpetually messy hair.

Tate looks like he might stroke out on the floor. Nick looks…well, kind of oblivious. It actually seems like he's watching me. Which isn't likely.

I turn around, searching for whoever Nick's gaze is aimed at, but I just see Stella. She's shoving papers in her locker now, still pretending to be deaf. I don't get it. The trio of jock junk behind me is the "trifecta of hot" around here, according to most. They're also *her* people, so this whole showdown is beyond weird.

But not interesting enough to make me late for my test. *Ugh*, where the hell are those notes?

"Maybe we should watch the videos again," Tate says, voice cutting like a blade.

"*Again*," Jackson says, obviously delighted with that particular word. "Oh God, oh God, *again!*" Jackson's voice drags out that last *again* in a way that tells me everything about the content of Stella's video.

I find my notes, but I don't feel triumphant. And I'm not as uninterested as I'd like. My throat's tight as I glance at Stella. She's perfectly still, like she's not even hearing this, but *everyone* is hearing this.

Time to go. Way past time. I chance a quick look over my shoulder to find a semicircle of students gathering, watching intently.

Jackson's eyes are black and bright, a weird contrast to Tate's grimace. And then there's Nick, who *now* looks completely shocked, like he's only just figured out what's going on here. I don't know, maybe he's the pretty-but-dumb type, but *come on*. This has had "torture session" written all over it since Jackson opened his mouth.

"We should go," Nick says, shifting on his feet and glancing at the ancient clock overhead. "We've got class."

"Too bad Stella isn't interested in class," Tate says. Jackson hums in agreement and—*crack!* I jump, my gaze darting to Stella's locker door, which is swinging right back open despite the impact of her slamming it shut.

All around, I hear people pause, conversations dropping into nothingness. Stella clenches her teeth so hard a muscle in her jaw jumps.

I look for an escape route and find Nick's eyes on me. His gaze feels like a question. And what the hell answer would I have? I have less than nothing to do with any of this. I reach back to close my own locker quietly and try to blend into the wall.

"I…" Despite her slamming, Stella's voice is strangely small and unsure. "I didn't—"

"Oh, it's pretty clear that you *did*," Jackson says.

"And that you enjoyed it," Tate says, that tension in his voice edging into something bitter. "So that's what you like now? Giving the whole world ringside seats?"

"Hey, whoa," Nick says softly, grabbing Tate's arm. "Let's go, man."

Stella shuffles her books, and I eye the onlookers like a cornered dog, looking for an opening. But the crowd has closed in tight. No one wants to miss this. Stella's not the kind of girl you feel sorry for, but God. This is awful.

Tate lunges from Nick's grip. "Is this what you're doing for extra cash now? I mean, I knew you were broke but—"

"Are you finished?" Stella asks, finally sounding like the spitfire she's known to be. "Or do you get off on humiliating people in front of an audience?"

"Apparently, you getting off *requires* an audience these days," Tate shoots back.

"You unbelievable ass. You don't even know…" Stella trails off, looking like the words are choking her.

The warning bell cuts through the tension and jerks me back to my senses. The crowd scatters and I shove my way through, desperate. People push in every direction, almost crashing me into the main players. I have to look right at them.

Tate's face twists as he leans close to Stella. "Would have been nice to know what kind of slut you—"

"Tate!" Nick cuts him off with a hand on his shoulder.

And just like that, it's over. The boys move off and everyone else is on their way and I'm heading down the hall on autopilot. Until I stop.

I look back. I don't even know why, but I do. Stella's still there. Something in me pulls tight as I watch her, her narrowed eyes taking in the dissipating crowd. A few people laugh as they pass her. Others look on with expressions of pity I don't really buy.

The truth is, people enjoy seeing girls like Stella suffer.

"Ready for the test?" Aimee, one of my fellow AP chemistry students, pauses inside our classroom doorway. She's smiling big and bright, proof that she escaped this entire mess.

I shake my head and force myself to return her smile. "Uh, yeah. I think so."

Aimee wishes me luck and moves inside. Everyone else is already in there. I can see Harrison lining up his pencils on the desk. I should be in there too.

And I will be. I just…

I look down the row of lockers again, thinking maybe Stella will still be there. That maybe, in the quiet, empty hallway, she'll be standing alone with her beautiful face crumpled up, needing… I don't even know what she'd need. Or why I think I should be the one to help, since I don't know her.

But it doesn't matter. Because the hallway is empty. All I can see is her locker door, still half-open.

CHAPTER TWO

. . . .

I stare at my fifty-year-old lab table and practice deep breathing while Mrs. Branson passes us our tests. She starts with the first row. Tim Gentry. Shay McAllister. Aimee Johnston. Harrison Copeland.

Mousy and whippet-thin, Harrison doesn't look like much, but if someone in this school is going to turn into the next Stephen Hawking, it'll be him. His GPA has landed him the number one rank in the class every year, so he's almost guaranteed to graduate in the top spot.

As long as he holds off Aimee.

Aimee's every bit as smart as Harrison, but that's not all. Pretty and popular, she's the student vice president and a beloved cheerleader. If she manages to overtake him, she'll be the first black female valedictorian in our school. Aimee's the one popular kid everyone loves. In the eighth grade, we took a class trip to a local nursing home. There was a deaf patient. It was awkward. The rest of us forgot about it on the bus ride back. She signed up for sign language classes. That's just Aimee.

Mrs. Branson drops my test on my desk and my happy thoughts wither. I use a single finger to drag the paper front and center. Showtime.

"You will have forty minutes total for both the written and lab portions," Mrs. Branson says, resuming her place at the front of the room.

Harrison mouths something to Aimee. It looks like "Good luck," but his eyes are sending an entirely different message. Aimee ignores him and focuses on her table, choosing a pencil.

Mrs. Branson waves at the room. "You may begin."

The lab portion is worth more, so I grab the small plastic supplies box and turn on my burner. It's a fairly simple recrystallization. I finish it quickly. I breathe a little easier then. I've still got twenty-two minutes. Plenty of time.

In the front, Aimee turns her paper face down and reaches for her box. She doesn't look at Harrison, but I wish she would because he's sweating bullets. He's hunched over, one hand furiously writing, the other crammed on his lap beneath the table.

If I didn't know better, I'd think he might actually be doing something vile under there. But he's not. He's holding something small and rectangular. It looks like a phone.

Because it *is* a phone.

I blink. I have to be wrong. It's got to be his wallet or maybe a lucky deck of cards or something. No way does Harrison Copeland, High Lord of Claireville Academia, forget the rules about cell phones and tests. It's a big deal. Automatic zero on the exam. Possible suspension. He wouldn't dream of having his phone out during a test, so it has to be something else.

And yet…

A second later he checks it, the soft bloom of light barely

visible. I look around, seeing nothing but bent heads. Is this actually happening?

"Miss Woods, kindly keep your eyes on your desk," Mrs. Branson says.

My cheeks go hot with an angry flush. I look back at my test, answering the next two questions in quick succession. I should double-check them, but I'm preoccupied with Harrison.

I answer another question and he looks down. Again. I've met friendlier pencil sharpeners, so I doubt he's chatting up a buddy between questions. Aimee measures something into her beaker with shaking hands. She wants this so bad she's practically vibrating, but Harrison's never going to slip. He's perfect.

Unless he's not.

My fingers itch, hand wanting to shoot into the air. Because someone should know. If our head-of-the-class-teacher's-pet is cheating, I can't just ignore that. But Harrison's lap is empty now. No glow. No darting eyes. Whatever I saw—or thought I saw—is long gone.

• • •

I skip the cafeteria during lunch. The little juice my phone battery had is drained now, so I decide on a granola bar in the parking lot to give me the chance to charge it. On my way back from the vending machines, I notice Manny and Tacey at our regular table, waving me over. I waggle my dead phone in explanation before turning away.

I head for the side entrance, which swings me right by the student store. It doesn't sell anything interesting and probably exists only to provide another volunteer opportunity for the students and free Lost and Found babysitting for the faculty.

Speaking of Lost and Found.

I pause just outside the store opening. A kid I don't recognize is at the counter, looking at his phone. Which sucks. I'd really rather drop this notebook off without an audience.

My bag turns heavy on my shoulder. It's like I can feel the notebook in all its disturbing glory. From the psychopath pictures to the Latin on the cover, this thing squicks me out. But I definitely don't want people seeing me with it. Or trying to pin it on me.

I take one last look at the Lost and Found tubs before I head outside.

It's bright and crisp—one of those perfect late fall days when the blue sky hasn't been lost to the bone-white ceiling of winter. I cut across the side yard, where a group of guys are tossing a football, guys from the team, which means Jackson, Tate, and Nick are in the mix. Of course. My whole day has been a unicorn ride through a field of rainbows, so naturally they're out here.

I keep my head down and try to move fast.

"Heads up, Nicky!" someone shouts.

Something thunks nearby. I hear a groan and then glance up through my hair to see Nick on the ground maybe twenty feet away. He's got a football cradled to his gut and he's flushed to the roots of his hair, but grinning. Jackson and Tate laugh so hard they double over.

Two and a half hours ago, they were eviscerating Stella in the hallway, and now they're having the time of their lives. Why am I even surprised? Cold fingers burrow into the base of my skull, reminding me of the evolution of this group over the years. If you were to look for a line in the sand, you'd find those boys on the side most people want. The side opposite of me.

In third grade, it was spies versus ninjas. What started as a pick-your-side game became an invitation-only club. In fourth grade, it was the seats in the back of the bus. By fifth, it was lunch tables. Year after year, the same kids found their way to the top of our small-town social stratosphere, while the rest of us wondered where we'd made the wrong turn. I stopped wondering freshman year. I have Kristen's special party invitation to thank for that.

I move fast, wanting as much distance as I can get between them and me. Two steps later, my foot catches on the grass. I stumble wildly, barely managing to stay on my feet. My backpack flies off of my shoulder, unzipped of course. It lands upside down and crap flies everywhere.

No one says a word. In seventh grade, this would have been a field day—insults slung from every direction. They think they've outgrown all that. Now, I just feel their eyes on me. I hear the ache of silence where laughter—or, even worse, pity—is hiding. A shuffle-hiss in the grass tells me someone's coming.

Nick. He's smiling down at me, but he's been on the right side of the line since they first started drawing it, so I don't trust him. He must see it on my face too, because the aw-shucks grin he's wearing droops into something awkward. Maybe even embarrassed.

I claw desperately at my stuff, shoving the notebook and my keys and every other damn thing I own back into my bag. I don't even know if I have everything, but Nick is way too close. I yank my bag over my shoulder and move in double time to the parking lot, wishing I'd taken another entrance—or maybe that I'd just stayed in bed altogether.

I've never been so grateful to see the unique slopes and angles of my old Subaru. The sun feels even more delicious inside the car. I soak in the heat, slouching down in my seat with a sigh.

Okay. Damage control. I open the mirror on my visor. Given the day I've had, I'm half expecting a human-girl version of the Kraken. It's just me though—long dark hair, big brown eyes. Mom says I look doe-eyed. Dad says soulful. I think I look like I'm perpetually on the verge of tears. Ironic, since I rarely cry.

I snap the mirror shut and my gaze drifts to my bag. I don't like it. Feels like I'm sitting beside the future potential serial killer of Claireville High. Which is…way more dramatic than it needs to be. It's just a notebook. For all I know, the kid's making it all up for a screenplay.

Still, curiosity picks at me. This is dumb. I need to figure out who this stupid thing belongs to so I can get over it.

I flip the cover to find the pictures have shifted in my bag. One corner of Anna's photo is visible, vacant eyeholes changing her smile into something sinister. I push them back into the folder. I don't think the pictures are going to tell me anything. Or maybe I just don't want to look at them anymore.

Either way, there are other things to focus on. Like all those stupid names. Or the Latin, which I could ask Hadley about.

I flip to November 2nd to get Shane's nickname from the accident entry. RJG. I know jack all about him, so it could mean anything. I've got to find something else.

I flip through the pages, looking for another mention. The only other mention of RJG/Shane is an ass smack in the middle of the hallway, but I wasn't there for that. And it's hardly newsworthy. But there are other, scarier things in here. Like the cretin sending crotch shots to freshmen, or whoever Tricky is and whatever goods he's dealing.

I'm guessing Tucker Smith for that one. Most of the kids around here are content to get drunk in someone's hot tub or maybe pass around an occasional joint. Dealing pharmaceuticals on school property is a bit big city for us.

I thumb through a couple more pages but stop on October 12th.

> LQ says he'll beat the shit out of Shutter if she doesn't
> shut her piehole

My arms tighten with goose bumps. That's me. Me and Manny. I'd given him a ride that day. It was a crap morning. Manny wasn't ready when I got to his place, and then on the way to school, he'd dropped the bomb on me that he was bailing on his post-graduation community college plans for at least a year. Told me not everyone had a fat education fund waiting for them like I did.

I was so shocked that I almost missed Hemlock Street. Spilled my coffee all over both of us to make the turn.

We fought the rest of the six blocks to school over the college thing and the money thing, even over the stupid coffee. And halfway down the main hallway, he said this. These *exact* words.

I can still see him shaking his blond head, coffee spatter staining the hem of his ancient Green Day T-shirt. I was sporting a matching stain on my jeans.

"I don't get why you can't just take a loan like you planned," I said. *"It's like you want me to nag."*

"Really don't."

"Then don't give up on college, Manny."

"You sound like a public service announcement."

"If you'd prefer, I could try a jaunty song about the merits of higher education."

He'd finally grinned. *"I'm gonna beat the shit out of you if you don't shut your piehole."*

It was a joke. That comment was the end of the fight, not the beginning. And anyone who knows anything about us would know that. Manny wouldn't hurt me. Not ever. He'd pound anyone else who tried.

We've been friends since before the beginning of time. We even dated briefly—a disastrous error in judgment for both of us—during sophomore year. If whoever wrote this thought what he said that morning was some sort of legitimate threat… I don't know, maybe the whole book is crap like this, stuff blown way out of proportion.

Maybe.

A quick scan of the pages reveals that I'm only listed once. Unless I've got more than one nickname. I search again, this time for Manny, who, for reasons I can't fathom, is LQ.

I find his nickname three more times. Once propositioning Candace for sex. No surprise there. Two other times in October. I spot the first one on October 7th.

IB paying LQ to clear some record up

And then on October 23rd.

LQ blackmailing Reese, possibly over attendance corrections?

A breathless laugh spurts from my mouth. I read the entries again. Manny. Blackmailing someone. Sure.

The idea's so ridiculous I throw the book back in my bag and close the flap. I laugh again. Look at me. Hiding in my car like I found Charles Manson's diary or something. Whoever wrote this is delusional. So desperate for drama, they're turning every little overheard comment into a conspiracy. And I darn near bought it.

I've been sitting here scanning a bunch of cryptic messages for what? My best friend's super-secret underground life of crime? Come on. Manny's life of crime includes Slurpees lifted from the Stop and Rob near his house and some seriously tasteless Internet browsing.

It can't be true. Can it?

My chest knots. *Manny, tell me you did not get mixed up in anything.*

My eyes are drawn to the bag, the notebook tucked inside. It's only two entries, but if anyone else figures them out, it'll be serious. God, I need to find out who wrote this thing.

There's a tap on my window and I jerk hard, my thigh slamming into the gearshift. I turn to my window and Nick holds up his hands, like he's trying to seem disarming.

I roll down my window. "Don't you know it's creepy to sneak up to a girl's car?"

"I wasn't exactly sneaking. I did knock."

I narrow my eyes, but he looks harmless. That's probably Nick's default setting though. He's standing here with his messy surfer hair and his dimpled smile, wearing a pair of shorts even though it can't be more than fifty-five degrees outside. The boy is so All-American he should be selling apple pie.

He's also enormous. Or at least it seems that way when he leans down to see me better. His shoulders are so broad they deserve their own zip code.

"I'm sorry," he says. "I didn't mean to scare you, Piper, I swear."

Suddenly, I remember his eyes on me in the hallway, and then his friends laughing today on the field. My defenses rise, sending the hair on the back of my neck upright.

"Adrenaline overload aside, I'm fine," I say, aiming for breezy and missing it by a mile.

"You sure?" he asks.

I tense. This whole situation is bringing to mind a lot of crappy makeover scenarios where some football-wielding tool makes a play at the smart but dorky art girl.

Not that I'm a dork. I'm a skirt-the-fringe type, maybe. An avoids-his-kind-like-the-plague type, definitely. But that's not the point. The point is he doesn't have any reason to talk to me. So everything about this feels like a setup.

"What are you doing here?" I ask him, looking around for his friends. Or maybe his girlfriend. This is exactly the kind of trap Marlow loves to set.

"You don't already know?" Nick tilts his head, smiling.

"No, I don't." Everything feels sharp at the edges. Intense. Like the air between us has a static charge and if I move—maybe if I even breathe—it will zap me.

He moves first, his cheeks tinged with pink as he reaches into his pocket. I watch him drag out a red wallet, realizing that it isn't just any wallet. It's mine.

He hands it over with another perfect, lopsided grin. "Uh, you dropped it in the grass."

Right. When I tripped over my own feet and almost face-planted into the ground.

"Well, I should get back." He looks toward the school, and I take a deep breath that smells like soap and fallen leaves and boy.

I know I should thank him. I really should. But I'm so stunned that I don't. I just sit there like a complete moron—a *rude* moron—until he's gone.

CHAPTER THREE

· ·

Tacey greets me at the door of the technology lab at
4:56 the next day. She pushes her long, curly hair away from
her eyes. "Didn't you get my texts after lunch?"

"Uh…" I trail off because I did *get* them. I just didn't read
them. As much as I love her, Tacey is strung like a caffeinated cat,
and after yesterday's drama, I needed a mellow day.

"Well, we have a major emergency," she says.

"I'm here now, so what's the big deal?"

"Come look for yourself," Manny says.

I walk around Tacey to the computer where he's sitting. At first it's
nothing new—our student website with the Claireville banner across
the top and student pictures scrolling down both sides. But then I see
the video playing in the box where our upcoming events slide show
usually plays. I step in a little closer, trying to focus on the rhythmic
motion and the grainy room. I can't quite figure out what's going on.

And then I do.

Heat flares up my neck, my mind suddenly blank. "Um, is that
what I think it is?"

"If you think it's naked people in the middle of—"

I put my hand up to cut him off. "Okay, I've got it. Why is it
on our website?"

He shrugs, so I look past him to another computer, where Connor is clacking away, Hadley sitting beside him, beautiful despite her obvious agony.

In my peripheral vision, I can still see bits of the video. A pair of legs. A nondescript footboard. Long, red hair.

The blood drains out of me so fast I grip the back of the chair in front of me before I turn around. Away from the screen. "This is Stella DuBois's tape."

Everyone in the room stares at me.

The way Tacey moves in—quick and light—makes me think of hungry wolves. "You already knew about this?"

"Yeah," I say, then wave. "I mean, not about it being up here, but I heard about the tape."

Manny, Connor, and Tacey all seem surprised. I think Hadley's too miserable about this to care. She's chewing her bottom lip hard enough to draw blood.

My eyes drift to the screen and my insides go squirmy. I know some part of me is halfway *watching* this mess. The photographer in me can't help but to notice the strange angle. It's contrived. Stella's on display, but the guy is off camera. It doesn't feel accidental.

Tacey answers her phone and stalks from the room, and Manny looks at Connor. "Think you can clean up the resolution?" he asks.

"You realize I'm busy doing something valid here, right?" Connor says. "Feel free to get off your duff and help at any time."

"This one's beyond my skills." Manny stretches. "But I'd like to figure out who this guy is. He seems awfully careful to keep himself out of frame, if you get my drift."

I move closer to him, a little because I'm backing his cause and a little because this might be less horrible if I'm standing next to my best friend.

He drops his voice so it's just for me. "This is really bothering you."

"You sure you can't make it go away?" I say, gesturing weakly at the screen. I know he hates messing with computers, but he is good at it.

"Sorry, Pi. Wish I could. But you know this school. This will be old news by tomorrow. Don't let it freak you."

I tug the back of his sweatshirt, so he knows I appreciate him trying.

"Give me a minute. I might be able to get the password from the keypass file," Connor says. He might as well be speaking Greek, but I trust him. Connor will probably wind up at MIT or something. But despite the geek-smarts, he's gorgeous and athletic enough to make any of the varsity teams. He and his girlfriend Hadley are kind of above all that though.

"It's not in there," Connor says. "What's taking her so long?"

Tacey opens the door again, with our technology advisor, Ms. Collins, walking behind her. Tacey gestures at the thin woman beside her. "Did someone ask for a password?"

"Connor?" Ms. Collins says, holding out a Post-it note with a shaking hand.

"What kind of idiot decided you shouldn't have that password?" Manny asks.

"The kind of idiot who knows what I can do with it," Connor says with a wink.

"I'm the idiot," Ms. Collins snaps. "It may be an independent website, but it contains school and student images and therefore a teacher needs to maintain security."

"Way to maintain," Manny says. I smack his arm.

Ms. Collins frowns so hard her whole face puckers. She's never been good at handling his particular brand of ornery. I think it's because she's so young. She took college courses in high school, so she's only three years ahead of us. Plus, she's got that whole tall, scrawny look—less supermodel, more praying mantis. Between that and her oh-so-obvious crush on Connor, she doesn't exactly command respect.

"I'm glad we found you," I say. I can't help it, I feel for her. She's never quite grown into her own skin. And if her teenage fashion sense was anything like the long floral skirts and baggy cardigans she sports now, I can't fathom she had an easy time of it around here. Come to think of it, I have no idea why she wanted to come back.

Ms. Collins smiles at me, then steps closer to Connor. Her voice—like her gaze—is just for him. "So, do you know how to take it down, Connor?"

"Already on it," Connor says, and a few clicks later, it's done.

"So, it's over? It's down?" Tacey asks, hands planted on her curvy hips.

Manny refreshes his screen and an error message appears: *We're experiencing technical difficulties. Check back later.*

"It's down," I say.

Tacey slumps over the table like Armageddon itself has been avoided. I don't feel like anything's been avoided. That video is still out there. No way are we the only ones who saw it.

"Now what?" Manny asks.

"Now the school board will investigate. Until then, the website will have to remain down. I'm very sorry," Ms. Collins says. She doesn't really sound sorry.

"Well, good luck," Connor says. "This file is totally buried and the source is encrypted."

"It's going to be like chasing a ghost," Hadley says. It's the first time she's spoken, and she's still so pale. Is she about to get sick?

"This is an independent, student-run website," Tacey says. "You can't keep it down."

Ms. Collins's lips thin into a hard line. "You use images and logos that are property of the school, so we certainly can."

I touch Tacey's shoulder because I know this will kill her. Tacey spent every waking minute over summer break working on this. She had a whole vision—a website for the students and by the students. Shutting it down is probably as harsh as giving her dog away.

"Do you think the police will get involved?" Hadley asks.

Connor puts a hand on her knee. "It's a good question. I mean, is Stella a minor?"

I remember the birthday cards taped to her locker earlier this year. "She's eighteen."

"Still, we can't be sure. We don't know how old…" Ms. Collins stops, obviously uncomfortable talking about Stella's mystery man. "Regardless, the website will stay down, and I trust that you'll all use discretion in this highly sensitive matter. We don't want anyone to think someone here is responsible."

"Why would we want our own site taken down?" Manny's jaw tightens. He's pissed.

"I just don't want to give anyone a reason to point fingers."

"It's cool," Connor says. "We appreciate the heads-up, Ms. C."

She blushes in response and then slips out quietly, leaving us alone.

Tacey looks up at the ceiling with a sigh. "She has a point. I did this for my college résumé, so I don't really want to advertise the scandal. We should keep it quiet."

"It's too late for quiet," Connor says.

"Why would you say that?" Tacey asks.

"Because he's smart." Manny smirks. "That video was up for at least an hour."

"So?"

"You know how I hate phrases like *going viral*, but…" Connor trails off and turns his laptop around so we can see the screen.

Screenshots, quick posts, little fragmented scenes from the video—Connor's right. It's too late to stop any of this.

• • •

The book is propped open on my desk, and I've got a notebook beside it filled with code names and possible descriptions. I didn't plan to spend my evening this way. But the Stella tape got me thinking. Maybe that book has something in it about the guy who was so careful to keep himself hidden, or about the tape itself. So far, I've found nothing, except page after page proving how much crap people are getting away with.

I thought long and hard about turning this sucker in, but what's the point? This isn't some threat-laced manifesto. All of this stuff already happened—if it's all even real.

My throat squeezes thinking of the entries about Manny. Blackmail. Changing student records. That's expulsion at the least. Maybe criminal charges. Seriously, Manny is way too smart for that.

But then I also thought he was too smart to wait on college.

I could just ask, but how would I do that to him? If this were my name and Manny reading it, he'd dismiss it no question. Because he's my friend and he knows I wouldn't.

No, I can't confront him unless I'm sure it's the truth. Which means I need to figure out what's real and what's not in this creepy thing.

My gaze skims the eerily uniform writing and the stack of white-eyed photographs beside it. I tip my head down, rubbing my forehead. I need a break from this thing. I feel icky touching the pages for too long. I flip open my laptop and search the Latin phrase on the cover.

Malum Non Vide: See No Evil

Weird title for a book that's pretty much dedicated to seeing evil. Maybe it explains why the photographs have no eyes? Or maybe it's just further proof that the mystery writer is a delusional psychopath.

Either way, it doesn't help. I need names. Real ones. So far I've got three.

Shutter—Me

RJG—Shane Haywood

LQ—Manny Raines

The initials are driving me crazy. What the heck does LQ have to do with Manny? And why does Shane get three letters? Unless maybe it's because he used to go by his first and middle initials: SK. It was weird even back in elementary school. SK doesn't exactly have the same ring as a TJ or a JD. It never made any sen—

Wait a minute.

I chew on the inside of my lip. Shane's initials are SKH. His code name is RJG. One letter off. I flip to Manny Raines. LQ. Same thing. Holy crap. I cracked the code.

I sit back, grinning. With all the Smiths and Taylors in the world, that's still a lot of figuring. But it's a start.

My phone buzzes and I glance over, groaning as soon as I check the caller ID: Tacey. Probably wanting to talk yearbook crap.

I toss it on my desk and head to the bathroom to wash my face first. The day has not been kind. The mascara I put on this morning is smeared half an inch under my eyes. I scrub it off and brush my teeth, mentally preparing for a high-energy phone call. All Tacey calls reach a certain level of intensity. I return to my room to find my phone skating dangerously close to the edge of my desk.

The screen informs me that I've missed four calls.

"Are you kidding me?"

A text lights the screen as I pick it up. I open it with a huff.

> Call me. It's an emergency.

I call, rolling my eyes before she even picks up. "Tacey, I really think you need to ease off the caff—"

I cut myself off when I hear her crying. Hard. It sends my heart into my throat. I make a nervous lap around my room as I wait for her to speak.

"Piper…" She falters, sucking in a shuddering breath. "Stella's dead."

CHAPTER FOUR

. . . .

I can't really remember everything Tacey said. Just fragments. Phrases like "maybe her music was loud." Words like "accident" and "train tracks."

Tragic.

That's what Tacey called it before she disconnected with a sniffle. People have been using that word a lot in the four days since that call. It's been a blur of sentimental phrases and long sighs from my parents. They're hugging me all the time too, stroking my hair back from my forehead, patting my hands. For now, all the quiet fights that simmer between them are forgotten. Buried because a girl they barely even knew is dead.

We didn't go to the funeral, a private affair held at the church her mother pastors. I thought the student memorial service would be easier, but now that I'm pulling into the parking lot, I'm not so sure.

Manny, who followed me to the community center near our high school, parks beside me in the parking lot that separates the two buildings.

He adjusts his collar, looking beyond awkward in an ugly tie, no doubt from his dad's meager collection.

"You look nice," I lie.

"You look miserable."

That's because I saw Stella before she died. I saw her in the hallway after she was ripped to pieces, and I walked away. I shrug and look at the road, where a young couple is walking a pair of yappy Sheltie dogs. Like it's any other normal day.

"Hell of a shock, right?" Manny says, the silence obviously getting to him.

"Is it?" I don't know where that came from. I think I meant to say something agreeable. But now that it's out, it makes me think. "Is anyone actually shocked about this?"

"If by *this* you mean Stella getting hit by a train, then yeah. I think people are surprised."

"Maybe they shouldn't be. That video of her went everywhere."

Manny pauses for a minute, but we're parked half a freaking mile away and there isn't anyone nearby. He still leans close. "What are you saying?"

His voice sounds like a warning, but it's not like I want to say any of this. It's a terrible word, too much like cyanide or genocide. So, I press my lips together and hold it in.

Manny isn't fooled. "You think she walked in front of a train *on purpose?*"

My breath escapes in a rush. "I don't know. I don't know what I think."

"So, talk. Talk to me. Which you could have done any day this week if you'd picked up the phone."

I bite my lip because it's true. We texted a little, but I just wasn't…ready. I've been processing all of this. Stella. That mess in the hallway. That stupid book and the things I found about Manny in it. For once in our friendship, I don't know how to go there. But I know it can't be now. And definitely not here.

But I have to say something. "I heard about the video…"

"Yeah, you were saying that in the lab. What was with that?"

I swallow hard, but the sharp thing in my throat won't budge. "People were talking about it in the hall before it even hit the website. I think it messed her up."

"A lot of girls regret these things after the fact. That doesn't mean they want to off themselves."

I grimace. "But who walks on the tracks without paying attention? Even if her music was blaring, she should have *heard*. You know how loud those trains are."

"And I know how loud my headphones are. Hell, it could've happened to me! I mean, she was upset, but Stella can handle herself." He nods at someone walking past us and lowers his voice to a whisper. "The girl was *not* suicidal."

"I know that, I just…" I sigh and the wind blows my hair into my eyes, so I tuck it behind my ears. "You weren't there, Manny. You didn't hear what they said to her."

"Wait, people were talking to her about the tape? When?" His voice is different. Tighter.

"In the hallway. It was bad." Tears well in my eyes, unexpected and unwelcome. "I was standing right there, Manny. *Right* next to her. I could have—I *should* have done something. "

Manny sighs, pulling me into a hard hug. "Hell, Pi, why didn't you call?"

"I should have done something," I say again, because I can't shake it.

He squeezes my arm. "Quit it. You barely knew Stella, so stop going there. We all do what we have to do to get by. You couldn't have known this would happen."

I don't say anything. Maybe what I did wasn't wrong, but it sure doesn't feel right. Not anymore.

"All that matters now is that we're here," he says. "To pay our respect."

I don't even know what that means, *pay our respect*. Like we're all going to pull out our emotional wallets at some big funeral cash register. I blink away the absurd thought, wet lashes brushing my cheeks.

"And what about that video?" I ask.

"Look, I know you should respect the dead and all, but you and I both know Stella had a wild side. Maybe the video was her idea."

"Don't," I say, because his words pinch my insides—mostly because they're true. It started sophomore year with whispers of Stella and Dean cashing in their V cards over the summer. It didn't stop there.

Manny's quiet again. I can feel he's trying to censor himself. It's never easy for him, but he knows me well enough to figure out how far gone I am right now. "Look, I liked Stella. I wouldn't be here if I didn't. But I'm not going to pretend she's some sort of virginal saint."

"No, she wasn't. But she wasn't an exhibitionist either. We took pictures of her." I even have one of them with me, for her locker. Thought I could put it up after the service. "I just can't see her agreeing to a *sex tape*. I mean, seriously, Manny—what if she didn't *know*?"

He runs a hand over his head. "Hell, I don't know. I don't know."

Neither do I. A rise of faint music from the doors tells us the service is starting, so we go. But the question won't leave me alone.

• • •

Eighteen minutes. I am only eighteen minutes into Stella's memorial service and I feel like I've been here two days. The event was planned for the students, but our auditorium isn't big enough, which is why they held it here. Six hundred seats and it looks like they're all full.

Tacey and Manny are on either side of me, and the video montage leaves her sniffing, him yawning, and me gripping my seat so hard that the metal edges crease my fingers.

I guess this is how we're supposed to do grief—with sad music and poetry that belongs on a greeting card. But apparently I'm defective. This whole service has filled me with the worst feeling, a prickling, crawling sensation, like I'm watching a show. Like the whole thing is a lie. Except for Stella's mom.

Her own red hair, now graying, is secured in a neat French twist, and her pale hands are wrapped around the bible in her lap. Mrs. DuBois has dark, deep-set eyes, the kind that probably pin churchgoers into the pews. Today they are a thousand miles away, searching some great unseen emptiness inside her. Looking for Stella, I guess.

An image of that locker door swinging back open flashes through my mind as her swim team comes up to joins hands on the stage. I squirm in my seat when they begin filing past the picture of Stella, each of them leaving a flower beside her smiling face. How's that for irony? A girl dies, and we cut flowers off from their roots so that they will die too.

Someone has to tap Mrs. DuBois on the shoulder to get her to take her own flower forward. She still looks so empty and lost. I can't look anymore. I slip out of my chair—I have to.

"Where are you going?" Manny asks.

"Bathroom," I lie.

"You're *leaving*?" Tacey asks. She reaches for my wrist and her eyes are so red. I don't get it. Half of the girls here didn't even know Stella, but almost all of them seem to be crying. Except me. "I'll come with you."

"I'm okay," I say.

"You shouldn't be alone," she says, but she's wrong. I *should* be alone, because I don't think I know how to do this right. Besides, Tacey means well. But I don't know if I can handle the way she is right now. I glance around, desperate for an excuse.

"I'll take her," Manny says.

I feel myself flush to the roots of my hair as he follows me out. It's ridiculous. I'm not five years old and we aren't together, but whatever.

I don't even bother with the bathroom, and Manny doesn't

ask. He knows it was a flimsy excuse. So I pace back and forth in front of a bulletin board advertising yoga classes, and Manny leans against the wall, tapping his thumb in time with the music inside.

"Why are you so relaxed?" I ask.

"Well, you've cornered the market on twitchy since you parked your car."

"This is just weird, all right? She's only eighteen, Manny. You're not supposed to die when you're eighteen. How can you be so calm about that?"

"It's a funeral, Pi. You want me to start throwing shit around?"

He's right. I sigh and press my back against the wall. He moves to stand next to me, slouching down until our shoulders are the same height.

"What's wrong with me?" I ask.

"How long do we have to go over it?"

I know he's waiting for me to punch his arm or kick his shoe or something, and when I don't, he sighs. "She kissed me once. Eighth grade at Shay's birthday. You had bronchitis."

I frown. "You never said anything."

"It wasn't any big thing. I was starting to crush on you, so I didn't want to jinx anything. But I'd never really kissed *anyone*, you know?"

I didn't, actually. I'm not too surprised. Manny's always on some girl conquest, but deep down, I kind of think he's like the rest of us—afraid to be rejected.

He swallows hard and nods. "Anyway, some guys had been

calling me out, saying they'd never seen me with anyone. They were giving me shit, and Stella…"

"She kissed you," I say, filling in the blanks. "To put them in their place."

"No, because my ninety-four-pound, eighth-grade self was so freaking hot," he says, and then he grins at me, freckles standing out on his nose.

"That's cool." I feel better and worse at the same time.

Inside, a new song starts up, and everyone's joining in this time. It's like being in church.

"You wanna go back in?" Manny asks.

"No," I say, the idea of it making my voice shake. "I'm going to go put up her picture."

He nods and I watch him retreat to the auditorium. His too-big suit jacket—probably his dad's—shifts awkwardly with every step and it makes me remember him smaller and younger.

My phone buzzes and I fish it from my pocket, expecting Tacey or maybe my parents checking in to make sure I'm okay. But it's an unfamiliar number.

Do you blame yourself?

I read the words once. Twice. I see Stella's locker door swinging open and I hear a train whistle, but neither are happening. It's all in my head. I force myself to take a breath and go outside. This text is a wrong number. It's not for me, and it's definitely not about Stella.

And then another message.

> Do you wish you'd done something? What if you still could?

I text back quickly.

> I think you have the wrong number.

> I don't have the wrong number, Piper.

CHAPTER FIVE

· ·

need to go inside. I'm going to get frostbite if I stand here staring at my phone much longer. But still.

I check again. No matter how many times I look, the five letters at the end of that message still spell my name. My fingers move to reply, to ask who this is, but I hesitate. Do I really want to know?

If this is a joke, it's not funny. And if it's a game, I'm pretty sure I'm not going to win. Every text I send gives this jerk exactly what he's looking for—a reaction.

In spite of all that, I'm still curious. But refusing to play along trumps curiosity this time. I shove my phone deep in my coat pocket and jog toward the high school.

There's a post-memorial reception here. If it's anything like my freshman year when Chase Timmons died in a car accident, it'll be a bizarre blend of light refreshments and therapy.

Cake? Cookies? Counseling? Or perhaps you'd like to go up to the open microphone and talk about your feelings?

At the main entrance, Mr. McCreedy hits the button before I can flash my student ID. He gives me a sleepy nod, and I walk past into the still mostly empty school.

I can hear some faint noise coming from the gym—probably

setting up for the big weird post-funeral party we're supposed to have—but I head to the stairs.

In a building like this, you can *feel* the quiet. It lingers in the shadowy stairwells and sends an old paper smell into the air. Even the posters—advertising everything from the upcoming production of *42nd Street* to the monthlong food drive—flutter as I pass them.

I swallow hard and fight the feeling that I'm trespassing. Unwelcome, even. It's just my nerves. The memorial, the creepy texts—they're putting me on edge and I know it. Still, every step I take snaps against the hardwood floors.

I climb the stairs to our bay of lockers. They're as they always are, identical to every other locker in the building, save the color of the combination locks. Mine is green—hers is purple. My mind conjures an image of her hand spinning that lock left and right. My ears still ring with the things I heard afterward.

I shake my uneasiness away and retrieve the picture I brought. Stella's got one hand near her face, tucking some of her pretty hair behind her ear. Her eyes are crinkled just a little at the corners and her smile is wide and genuine. It's not perfect quality, since I had to print it at the drugstore on the way in, but it's not hideous.

And it's a good shot. An honest shot.

I tape it carefully to Stella's locker. There isn't anything else I can do now. I try to tell myself there wasn't anything I could do then either, though I'm not sure I believe it.

I hear footsteps and turn to see my friends coming toward the lockers. Memorial must be over if they're here. I scan their faces—Manny, Tacey, Hadley, Connor—the entire yearbook staff. Unless you count Ms. Collins. And, sadly, no one does.

"Hey," I say.

"It's beautiful," Tacey says, nodding at the picture.

Her eyes are rimmed with red, but otherwise, she looks like Tacey always does—professional, put together, and very conscious of her ample hips. She's tugging at her suit jacket now, trying to cover her curviest section.

Hadley gives the photo a good look, lacing her fingers with Connor's. "Thanks for doing this."

I shrug. "It was Manny's shot, actually."

"He occasionally has decent ones," Tacey says with a wink.

Manny just rolls his eyes. "Let's go get snacks."

"And crappy punch." I sigh and link my arm with his, heading for the cafeteria.

Ten minutes later, I'm holding an uneaten banana and a cup of Sprite—an upgrade from crappy punch—as I stare at the memorial book Harrison and Mrs. Branson are signing.

There are a few students at the tables. I spot Tate, looking hollow eyed and pale at a table by the window. Nick is sitting near him in a loosened tie. His gaze flicks to Tate every few seconds and both of their cookies lie untouched on their plates. I tilt my head, spotting a hand on Nick's arm. Someone's between them, dabbing her eyes.

No. Not someone. Marlow. How could I forget?

A memory flashes through me. A hard shove between my shoulders. My knees cracking into the concrete. And then a little girl, cooing at the teachers to come quick—quick because *"Piper is hurt."*

Over and over, for a week, she did this. Finally, I found my voice, but it was Kristen then who slid to Marlow's rescue, telling the teachers no one pushed me. And that was just the start.

I turn my gaze away and the memory withers.

Connor and Hadley sit down across from us, and I smile at them, grateful that they're blocking my view. They should be in magazines, they're so pretty together. Connor's dark and lean, and Hadley's like a porcelain doll, with ivory skin and enormous hazel eyes.

"So, how is everyone?" Hadley asks, offering a sad smile.

I start peeling my banana, hoping Tacey will take the lead on responding. She does, scooting forward on her seat. "I think we should talk memorial page."

"Oh," Hadley says softly, looking down at the orange she's peeling. "It seems soon."

"It's fresh in our minds now. We can get interviews, candid shots from her friends."

"No." This from Manny. We all stop, surprised. "You're not going to make a project out of her. I'm not cool with that."

I slouch in my chair and try to find something to say. Everyone's looking at me now because I usually am the resident Manny handler, the one who softens his asshole comments and talks him into being more reasonable. Except this time I can't do either.

"I agree. It's too soon." And then, because I can't deal with more talking, I stand. "I've got to go grab a memory card from my locker and get home. I'm behind on a bunch of work."

"We can do the memorial later," Tacey says. "When you feel better about it. I swear I'm not trying to sensationalize this or whatever."

"Yeah," Manny says, not sounding convinced.

I try a smile for her, but it's pathetic. "It's fine. I just need to go. I have that paper due."

Which is true. But it's not why I'm leaving. I'm halfway down the hall when my phone buzzes. Same number as before.

> I know you wanted to help her. You still can.

Something hot tears through my middle. I pull up my phone keyboard.

> Who is this?

> I can't tell you that, but I can give you a chance to do right by Stella.

> Stop texting me. I'm not interested.

> Don't act like you don't know what happens around here. I know you saw what happened to her.

> It's too late to help her.

> That doesn't mean they should get away with it.

This message feels different. Part scolding and part…invitation? The words needle through me, full of cold promise. I want to ask what he means. And I want to know who this is.

They saw me in the hallway that day. That much is obvious, but that also narrows it down to practically anyone in the school. So why text me and not someone else?

Don't act like you don't know what happens around here.

The notebook flashes through my mind with its precise letters and lined pages. Goose bumps rise on my arms. The book. Whoever's texting me must have seen me with it. I flipped through it in homeroom and in the parking lot, so anyone could have seen.

But it wasn't just anyone. It was someone who knew what was inside that book. Someone who'd read it. Maybe even the person who wrote it.

I pull out my phone, finally knowing my response.

> This is about the notebook, isn't it?

There's a long pause after that. Good. About time I'm not the only one caught off guard.

> Maybe. Does it even really matter?

Bingo. Now I know who it is. Sort of.

> Your sick little diary can't help Stella. Or anyone else.

> Maybe not, but we can. Send me a name. Help me make someone pay.

The words send a chill up my spine. I don't know if it's temptation or alarm I'm feeling. Either way, I'm pretty sure this conversation is a bad idea, so I pocket my phone and thunder up the stairs to my locker.

I stop in my tracks when I see Tate and Nick standing in front of Stella's picture. My stomach seizes, threatening to dump the meager breakfast I ate. Their backs are to me, so I duck into the alcove of a classroom door, careful to keep my sneakers from squeaking. I press myself into the shadows with my heart hammering behind my ribs.

Tate is standing closer to Stella's locker. Even from here, I can see his shoulders bunched tight under his dress shirt. He looks like he's going to punch the locker. Or maybe Nick.

He's mad about her dying? Last week he seemed like he'd be happy to kill her himself.

Nick keeps watching him, his hair swept away from his eyes in a slightly more organized version of his normal mess. He finally claps a hand on Tate's shoulder, one that's shrugged off hard and fast with a look that probably roughly translates into "Eat shit and die."

"Don't," Tate says. And then he turns to walk toward me.

Yeah, I'm busted. I slide away from the alcove, so I won't look like I'm hiding. When Tate gets close, my whole body tenses. I force myself to look at him. Maybe it'll remind him that I was *there* when he attacked her in this hallway, that I heard every awful word.

I lift my chin and he hesitates for a beat. I want to do something—anything, really. But I don't. I watch him walk past while everything he said that day burns me from the inside out.

Tate takes the tension with him. After he's gone, I deflate against the wall. So much for my tough-girl attitude. Nick scuffs a foot against the floor and I startle at the sound. I make my way to my locker, even though I don't really care about the stupid flash drive anymore.

I open my locker and grab what I need, cringing at the groan of the metal door. Everything feels so loud, but Nick completely ignores me—his gaze is fixed on Stella's image.

Maybe I should say something. We can't just stand here pretending to not notice each other. Can we?

He's obviously not in a talking mood either. But I don't want to leave. I feel…not finished or something. I keep staring at my locker door, my hands going slick with sweat at the idea of an it's-so-sad-about-Stella conversation with Nick Patterson.

"You seen Tate?" Jackson's voice booms from the back of the hallway, making me jump.

"He took off," Nick says. He sounds tired.

"He's still freaking out?" Jackson's laugh makes me think of dark, slithery things. I don't want to be in the same zip code as this guy, but when I turn to leave, he's directly in my path.

Nick exhales loudly. "Everybody's shook up, man."

"I'm not." Jackson shrugs. "Don't look at me like that. Losing it won't change things."

They're talking like I'm not even here. I'm like wallpaper to guys like this. Invisible. But I'm not okay with that today. If they want to chat about Stella, they can talk to me too. I lean against my locker and glare at Jackson, but he barely spares me a glance.

"I'm not trying to be a dick, but she wasn't some first-rate citizen." He turns to me. "She's not a good girl like you, Piper."

Pretty words delivered on a razor-blade voice.

"Wow," I say, arching my brow.

He throws his shoulders back and his eyes turn flinty. "You got a problem, picture girl?"

Nick steps closer to me. "Leave her alone, Jackson."

Yeah, hell no. I shoulder past him. "I don't need a rescue, thanks."

"You heard her," Jackson says. "She's a big girl. She can handle the truth."

I swallow my irritation—and maybe a little fear too. Jackson stands there, his neck corded and tight like rope. Then, he flashes a chilly grin and turns back to Nick.

"Look, I went to the girl's memorial thing. I laid a flower down and lit a damn candle and all. But now I'm moving on."

Moving on? He started this whole thing! Unbelievable. This tool obviously doesn't feel a morsel of regret about that day. And what did I expect? Contrition? Tears? Jackson Pierce is not the kind of guy who's going to learn his lesson.

I shoulder my way between them. Nick touches me as I pass, long, calloused fingers curling gently around my wrist.

"Piper," he says.

I spin to him and open my mouth to say something snarly, but he looks every bit as torn up as I feel. And he's staring *so* hard, like there are things he wants to say. But I can't hear those things or have him looking at me. I don't want him to see everything I'm feeling.

This is easier with my camera, when there's a lens between me and the rest of the world.

"I have to go," I say, but he doesn't release me, and I can't stop staring at his eyes.

Jackson makes a low whistle. "Hey, not judging or whatever, but if Marlow sees this, she's going to go apeshit."

It's like being thrown in a pool in October. Nick drops my arm and turns to Jackson, and I start walking, my blood roaring in my ears.

"You need to learn to shut your mouth." Nick's voice is low and dangerous.

"Don't get your panties twisted," Jackson says. "You want to play the field, I'm all for it."

I move fast, trying to get out of this hallway and away from both of them. My heart is banging hard, like I've been sprinting. I stop past the corner to get myself together, to breathe.

"What is your problem, man?" Nick asks, clearly assuming I'm long gone. "This isn't about a piece of tail. She was obviously upset!"

"*My* problem?" Jackson snorts. "Look at you, Nicky! One stupid slut offs herself and now you're concerned for the entire female gender!"

I hold my breath because somehow, even after everything, I'm shocked. My feet move. I don't know how, but they take me to the nearest bathroom. The far sink is dripping and the glass blocks behind the mirrors are filtering milky winter sunlight into the room. I lean against one of the walls, and the mirror above the sink reveals a reflection I can barely stand to look at.

How am I going to handle children starving in Ghana or drug violence in Mexico if I can't handle a seventeen-year-old jerk in my high school hallway? The girl I'm supposed to be is stronger than this. *That* girl would have stood her ground, maybe said something. She sure the hell wouldn't be hiding in the bathroom.

I lift my chin and dare myself with a single look. Because if I want to see the truth in this world, I can't be a girl who hides.

Send me a name. Help me make someone pay.

I slide my phone out of my back pocket and type the letters slowly.

Jackson Pierce.

There is one moment when I hesitate, my thumb hovering over the Send button. I could still keep my head down. I could delete this text and forget about what Jackson said.

I press Send.

CHAPTER SIX

· ·

Dead leaves crunch under my feet as I gaze up at the oak trees behind our football field. I don't need to check my phone to know I'm late. The bursts of trumpet and the smell of cotton candy tell me it's getting close to game time.

I don't even care. I've spent the last two days jumping every time my phone rings, staring at the notebook night after night, picking up my phone to call Manny, and putting it right back down.

There haven't been any more texts. Part of me thinks it's over, that whoever was behind the creepy *Avenge Stella* texts thought better of it. This should be the end of it. It really should.

Except I can't stop wondering who it was.

I tried reverse searches on the phone number, but that got me nowhere. The phone is probably a throwaway. Since I'm pretty sure you can buy those at every freaking store in the Midwest, that's as dead as an end can get.

Which leaves me with the book. I've gone over those texts, and I'd bet money it's the same person behind both. He knows I have it—I can't think of any other reason I'd be involved. But other than the weird handwriting, there isn't anything special to see in it.

Well, there is the Latin title, but there are two separate Latin classes, and from what Hadley says, the first year doesn't move past what you can figure out on Google translator. Of the people she mentioned in her group, no one stands out. Hadley might be able to offer a couple of suspects, but I'd have to tell her about the book. And I'm not going to do that.

It would probably give her nightmares. And, worse, she might figure out the stuff about Manny. I don't want her thinking badly of him if it isn't even true.

Which you could find out if you'd ask him.

I wince, because I really can't keep ignoring this conversation. Then again, he's barely even answering texts right now, and this is definitely something I want to ask in person.

But not right now. Right now the only thing I'm going to let myself think about is this light. It's a rare thing in November, a sunset that turns everything the color of honey. Light like this doesn't wait, so I can't either.

I adjust my neck strap and lift my camera. The sun is dipping low in the sky, lingering just above the roof of the school. My phone buzzes, and I'm sure it's Tacey reminding me of the time and asking where the hell I am. I don't answer. Right now, with my camera, I feel like I'm finally peeling off blinders. This is how I see the world best.

I take a few shots before shifting to a wide angle lens. The band starts its first warm-up on the field. There's still time. I focus on the line of trees behind the stadium. I snap a few shots of the leaves overhead before focusing in on the trunk. There are hundreds of initials on these trees, scars carved into the bark with pocketknives and ballpoint pens—hearts and plus signs and declarations of forever.

Not that it means much. My parents' names are on this tree and they sure don't look like forever anymore. Still, it's kind of beautiful.

"Aren't you supposed to be getting the band?"

I turn and take a few shots of Tacey. She's one of the most photogenic people I know. She always argues with me on that, but that's just because she's too damn obsessed with the size of her jeans and the circumference of her waist to notice that the light always hits her face like it's meant to be there.

She holds her ever-present phone in front of her face and then lowers it down an inch, revealing narrowed eyes. "I'm serious, Piper!"

"I know you're serious. You don't have any other gear."

"Would you stop being artsy and come on?"

I sigh but follow her, pulling on my fingerless gloves that won't do near enough to fight the chill I can feel the sunset bringing. Can't take pictures with my fingers covered though.

"We need to get some good ones of the new uniforms, so don't be afraid to get close."

I smirk. "Am I ever?"

She hums agreeably. "Oh, I checked your basketball shots. They were awesome."

"Yes, nothing says 'fine art' like shots of armpits and blurry nets."

"It's the yearbook. They like that kind of crap. Next year you'll be in some artsy college and you can take all the depressing pictures your heart desires. Now, tell me the truth. Do these jeans look looser? I've lost four pounds."

"You look great with or without those four pounds."

I follow her down the asphalt leading to the stadium entrance. The concession stand is buzzing, people lined up for hot chocolate and popcorn and the cotton candy they spin right there. I give it a longing look and Tacey shakes her head.

"No chance, Woods. We need to get the band. Make sure you get the hats—"

I stop then, forcing her to turn to look at me. "I was hoping to avoid the hats."

"Well, don't. The school board spent serious money on those hats."

"They have feathers, Tacey. *Feathers.*"

"It's just business, okay? The PTO wants a feature page on the new uniforms, and they donate a hefty chunk of cash toward yearbook production—"

"So we sell our souls to make them happy?"

Tacey sighs, tugging at her ponytail. "Look, I know it's not your dream job. I know it's not super artistic."

I feel a pang of guilt. It isn't my dream job, but it *is* hers. She lives for this kind of stuff.

"It's fine," I say. "Seriously. I'll get the hats. I'll even do half time. It'll be velvet and feathers everywhere."

She looks back to her phone, a long curl sliding over her shoulder. "Perfect. Now, I need to go find Manny. He's avoiding my texts."

I wave her off and slip into the quiet space beneath the bleachers. There's a hallway here that leads to the locker rooms and equipment storage. It'll be swarming with players and cheerleaders soon, but right now, it's mostly empty. So I take advantage, snapping a few more pictures, of the brick wall and a football player talking on the phone, equipment only half on.

My phone chirps with a message. I juggle the phone into my free hand and pull it up.

> Jackson goes down Tuesday morning. Bring camera and be early.

My fingers turn to ice, but the message remains, as bright and sure as the promise in those words.

"Taking pictures of equipment closets?"

I jump and my phone drops. It's caught before it hits the ground.

"Rescuing your stuff might be my superpower," Nick says.

I should smile, but I can't. Because the text message is still glowing on the screen, right where Nick can see it.

• • •

His smile falters, and I'm sure it's partly thanks to the stress that's tightening my face like a vise. I command myself to grin, but it's a feeble attempt. Mostly I'm trying to stare some sort of subliminal message into him. *Do not look at my phone. Do. Not. Look.*

"Uh, here," he says, offering the phone without incident.

Too freaking close.

I reach for it, my hand slapping over the screen. My fingers brush his palm as I take the phone. I notice the feel of it—the feel of him—way more than I should. Nick clears his throat and looks every inch as awkward as I'm feeling.

"So, what were you taking pictures of?"

"Huh?"

He points his thumb toward the wall of the stadium, shifting on his feet. "I saw you out there earlier. You were taking pictures of trees or…something."

I push myself through the fog, back into the real world, where I know how to form words. Whole sentences, even. "Sorry." I scratch my head. "Yeah, I was just playing around."

"You going to study photography in college?"

"Yeah. You?"

"Computer science, probably. Did you do any college tours this summer?"

I open my mouth to answer and then snap it shut.

What the hell is this? Why is Nick Patterson—standing here in his tight football pants and his Under Armour shirt—talking *college plans* with me? And while we're at it, why am I still out here? Because hanging behind the bleachers to chat up a football player isn't me.

"You don't like talking to me very much, do you?" He's looking me right in the eye, shoulders relaxed and voice even.

I, on the other hand, feel like a rabbit dodging an oncoming lawnmower.

"No. Yes. I—" I cut myself off, feeling my cheeks flush as I look up at him. "Why would you think that?"

I expect him to shrug or blow it off. Change the subject. It's the guy thing to do, right?

"For starters, you glare at me a lot."

So much for dropping it.

"I don't…" But yeah I do. I'm glaring right now. I bite my lip and force the laser beams out of my eyes with a chuckle. "That's not intentional, I swear."

"I'm guessing there's still a reason, though?"

I shrug. "I guess I don't get this."

"Don't get what?" he asks.

"Why you're suddenly so helpful and interested and *chatty*."

"Is it a problem?" he asks.

"Since you probably couldn't have pointed me out in a lineup until this week, it's a little weird."

"I wouldn't bet on that if I were you," he says, and there's a teasing gleam in his eye.

I shake my head, thrown off by his comments and his dimples. "Okay, fine. So what gives? What's the point here?"

"I didn't realize there needed to be a point."

He smiles and every single part of me notices. Not just the smile—all of him: the line of his shoulders, the size of his hands, the clean, soapy smell coming off of him. Nick steps a little closer, his cleats scraping against the cement. I take one sharp breath. And then another.

He's flirting with me.

Wait—*he's not single.*

He is a not-single football player dating a girl who has delighted in my misery for years. More importantly, he's friends with Jackson Pierce and Tate Donovan. He stood in that hallway and let them rip Stella to pieces.

Oh my God, is that why he's talking to me? To protect them?

I feel the blood drain out of my face as I meet his eyes. "Is this because of Stella?"

"I'm sorry?" he asks, looking lost.

"Stella," I say, and her name feels like a hot coal in my mouth. "That morning in the hallway. You were there when Jackson and Tate—you saw me there. You started talking to me after that."

He frowns. "I started talking to you when I found your wallet in the grass. I had no idea that day would…"

"What, did you think she'd just bounce right back?"

"I don't know what I thought. The whole thing was news to me. They hadn't even told me about the tape."

"But they're your friends. Your *good* friends, right?"

The kind of friends you'd protect.

I don't say the last part, but he must see it because he shakes his head.

"That day has nothing to do with why I'm here. Look, I know that was a mess. It was a mess before that day, before the tape even existed."

"Well, then I guess it's perfectly okay for them to terrorize Stella the day before she happened to walk into a train."

He blanches. It's like watching a cloud pass over the sun. "None of us dreamed—no one's okay with it. You have to know that."

I'm fired up now, moving closer with my fists clenched. "The only thing I know is that you're standing here dangerously close to defending them!"

Nick's eyes move past my shoulder. I turn to glance behind me, where a group of tenth graders is watching with interest. They notice us looking and keep moving, but I don't miss their snickers or the tightness in Nick's jaw.

I nod and look down at my feet, my ratty slouched boots across from his muddy cleats. The space between our toes feels like a canyon. We're on different sides of the world. Always have been. Probably always will be.

"I wish I could change that day," he says. "Maybe you do too. But we can't."

Yeah, maybe not. But come Tuesday morning, something's going to change. And I can't wait to be there to see it.

"Nick?"

We both turn at the new voice coming from the direction of the locker rooms. Marlow is standing in the hallway, and she isn't alone. Jackson is with her.

Nick's eyes linger on me longer than they should before he walks away.

"Hey," he says to Marlow. "Sorry, I got caught up."

She reaches for his hand when he approaches, and I watch their fingers intertwine. I watch it with way too much interest, because there isn't anything to see here. Not really.

She murmurs something quietly, too soft for me to hear. Something that makes me think of too many whispering moments just like this, pretty, lined eyes watching me—picking me apart piece by piece.

Nick shakes his head and enters the locker room. And Marlow heads to her regular seat in the stands like a good little girlfriend-bot. Jackson stays, watching me with coal-black eyes.

I lift my chin and refuse to budge my gaze until he ducks into the locker room. My heart is pounding like a drum long after he's gone.

A hand brushes my arm. I jerk so hard my teeth snap together.

"Whoa, jumpy!" Manny says. "What's wrong with you?"

I still can't unclench my hands as I nod in the direction they went. "Jackson Pierce."

Manny scoffs. "Douche. Did he say something to you?"

"No. Forget it. I'm just pissy."

"So, business as usual?"

It makes me laugh, so I sling an arm through his. "You're lucky you're funny."

"Seriously, are you all right?"

I wave it off. "Fine. Really."

"Because I will pound him if you ask. Probably even if you drop a good hint."

Manny couldn't pound Jackson's big toe, but I love him for being willing. I look him over—familiar brown eyes and a freck-led nose that crinkles up when he laughs. He's my best friend. No more excuses. I've got to talk to him about that notebook—hear his side of all this.

He deserves that from me.

"What are you doing tomorrow night?" I ask.

"Saturday? Mooching food at your place, if your mom's cooking."

"Good," I say. "I have something I need your opinion on."

CHAPTER SEVEN

· ·

Manny flips through the pages carefully, his face unreadable. I pace grooves into my carpet and wring my hands until he finally rolls his eyes at me. "Sit down before you hurt yourself."

"So?"

"So what? This is a hot mess you've got cooked up here, Pi."

"It's not mine. I told you—I found it."

"Then unfind it," he says, tapping at one of the pictures. "Because that is some Grade A scary shit right there."

"I totally agree."

"And what's with this handwriting? No one writes like this."

"Someone obviously does. I'm thinking of volunteering in the office, so I can file tests or something."

He shakes his head. "Won't help. I work in the office. Everything's electronic and the grade stuff is on pretty tight lockdown."

I chew my bottom lip, feeling the questions bubble to the surface. "What about the attendance office?" My voice is much softer than usual. "Did you get in there?"

He hesitates, his eyes narrowing. My cheeks go hot, and I flip to the section of the book that led me down this path. He reads the first entry—the one about us—and then I show him the next. He doesn't deny a thing. Instead he sits down in my office chair, arms crossed over his chest.

"Is that why you didn't throw this thing away?" he asks.

There are a million reasons for that, but I nod and he scratches the back of his neck.

Then he just sits there, picking at a rip in the fabric of my desk chair. He's looking at his knees or the floor or something that definitely isn't me.

I sigh. "Would you say something?"

"What do you want me to say? 'Don't worry'?"

"No, I want you tell me that it's not true. Or that it is true. I want you to tell me why I'm reading about this in some whacko's diary instead of hearing it from you."

"Well, it's not like I knew a whacko was keeping tabs on me."

"Manny, I'm serious."

"So am I."

I throw my hands up in the hair. "Would you answer me already? Are you messing with student records?"

He rubs a hand over his head and presses his lips together. And then, finally, he spills. "Yeah. A couple of times. It's done now."

I sink onto my bed. "It's done? How did it even start?"

"I was working in the attendance office. Scanning permission slips and cleaning viruses off of computers for them. It was easy." Manny shrugs.

"It could get you expelled! What were you thinking?"

He shakes his head and jabs a finger at the book. "You're one to talk, since you're sitting around with stolen property."

"Not even *close* to the same."

"So, that means we're back to the Inquisition, huh? Ever since I told you I'm not going to college—"

"Wait a minute, what? I thought you were putting it off. Now you're not going?" He doesn't answer so I huff. "Seriously, Manny? *This* is your new plan? Petty crime for hire?"

"It's real easy for you with your tuition check just waiting to be signed, but not all of us have your options! Sometimes there aren't any good choices, okay?"

"There's always a good choice," I say.

Manny just laughs at that, standing up and pushing his chair against my desk. He grabs his coat from my bed and heads for my bedroom door.

"Wait, don't go. I'm sorry. I just worry because I care."

"Well, don't," he says. "Believe it or not, I'll survive even if I have to, *God forbid*, follow in my dad's skilled trade footsteps."

I bolt to my feet. "Don't act like that. You know I love your dad. He works harder than anyone I know. But why is it so wrong for me to want more for you? I know you, Manny—you're not going to be happy in a job like that. And I'm not talking Ivy League, here. I'm talking community college, so you can do what you want. *Go* where you want!"

"You don't get it, do you? It wouldn't matter if it was thousand-dollar-a-year college. We. Don't. Have. The. Money. There is no college fund. No savings. Most months there isn't enough to make ends meet. But you wouldn't understand anything about that, Pi."

I drop my head, tears welling in my eyes. "I'm sorry."

But he doesn't hear me. He's already gone.

• • •

Tuesday morning—and whatever's going down with Jackson—comes too fast. Still, the coffee I grabbed on the way into school was maybe not my best idea. I haven't been sleeping well after the Manny debacle, but now I'm a jittery mess. God knows how I'm going to get a decent shot of whatever the heck is about to happen.

I almost bump into Harrison in the hall. He looks at the camera around my neck and the coffee in my hand and then finally at my face. We exchange something that passes for pleasantries, and I wonder again about that glow I saw under the desk.

"Morning, suckers!"

Two words and my stomach clenches like a fist. I whirl to see Jackson walk in, high-fiving one of his fellow A-listers without breaking conversation with Nick.

I pitch my coffee and lift my camera but kind of stop halfway because I don't know what I'm supposed to be getting here. Nothing's happening.

My chest tightens and people stroll past. I click my shutter for show, collecting random pictures of the trophy case and the drinking fountain, or someone's nostril. Who knows? All I really see is Jackson and Nick walking right on by.

Maybe I read the text wrong. Maybe he lost his nerve?

Or maybe it's all a big fat joke, and you're sitting right at the center of it. Again.

Freshman year flashes back, the year Marlow and Kristen tried to *make up* with me for all the shoving and middle school teasing. Kristen invited Tacey and me to a party at her apartment clubhouse—said it was high school now, time to mature and let bygones be bygones, but we still knew the score. This was a popular-kid party. They were inviting us over that invisible line.

When we got there, we heard them laughing about some poor girls they'd invited, losers by the sound of it. Tacey had lifted her chin, feeling proud to not be the butt of the joke, for once. And then they'd said *chubby girl.*

She figured it out before I did. I didn't get it until they mentioned her *hippie friend.* My fingers fluttered down the braid in my hair and then over my hand-beaded bracelets. Two words and just like that, I was eight years old again, pushed knees-first into cement steps.

Tacey cried the whole way home. And I bit my tongue until I tasted blood, silently swearing to never so much as look at their kind again.

In the here and now, Jackson and Nick hit the corner of the hallway. Nick looks back then, his green eyes begging me to break every vow I made that day. He's one of them. But it's hard not to like him just a little when he smiles.

The faint echo of the train whistle outside jerks my attention away from the boys and my memories, dredging up the image of Stella's face. Good. I need to remember her. I'm doing this for her. Because I wish so badly I'd done it when she was still here.

Too bad it doesn't look like it's going to happen. As far as I can see, nothing's going down with Jackson Pierce.

I drift away from the stairs, adjusting the strap of my camera bag on my shoulder with a sigh.

Stupid. I should have known better than this, but I didn't. I dragged myself out of bed so I could be here, ready to…I don't know, *make things right* or whatever. As if I could ever make any of this right. I plod toward my locker, pausing when I hear laughter from one of the classrooms.

Bits and pieces of a conversation trail filter into the hall.

"Oh my God, he didn't!"

"He did—I was there. I think Alex cried after that mess."

"Geez, really?"

I don't know the voices, but they sound pretty excited. I should be curious—everyone else obviously is. I force myself to peek into the classroom, but there's not much happening. A crowd is huddled at the front of the room, focused on the television that projects special programs or our weekly school newscast.

Something's playing, but I can't see what it is, really. Terrible quality, maybe cell phone video. I'm too far away to tell. The group closes in tighter, blocking the screen, and I head down the hallway. I just want to get to my locker.

The next room I pass is still dark, but I can see the blue flicker of the television. Which isn't that weird since our school televisions can be programmed to power on together. Maybe a newscast was launched at the wrong time. There are even more people in the classrooms at the end of the hall. In a math room on the right, people are laughing.

Wait a minute. Is this about Jackson? It isn't what I was expecting, but then a particularly loud burst of laughter draws me to the math room. I spot Connor inside. As riveted as he is to the screen, I'm starting to think this might be it. I step inside, spotting more familiar faces. Aimee Johnston, Isaac Cooper, Nick Patterson, and—*bingo*. Jackson Pierce.

Connor catches my eye and points to my camera before giving me a thumbs-up. He mouths "Lucky" to me, like this was all just random chance. If only he knew.

"This is genius," Isaac says, shaking his head at the TV. He looks over at Jackson, who's scrambling, searching the tables.

"Where's the damn remote, Cooper?" Jackson's laugh is weird. Like a bark. Or a cough.

There are probably fifteen kids circled around the screen, everyone huddled in tight except for me and, now, Jackson, who's walked away from the rest of them. He's standing against the back wall of the room, arms crossed tightly and something that isn't even similar to a smile stretched on his lips.

Whatever this is, it's about *him*.

I check the TV. Not a newscast—way too grainy. Like a home video or surveillance tape. Yeah, it's security footage from our high school—the gym, some of the classrooms, even the cafeteria. We all know about the cameras installed last year, but I don't think any of us thought they kept the tapes.

The first scene shows Jackson sashaying, limp-wristed, past Tim Corning, one of our soccer stars who announced that he was gay this past spring. The next scene is in the cafeteria, high-lighting Jackson again. He's gesturing wildly at his crotch behind Marlow's back.

"God, you're such a pig," Marlow says from somewhere in that tight crowd. She sounds way too pleased about it.

Jackson answers with a flirty smirk, and Marlow's lips curl in a way that makes me think of a cat with a dish of cream. It also makes me wonder why Nick, who's looking right at her, doesn't seem bothered in the least.

But then the screen changes again, and Jackson's slamming his fist into a locker, looking like a pissed-off bull on speed, though there's not another soul in the hallway. A sprinkle of awkward laughter filters through the group, with a softly muttered, "Nice temper tantrum."

The scenes flash one after the next. The whole thing is an unbelievably well-edited mash-up tape of Jackson Pierce being an absolute jerk. This is nothing like what I expected.

It's so much better.

Feeling a surge of vengeance for Stella, I raise my camera, slink-ing into the farthest corner of the room. My breath goes still in my lungs. I adjust the lens and begin.

My shutter snaps over and over, capturing images quickly. Jackson's red face, tendons straining in his neck; the television screen, the kids laughing, and then the same kids pointing when the scene changes again. Isaac juggling the remote to keep it out of Jackson's reach. I capture image after image, but all I see is Stella.

Mrs. Durmond walks in and demands the controller before she really even looks at the screen. Everyone gasps, I'm guessing because of Mrs. Durmond. I'm wrong. They're still looking at the screen, but it's obvious no one likes this joke. I drop my camera to see why. In this scene, Jackson's imitating Chelsea Timber's awkward, shuffling gait down the hallway.

Apparently, even Marlow and her ilk have a no-fly zone. And a girl who struggles to walk because of cerebral palsy is on the wrong side of the line. Especially Chelsea, who has harbored a well-known crush on Jackson since junior high.

Girls look at Jackson with revulsion, and Nick looks at him with obvious disgust. Even Mrs. Durmond stops her search for the remote to gaze at Jackson with her hand at her throat. I get that photo just right, the press of her fingers against her pearls, her eyes wide with horror.

Every second of this scene feels like it's stretching on forever. Until Jackson snaps, flying through the crowd and leaping at the TV. He slaps the control panel. Plastic cracks and the crowd jumps. Connor narrows his eyes and edges in front of Hadley. I hadn't even noticed her before.

"Mr. Pierce!" Mrs. Durmond's voice filters through the sudden quiet. "Let's take a walk to the office. Now."

And just like that, it's over.

I feel the warm rush of triumph through my limbs. I didn't miss it. I could have, but I didn't. Best of all, I don't think anyone's seen me except Connor. Everyone is too busy looking at Jackson as Mrs. Durmond walks him to the door with brisk steps and a hard frown on her face.

Once they disappear into the hallway, I back toward the door, ready to make my escape. My smug grin fades when I realize I was wrong about not being seen.

Because Nick is looking right at me.

• • •

I slip from the classroom and move fast, half-convinced Nick will follow me. He doesn't. Or at least, he doesn't come sprinting wildly down the hall and up the stairs after me, which is about what it would take to catch me.

I stop on the second landing, camera pressed to my chest to secure it. No one will be up here yet, so I lean against the wall and grin at the stained-glass window. Even here, surrounded by dark wood and long shadows, I feel light and bright, like a balloon about to take flight.

A message comes into my phone, a startling buzz against my leg that makes me smile.

It's him. Or her. I don't really know, I guess, and I don't care. This total stranger is officially my freaking hero. I read the message waiting for me.

How's that for justice?

I laugh out loud, but when I move to text back, my hands still shake, fumbling over every letter.

> Tastes pretty sweet.

> Get good pictures?

I scroll through them on my camera, admiring every shot. There's one of Jackson's face, his white teeth obviously clenched between his lips. Yeah, they're good. Really good.

I let my camera drop down on the strap around my neck.

> Yes, I've got them.

> Good. Now you can make your own little book. Or add to the original if you like.

My laugh isn't so quick this time. I don't really like this part, this undeniable reminder that while he's a stranger to me, he knows *exactly* who I am. But I guess if I have his book, we're both even in a way.

Another text arrives, jarring me.

> So, what's next?

I bite my lip and look around, though of course no one's here. I sink to one of the cold steps and tap out a reply.

> For Jackson? Hasn't he suffered enough?

> Unlikely. But how about someone else?

Worry nags at the back of my mind. I could be caught. Another text comes in, one that seems to read my mind.

> Come on, Piper. This is bigger than Jackson. We could change things. Make it better.

Could we? Could we stop people like this? Adrenaline flares through me at the idea. But fear is close on its heels. This could be trouble for me. Big trouble.

I pull my legs back in, my ears perking to a new group of students heading down the main hall. It's getting closer to first bell. I should probably get something to eat, brush up on my Spanish for the test this week or something. I haven't even slapped on any makeup today. I think about a lot of random things like that—a lot of perfectly legitimate reasons to ignore the text on my screen.

Another message arrives.

> Guess I was wrong about you.

I peck back quickly.

> I need time to think.

This time, I don't wait for a reply. I power off my phone, telling myself that the battery is low. Which is true. *Ish*. Except that I have my charger in my camera bag and I've got technology lab later and could charge it there.

Ten minutes later, I've got my books for the day under my arm and a half-eaten granola bar in hand. I'm waiting at our usual breakfast table when Tacey arrives, pink-cheeked and looking scandalized.

She slides in beside me with an enormous coffee and a folder with an extra credit history paper under her arm. I'm convinced she never sleeps. "Hey, early riser. Did you hear about Jackson Pierce?"

Before I can answer, Manny arrives from the other doors, walking a wide arc around the empty chair beside me to sit by Tacey. All's definitely not forgiven. "You guys talking about Jackson?"

Tacey sags. "You heard?"

"Jackson's benched," he says.

Tacey practically slams her cup down but speaks in an exaggerated whisper. "No. Way."

Manny nods, stretching his arms overhead like it's all old news to him. "Yep. Coach Carr was in the office with the principal. They talked for all of five minutes before Coach said under no circumstances would Jackson set foot on the field this year if he has anything to say about it."

"I don't get it," I say. "I thought football was over."

"Baseball, baby." Manny says it to Tacey, even though I'm the one who asked. "Pierce is ridiculous on the pitcher's mound. They were talking college scouts, scholarships. And he can kiss it all good-bye."

I never considered him as a scholarship contender. I don't know much about the Pierce family, but since he drives a fifteen-year-old pickup truck, I doubt they're loaded. Am I really okay with maybe taking away his shot at college?

A voice reminds me that I *should* be fine. It sounds a whole lot like Stella DuBois. And I'm pretty sure I agree with it.

"That's…huge," Tacey says with wide eyes.

"Things like this should happen every day," Manny says, looking dreamy. "It's like Christmas. There's Connor. I'm going to fill him in."

I don't call after him to tell him that Connor was there. Come to think of it, I didn't tell him I was there either. Not that he would have listened if I did. I'm clearly persona non grata right now.

Manny meets Connor in the middle of the cafeteria. They share a fist bump, and even from here I can see how animated Connor is. People all around are buzzing, and why shouldn't they be? Jackson Pierce, reigning king of the upper echelon, just got smacked down a *whole* lot of notches. After how many years of us all putting up with his crap? Too many.

Yeah, this needed to happen.

I pull out my phone and navigate to the message I closed earlier. Because maybe Manny's right. Claireville High could stand a little more justice. And since no one else seems to be offering, maybe I am the girl for the job.

Because Jackson's not the only one who turned Stella's world upside down that morning.

I send a text with Tate's name and have to bite my lip to keep from smiling. That's when I see him. Standing in the doorway with his arms crossed and his backpack at his feet.

Nick again. And he's staring right at me for the second time this morning.

Whatever this is, I'm ready to deal with it. Nick's eyes are flashing in a way that tells me he knows *things*, so I should be freaking out. I don't know why I feel so calm. I don't know why I get up at all, crossing the cafeteria with long strides.

CHAPTER EIGHT

. . . .

I'm pretty sure Marlow will lose her mind if she finds me in close proximity to her boyfriend again, but I'm over that. I don't stop until we're maybe four feet apart.

"Nick Patterson," I say, inclining my head.

He smiles. "Piper Woods."

He smells like laundry detergent, and his thumbs are hooked in the pockets of his jeans. We stand there for a minute, until I feel too stupid just gazing at him with an amused expression carefully settled on my face.

I clear my throat. "So, are you doing a little recreational stalking here?" Okay, too much. I really need to filter. Or maybe muzzle altogether.

"Stalking? Wow." The corner of his mouth curls up and my insides flutter. Okay. Weird. But it's a weird morning, so I'm not going to dwell.

I laugh a little awkwardly. "Sorry. But did you want to say something?"

"Not sure I should. I mean, we're not friends. Right?" He looks awfully friendly for someone who isn't.

I grin back. Can't help it. I point at our table, where everyone's watching with interest. "See my table? It's situated somewhere between Art Land and Mathlete County."

He tips his head, his chin jerking toward his own table. "So, let me guess, I live in Jock World? We're not friendly neighbors?"

"It's a long-standing boundaries dispute."

"Our own little Gaza Strip?"

"Exactly." I really wish I could stop smiling.

Wait a minute, is this flirting? Again? Because his smile matches mine, and I'm way, way too aware of how green his eyes are. Crap, it *really* looks like flirting.

I stumble back a step, feeling the smile slide off my face. I need to regroup. This isn't normal. Not for me. Boys with girlfriends do not float my boat. They don't even hoist the sail, so I've got no idea why I'm suddenly playing eye-footsie with this one.

"Nick?"

Marlow. Ah, nothing like the shriek of a harpy girlfriend to bring me back to my senses.

My shoulders tense, but Nick doesn't move.

"You should go handle that, right?" I ask him.

"What do you mean?" His voice hasn't just chilled. It's positively arctic.

"Well, isn't that your *girlfriend*?" I say, though I don't mean to put so much emphasis on "girlfriend."

He blows out a breath, looking frazzled. "Hell if I know."

He doesn't look at me again, just shoulders past me on his way to Marlow. The fight that follows isn't exactly loud, but I'm tuned in like a specialized satellite dish. I know I need to be as far away from this as possible, but I just keep standing there, my hands curled into fists and my breath coming too fast while Nick tries to move Marlow somewhere more discreet.

Too bad she's bent on a scene.

"Is this what it's going to be?" she asks.

Nick's voice is low and unmistakably angry. "You really want to do this in the cafeteria?"

"Well, you seem to think it's the place to hook up with another girl. And, *really*, Nick? Piper Woods?"

I can feel the heat climbing fast up my neck and cheeks.

"*You* wanted to break up," he says, as softly as he can. "Again. Which I think makes this episode four."

"Well, I changed my mind."

"Yeah, well, I didn't. And believe it or not, I do have a say in this."

"You know what, Nick? You don't have a say in anything. Because we're done."

Marlow flies past me, trailing perfume and righteous indignation in her wake. Nick looses a disbelieving laugh before heading to the opposite door. And me? I just stand there while my heart makes every effort to pound its way out of my chest.

Tacey walks up, and I force myself to unclench my jaw. She touches my arm, and I look up, finding her eyes wide.

"Did I just hear Marlow break up with Nick?"

"I'm not sure. Sounded mutual," I say, cheeks hot and palms slick as I tug out my phone, checking the time. "We should go. It's getting late."

Her hand on my arm stops me. "Piper, she said your name. Do you have something to do with this? With that?"

The words slip out of me unbidden but absolutely true.

"I think I might."

. . .

Tate's too obvious. We can't make this all about Stella.

The response to my text comes in when I'm flipping through the mail on my dining room table. I abandon the latest issue of *Popular Photography* to read it again.

How is this *not* about Stella? Why should Tate get away with everything he said if Jackson doesn't? Just because he doesn't make my skin crawl quite the same way doesn't make him any less guilty.

I finally reply.

I thought we were doing this for Stella.

What happened to Stella is done. We need to focus on the future. On who we can still save.

It's scary. Tate was as obvious as Jackson, but finding someone else? I feel an uncomfortable weight settle in my middle.

Still, maybe he's right. Maybe stopping this kind of crap before it turns tragic is the whole point.

I sigh, staring down at the phone. Knowing that I'll never be able to live with myself if I ignore the opportunity.

> I need time to find someone.

> By 7 Friday. I need time to work up a plan.

I toss my phone facedown on the kitchen table with a sigh. Mom takes a seat across from me, a big mug of tea in her hands.

"Tacey driving you crazy?" she guesses.

"No, it's nothing," I say, pushing my hair behind my ears and smiling. "How was Idaho?"

"Good. No paperwork issues," she says. Mom's an adoption liaison. She's told me more than once that the movies have it all wrong. The only real drama in adoptions is missing signatures and transposed numbers. She nods at me. "I got you something."

She heads to her briefcase and sorts through what seems like a thousand papers tucked in beside her laptop. She pulls out a slim, familiarly shaped rectangle and I scoot to the edge of my chair, my fingers practically itching for it.

It's silly. I know it's only a postcard. But it's our thing. She always looks for a special print, one that will appeal to me.

"Well, are you going to look at it?" she asks.

"Of course I am." I flip it over.

It's an ancient barn, half-collapsed and wood gone gray, but it's nestled in this impossibly green valley with a cloudless, cobalt sky stretching overhead. I love the visual of stark decay in this lush setting.

"It's genius," I tell her, smiling. "Perfect."

"You've taken better," she says, as she always does. And when she looks at me, the set of her chin tells me she absolutely believes it.

We share a smile, and then my dad comes in from the garage. The studio. The cave where he spends his time when she's home.

"One of these days, she's going to bring you a real souvenir," he says.

The words might as well be a pinch on the arm. He knows better. But when I give him a look that tells him as much, he winks at both of us. "Settle down, ladies. I'm teasing."

Mom's face drops, but she keeps her voice friendly. "I thought we could do Chinese."

"Ah, I'm sorry, I can't. I've got a meeting."

"A meeting?"

Dad runs a hand over his hair. "Yeah. With the university."

She brightens and asks something about whether or not he'll be teaching again, and he says something that doesn't really confirm or deny it, and I pick at my nails and wish I could transport myself to pretty much anywhere else on earth. Mom's tensing up across from me, and I can hear my dad's hands squeak on the back of my chair, he's gripping it that tight. I feel the irony of my placement, wedged into the distance between them.

The doorbell rings and I bounce to my feet, thrilled to have a reason to go. "I'll get it."

Tacey's standing outside, wearing a ridiculous pink-and-black tracksuit that no one who doesn't live on the Hollywood A-list could get away with. She stretches up on the balls of her equally hideous and obviously new sneakers. "Want to go for a run?"

My brows arch so high I think they brush my hairline. "Not unless there's an ax murderer standing behind me."

She stops the stretching and frowns. "You know, you could stand a few more healthy choices in your life too. I'm at six pounds and counting."

"I'll listen when this starts being about health and stops being about your dress size," I say. "You're gorgeous. And women everywhere would kill for your rack."

"Yes, but they want it on top of your legs," she says.

"With Marlow Crane's face." I smirk and then glance back at my house. Like I'd want to wade back into that cold war.

"All right, I'll come with you—"

"Yes!"

"—but we *walk*. And I'm bringing my camera."

"Fine. Then we're talking about homecoming layouts."

"I can handle that."

Tacey checks her curly ponytail with her hand. "Good. Go, quick, before I freeze out here."

I zip back inside to tell my parents and grab my camera. We're not even at the end of the block before Tacey gives up on me having any useful input on yearbook business. After some silence, she heaves a weighted sigh.

"All right, I give. I get that you want to go to Darfur and take pictures of people dying in gutters, but what do you have against homecoming? Every time I bring it up, you zone out."

"I don't have anything against it. I just don't have anything for it either."

"Which makes no sense. You do remember that you went to prom last year, right? You wore a dress. It wasn't the worst time of your life."

"Yes, Crazy, I went with you. And mashed my fingers in Manny's car door." It was the climax of a pretty dull night, and the only part I remember with any clarity. "But it's not homecoming, I swear. I'm…distracted."

She nods. "I think you need a date."

"I don't need a date."

"Going out can be fun. When's the last time you had a date?"

I shrug. "I went out a few times this summer."

"Eric doesn't count."

A mental picture of him flashes through my head—dark hair, slender fingers, and a low, soft voice like an old song. I shake my head, irritated on his behalf. "Eric totally counts."

"He only lives here in the summer when he's spending time with his dad," Tacey says. "I'm talking about someone with potential. Someone like…Nick Patterson."

She keeps right on marching, her arms pumping as if she doesn't know I'm staring daggers into the back of her head.

"Yes, that's a swell idea. I'll go on a date. With Nick. Maybe I can pick up some pom-poms and we can talk about his wide receivers."

"First, don't try to talk football. It's tragic. Second, don't act like the cafeteria situation didn't happen. Plus, he's been watching you for at least a month. There's something there."

"Tacey, have you even met me? He is a football player. A *football player*."

"So? He's a seriously hot football player, and what do you have against athletes anyway?"

I walk faster, until I have to hold my camera against my chest so it doesn't bounce. "You of all people should know what. Forget that. Let's talk about you for a minute." I stop suddenly, pointing at her ridiculous outfit again. "What's going on with this getup?"

She stumbles over her feet, a flush creeping up her neck. It's not like Tacey to be quiet. Not ever.

"Tacey." I say her name like a teacher calling her out for texting in class.

Her shoulders bunch around her neck, and then she blows out a huge sigh. "Fine, I was at the mall. Kristen was there with Candace and a couple of other girls."

I frown. The stripes on that tracksuit, the fit—it's all wrong for Tacey. And Kristen would damn well know it. "The same Kristen who baited us to that party?"

"It was three years ago, Piper! How long are you going to hold a grudge?"

"I'm not holding a grudge. I'm choosing to learn from my mistakes!"

"Well, I don't want to live in the past. They were nice to me, okay?" She says it like that because she knows I'm probably not going to believe her. And she's right. I don't. That tracksuit is a fashion assault and Tacey's the victim. It isn't the first time I've seen Kristen do this, but how do I say that to her?

Tacey feels bad enough about her body. How many pictures have I shown her where her cheekbones and wide smile just pop, and yet she'd point at her chin or arms with a groan?

Tacey takes a breath. "She said it looked perfect. She even told me about this fashion club she's going to start in school, 'Putting Your Best Foot Forward' or something like that."

"Are you even listening to yourself? Tace, I love you, but this is Kristen. You're not only believing her, but you're also taking her advice to buy what I'm guessing was a two-hundred-dollar matchy-matchy outfit? I thought you said your parents were bro—"

"I paid for it with *my* money!" she says, eyes hot.

I bite my lip, because I shouldn't have gone there and I know it. "That was crappy. I'm sorry. It's just—you're better than that, Tace. Than them."

"But I'm not better than them if I care how I look? If I want to feel good about myself?"

"Of course I want you to feel good about yourself! But it's Kristen. She's mean and she steals almost everything she wears."

"I know how Kristen is. I know what she does and I'm not cool with it." She stops, adjusting her ponytail. "But I don't have your unshakable confidence. It's just…when she's nice, or even pretending to be nice, I feel like it's my chance to prove it to her."

"To prove what?"

"That I'm not the pathetic little nobody she thinks I am."

My heart sinks and then burns. Why does someone like Kristen Green get to determine who counts and who doesn't? How does that even happen?

I step closer to Tacey. "I'm sorry. I shouldn't have said that about your parents."

"I'm familiar with your brand of tactlessness." She winks after she says it though, and then takes a right on a street beside the railroad tracks.

My eyes are drawn to the rise of grass and gravel, one slender gray-brown line of track showing through where the trees are thin. Tacey's new sneakers slap rhythmically at the asphalt. It makes me think of Stella's steps that night, what they might have been like.

Would she have raced forward or dragged her feet? Would I have heard the tinny strains of music coming from her headphones as she passed?

I look over at Tacey, her hands brushing unconsciously over her middle even now. With me.

I bump her lightly with my shoulder. "For what it's worth, I think you have a great sense of style. And I still say the camera loves you."

Tacey smiles. She opens her mouth to say something, but then we hear a train whistle.

The sound cuts through me, winding my insides until I feel tight and breathless. Tacey shivers, looking over at the tracks. I don't have to ask to know she's thinking about Stella too.

We both kind of stumble to a halt, staring at the approaching train. When that whistle wails again, I ache down to the center of my bones.

Don't think about her climbing that gravel hill, her long hair whipping all around. Don't think about the scream of the train brakes, desperately trying to stop.

I slide my phone out of my pocket and pull up my text messages. I don't know why I'm doing this now. Maybe I just need a distraction from the steady, rumbling approach of the engine. Or maybe I think it's a sign, some way of Stella telling me this is the one I should choose.

My fingers are surprisingly steady as I make my next choice.

> Kristen Green—Shoplifter/Egomaniac/Mean Girl

I send it as the train rolls by, shaking the tracks and vibrating the ground around me. The wind is cold enough to hurt. I put my face right into it and watch the cars fly past, making my eyes water. The whistle—so loud it rattles my teeth and hurts my ears—leaves wispy images of a red-haired girl as it fades away.

I hear you, Stella. I hear you and I'm trying to make it better.

• • •

"Well, I'll be a monkey's uncle."

I grin even before I'm inside the school office. I know Manny's dad's voice as well as either of my parents'. It's the voice of the guy who has served me burned grilled cheese sandwiches and those little plastic tubs of juice that he always made me swear not to tell my *earthy mama* about. His phrasing, not mine.

"Hey, Mr. Raines," I say.

He looks at me from behind a row of security monitors in a cubby beside the secretary's desk. "Pied Piper," he says, reaching over the short cubicle wall to ruffle my hair. "Been to Botswana yet?"

I brush my hair back into place. "The parents insist I graduate first. Annoying."

"Parents," he says, with an eye roll and a wink. Being a single dad means the Raines house isn't big on coasters and homework charts. Still, Mr. Raines runs a pretty tight ship.

He's exactly what Manny will look like in twenty-five years—wiry and freckled, with blond hair gone ashy.

"I thought the last bell rang," he says.

"Yeah, I was just dropping off a homeroom folder for Mr. Stiers."

Mr. Raines nods absently, stretching to run a cable from the unit under the monitors to a laptop he's carrying. I leave the folder and wince when I see him hobble out from beneath the desk, looking pained. He's had a bad back for years.

"Can I do anything for you?" I ask.

"Nah," he says, "unless you want to trade backs. So, what gives with this? Is video-mockery the new, big thing?"

Oh my God. He's here because of the Jackson tape. Because of me.

"Hard to tell." The smile stuck into Mr. Potato Head is more genuine than the one I flash him. I shouldn't be surprised. Of course he's here. He installed the cameras, didn't he? So, if the cameras get breached, who else did I think was going to get called in to beef up the security?

That's right, I *didn't* think. I just wanted Jackson taken down, fallout be damned.

"Well, I better get going," I say, my mouth feeling like I've swallowed a fistful of sand. "I've got loads of studying to catch up on."

And now I'm lying to the man. My ticket to hell should arrive any moment.

"Get my kid to study a little, will ya?" he asks.

"I'll do my best."

I slip away, feeling like something that should be scraped off a shoe. And then, of course, I run straight into Manny.

"Hey!" Too bright. I clear my throat. "Did you see your dad?"

"I tried not to," he says, and then smirks. Relief floods my senses. Okay, we're speaking again. It's something.

"He's hard to miss," I say lamely.

"I brought him a coffee. Speaking of the old man, you won't believe this crap. They aren't even paying for this."

"How? I thought he got bonus pay for this kind of thing?"

Manny clenches his jaw. "They're claiming it's part of the contractual obligation for maintenance. I'm claiming bullshit."

I nod and cross my arms, feeling my palms go sticky with sweat. "Hey, listen, about the other night—"

"Can we just…not?"

95

"Yeah, we can." I bite my lip, looking for something else to talk about. "So, do you still want me to come over to help edit those football shots?"

Manny's shoulders tense. "Can't. I'm swamped. But I left my memory card in the technology lab safe. In case you want to paw through my shots. Maybe they'll help."

"Okay." I sound like I'm about to cry. I feel like I'm about to cry.

Manny plunges his hands into his pockets and offers a crooked grin. "I swear I'm not mad. I'm over it."

"You don't seem over it. You won't even let me say I'm sorry."

A text message comes into my phone and I reach for it. Manny takes the opportunity to walk backward. "How about you make it up to me? Friday? Dry Dock?"

"Deal."

I wave at Manny and pull up the message.

> Kristen it is. I'll be in touch.

I still wish it were Tate. I'm doing this for Stella, and it doesn't feel finished with Jackson. When Tate pays—that's when it will be done.

Will it?

I don't like the question and I hate the answer. That's the problem with this place. What happened to Stella, that stupid freshman party, the crap Jackson pulls—it never ends around here. Because no one bothers *to* end it.

Until now.

Jackson suffered plenty last week. And if my little texting partner comes up with something creative for Kristen, she might finally get a taste of what she's been dishing out. At the very least, people will see her for what she really is for a change.

I round the corner to the lab and push the subject out of my head. The lab sits in the newest part of the building, a small, modular block of rooms added to the back of the old school to accommodate intervention studies and specialty classes. The halls here are bright and sterile, but I've always hated the boxed-in feel, all low ceilings and dull, practical carpeting.

Still, it's quiet. Most of the classrooms are dark now, doors shut until tomorrow.

I pass by the art room and slow down. I can see someone hunched over one of the tables in the soft light filtering through the windows. He isn't moving a muscle or making a sound. And I know who it is. Not just from the stretch of his shoulders or the way his hair flips up a little around his ears, but also from the way my whole body seems to thrum with this weird energy—energy that seems to be very specific to *his* presence.

I put my hand on the door frame and force myself to speak. "Nick?"

CHAPTER NINE

· ·

He spins on the seat of his art stool, and I swallow hard. I'm alone in the semi-dark with Nick Patterson. Not how I imagined my Monday afternoon.

"What are you doing in here?" I ask, because I don't exactly see him as the secretly-expressing-my-inner-Monet type.

"Avoiding." He shrugs. "I like this room, the way it smells."

Like wet clay and mineral spirits? *Okay.*

My face must reflect my thoughts because he twitches his head toward a wall of easels. "My mom used to teach art. She still does weekends at the community college."

"Oh."

He nods, looking distant. Almost spacey. "Marlow and I have been on and off since summer. I thought you should know."

"Oh."

Titillating replies, Woods. Maybe you could try two entire syllables next time.

It's still better than anything that resembles the half-choked terror or weird thrill I'm feeling. Not that it matters to me. The state of Nick and Marlow shouldn't even be on my pertinent-information radar.

He's still sitting there blankly, like he just mentioned the weather outside and not the end of his relationship.

I clear my throat and force myself to step into the room. It feels like leaping a gorge. "Uh, are you okay with it? The breakup?"

"This is the fourth time, so I've adjusted," he says. He smiles and comes to life, dimples curving his cheeks. "Honestly, we knew it was inevitable for months. Could have done without the drama though."

I should say something. "Well, you've both got a good…support network. I'm sure things will settle down." Wow. How very Hallmark of me.

I gesture vaguely at him when he doesn't say anything. "I mean, you both have lots of friends, right?" Ugh, I really suck at this and just need to stop.

Nick rolls his shoulders. "Yeah, that doesn't always make it easy."

My goodwill vanishes. "Right," I say. "The *trials* of popularity."

I see a flicker of irritation cross his features, but he pushes away from the table and stands up, obviously trying to stay unruffled. "Maybe we should talk about something else."

"Like what?"

He moves slowly toward me, and I swear the temperature jumps ten degrees with every step he takes. "Like the pictures you took of Jackson last week."

My whole body—heart and lungs and just everything—stops. There's this hollow silence in the room, and I want to fill it up. Finally, a tinny laugh dribbles out of me.

"I…" Yeah, I've got nothing. Absolutely nothing.

Nick moves around the last row separating us. He leans back

on the table across from me, and I notice our feet again. Boots for me—tall ones today. Nikes for him. Of course.

Nick looks utterly relaxed, completely at ease while I stand here twitching.

"Somehow I don't think you took those for the yearbook," he says.

"Well, it'd be a more honest look at senior year, wouldn't it? A moment that illuminates reality."

"Illuminates?" He smiles. "Jackson might pick a different word."

I cross my arms. "I'll bet he would."

"Can I see them?"

"*Why*, so you can try to get me to delete them?"

His smile vanishes. I swallow hard as he stands up straight, and man, he is *towering* over me. I force myself to look up at him and ignore the fluttery, breathless feeling in my chest. I've got no clue why this guy's eyes work voodoo on my lungs, but they do.

"Do you really think I'd do that?" His voice is almost a whisper.

"I don't know what you'd do," I say, just as softly, but I don't tell him what I do know. Like how far his people will go to stick together. And what they've already done to me.

"Then maybe you should ask instead of assuming."

"Okay, fine. Would you?"

He just shakes his head and walks past me. I slump hard, trying to steal the strength from the wall. Nick stops at the door, the false light from the hallway casting yellow-green highlights over his face.

"You ever hear the saying, 'Don't judge a book by its cover'?"

I scoff. "Of course."

"Same principle applies to football jerseys, Piper."

• • •

In my entire life, I've never been this early to an assembly, but according to the text, this is where Kristen's going down. I've always pulled the yearbook-team card for these. I snap some pictures in the hallway, and hope to slip away before the doors close. It's easy to go unnoticed, especially if you're holding a camera and generally viewed as a non-problem student. For the record, we still assemble, but we do it in the technology lab, usually after Manny sneaks out to bring us coffee.

Speaking of Manny…

He strolls up, looking at me like I've just grown a second head. I'm probably the first senior to get in line for assembly in the history of the school.

"Hey!" I say. Still too chirpy.

"Hey back," he says, looking at the door. "What are you doing?"

"I figured I'd head in a little early," I say.

"Why are you heading in at all? I'm grabbing coffee. Want to come?"

I chew the inside of my lip. I do want to go with him. More than anything, I want to criticize his driving and dredge up some old jokes. I want to fix this weirdness that's been lingering since the college mess—and the notebook.

"I can't," I say. "I'm sorry."

"I know. You're not a slacker like me."

My stomach twists. Hurts. "I didn't say that, Manny."

He puts up his hands defensively. "I know, I know. Don't start. I shouldn't have said it."

But he did, so I'm taking the opportunity. "I was worried about you. I'm still worried, but I'll keep my mouth shut."

He smiles at me. "You really needed a little sister to look after or something."

"I'm not trying to mother hen you. I just believe in you."

"Well, that's mistake one." He kicks my shoe and chuckles. "I'm not planning a life of crime. It was a one-time thing, and I had my reasons. We all do shit we're not proud of when we're pushed hard enough."

The auditorium doors click open and he bumps my arm with knuckles. "That's my cue. Friday, then?"

"Definitely."

Manny waves as Coach Carr ushers me inside with the freshmen. He's headed for caffeine and sunshine, and I'm being herded into the seating area like cattle.

Everyone immediately climbs toward the preferred seats, high in the back of the auditorium. Those are the places teachers don't pay much attention. I choose the center section, lower level. Not a popular address by any stretch, but closer is generally better when you need to take pictures. Question is, what the heck am I taking pictures of?

I take a seat in the sixth row from the stage, close enough to get whatever might happen, far enough back to go unnoticed. I hope.

Students continue to arrive from all the class levels. I change my lens and settings, knowing I'm going to have to pull this off without a flash. It won't be my best work. My palms are damp on the base of my camera, but I force myself to act natural, snapping shots of the students taking their seats and of Principal Goodard when he steps up to the podium.

He greets us with a Claireville High welcome and makes some comment that I assume relates to the football season, given the volume of the cheers that erupt. My heart begins to pound as I watch the stage, but Kristen's nowhere in sight.

A couple girls provide details on the winter formal, and I force my feet to stop jittering. One of the football coaches pitches an off-season development camp. The girl next to me asks me if I can stop tapping my fingers on the armrest.

Finally, someone gets up to talk about the gardening club, and my body goes absolutely still. Because I get it now. I know why it's happening here.

Tacey's words echo through my mind as the presenter flips through a slideshow presentation with butterfly gardens and ornate topiary mazes.

"She even told me about this fashion club she's going to start at school…"

Polite applause ripples through the crowd as the student sits down. A junior stands up next, Ethan Crawford. He's small and lean with a shock of blue and black hair and an irresistible grin. He starts talking about the skateboarding club, with big arm gestures and promises of unprecedented parties, which ticks Mr.

Goodard off plenty. I actually dare a picture of him—thin lipped and glaring—mostly to check the light.

It's all right. Not perfect, but stage shots are tricky.

"Thank you, Mr. Crawford," the principal says, cutting Ethan off. He points to the side of the stage, and I scoot forward. Even before I see her, I somehow know she's next.

I raise the camera into position. And there she is, Kristen Green, dressed in a red skirt, black boots, and a sweater that looks expensive. She beams out at the crowd and picks up the remote for the projector. She waits for the slideshow to begin and I wait for…well, I'm assuming for all hell to break loose.

"Good morning, Claireville High," she says with a smile designed to sell things. She unhooks the microphone from the podium like she's on stage all the time. Giving speeches. Talking to contestants. Whatever.

She walks to the side of the podium, so that she's illuminated head to toe in the spotlight. Her smile turns a little flirty as she cocks her hip. "So, tell me, everybody…how do I look?"

Predictably, most of the boys in the audience—and a few girls that I'll assume are her friends—applaud. I ignore the smattering of lingering whistles, keeping myself absolutely still. Poised.

Kristen beams as she draws the microphone to her lips again. "I'm here to talk to you today about one of my many great passions—my commitment to personal style and presenting your best self."

And I'm here to talk about dry heaving.

A slideshow starts and I focus the lens, pulling in tight to the screen. But it's just a bunch of supermodels strutting down various runways. I pull back from the camera and frown, listening to her drone on about the importance of looking your *best* to feel your *best* and how one's commitment to fashion is the *best*... I tune her out, because I'd rather chew broken glass than listen to anyone who uses the word *best* this much.

She moves back behind the podium. She's got to be almost done and nothing's happened. What gives?

"In January, I'll be heading up a fashion club," she says. "It'll be the perfect opportunity to correct your fashion tragedies and step out with your best foot forward."

I feel my teeth grind at the *best*.

Kristen flips her hair and smiles wide. "Be sure to stop by. Trust me, some of you could *really* use the help."

She gets a few laughs, but she also gets a bunch of people looking down at their outfits, hoping they aren't the ones she's talking about.

"The Best Foot Forward Club starts January third," she says.

She flips the slide, and I can't really read the information because suddenly, things are raining down from the rafters. Rags. Or towels. Some kind of cloth. I don't think; I just shoot, snapping picture after picture. I pull back the camera to find one perfect shot, a pair of jeans sailing down toward Kristen's horrified face.

It's clothes. Clothes are falling all over. Goodard is shouting and teachers rush on stage. A banner unrolls overhead, stretching almost the width of the stage.

It reads: *Five-Finger Discount Club—Join Today!*

I stand up, taking as many pictures as I can. I get Kristen's wide, shocked eyes as she holds a red-inked pair of jeans that look to be her size. A baby blue T-shirt I remember seeing her wear last week catches on the podium and dangles.

Principal Goodard holds up a white sweater with the word *STOLEN* emblazoned across the front in red. All of the clothes are marked with that same red ink. Words like *SNAGGED, LIFTED, TAKEN* silently judge the fashion princess.

It's amazing. Better than amazing. People are pointing and whispering, and I have no idea how anyone pulled this off.

This couldn't be set up in advance. *Someone* is here running this.

The teachers are looking up at the catwalk, but I know better than that. Someone capable of that book—someone who looped Jackson's videos—isn't going to wait up there to get caught. Sure enough, at the far side of the stage, I see a dark figure climbing fast down the opposite ladder. All I can see is black. Every stitch of clothing on this guy is meant to conceal.

But it's *him*. That's my mystery partner. My heart catches, lodging itself into my throat as his feet hit the stage floor. I'm not the only one who sees it.

Goodard points. "Stop! Immediately!" Then he breaks into an awkward jog across the stage, dropping the shirt he's holding and slipping in his dress shoes. The laughter in the crowd swells into a roar, and I can see that whatever figure had been in those shadows is long gone.

Teachers begin filing down the aisles, dismissing us with firm instructions to return to our classrooms at once.

On stage, Kristen watches the crowd, her face sheet white. I see her raise the microphone in her hand and my throat feels even tighter. I don't want her to speak. I know she'll only make it worse, and this feels bad enough.

"I—I didn't steal these!" she says, sounding just like you'd expect a desperate liar to sound. "I didn't. I didn't do this!"

"Yeah, right you didn't!" someone shouts from behind me. I can't spot the guy who says it, but Kristen obviously does. Her face drops. She tries to argue but can't manage a word.

"Just own it," a girl in the left section says. "You got busted."

"Finally," someone else adds.

I force myself to take another picture of the principal returning to Kristen, obviously unsuccessful in catching anyone. He pries the microphone from Kristen's hand and wraps a comforting arm around her shoulders. They start heading off the stage, and Kristen trips on a shirt, almost going down. When she looks up, I snap one last shot of her red-rimmed eyes and glistening cheeks.

This one doesn't feel quite as good.

• • •

I volunteer to help with assembly cleanup after school. As much as I'd like to pretend this is only an act of kindness, some guilty twinge in my gut tells me I have other, more selfish reasons. My partner was here and I'm hoping he left something behind.

Before today, it barely felt like a real person, but there's something about that dark figure slipping down the stage ladder. The memory of it is crisp like a picture, but still tells me nothing.

I wasn't close enough to make a good guess on height, and it was too dark to see much else. Which is frustrating. I need to know something about this guy. I saw a police officer in the administration office today, and it turned my bones rubbery.

Breaking into school security tapes is one thing, but if the chatter in the hallways is right, this time, my partner broke into Kristen's house. It's just clothes—clothes she didn't even buy—but it still feels bigger now. Scarier.

Maybe it's time to take a step back.

But I walked away from Stella and she died. I can't do that again. Not ever.

Of course the book is another option. I could turn it in. But what would happen? I mean *really*? Unsettling as it is, it's nothing but code names and a whole lot of hearsay. If the school got their hands on it, we'd end up with a Very Special Assembly, where we talk about feelings and fairness and breaking down the boundaries between social and cultural groups. And we'd file straight out of that assembly and right into the same old routines.

Nothing would change. That book is not enough to fix anything.

But what happened today with Kristen?

Maybe it can.

I push the doors open to the auditorium. There's only one thing I'm sure of: I need to know who's texting me. I know what this is about for me, but not for them. And I need to understand that. That's what great photographers do. Good photographers look. Great ones *see*.

A medley of voices drifts down from the top of the steps. I stop short on the stairs, frowning at the girly chatter. I climb until three pairs of feet come into view. Freshmen, I think. All of them sporting pairs of nearly identical overpriced boots.

"Poor Kristen," Gray Boots says.

"I *know*." This from Taupe Boots.

"She was crying in the bathroom." Brown Boots is tapping her right foot.

"That's terrible! So what if she lifted stuff? Maybe she has that one disorder," Taupe says.

"Kleptomania?"

"Exactly!"

"I stole a pack of gum once from Walgreens."

"I bought study flashcards from Charlie Devin last week. That's kind of the same."

"No, it's not. Everybody does that. Tate Donovan pays that smart kid to write his history papers."

My spine stiffens. Tate's paying for papers? Huh. Wouldn't have guessed that.

Brown rises up on her toes. "Omigod, Tate is so beautiful. I'd pay *him* so I could write his papers."

"God, Cara, dream on. He's elite."

"Hey, I won't be fifteen forever."

"But he'll always be Tate Donovan."

Someone sighs. "I'm still jealous that Harrison gets to write his papers."

They laugh and I choke on air, the floor tilting sideways beneath me.

Harrison? Harrison is writing Tate's papers.

The text message flashes through my memory. *Tate's too obvious.* I didn't think about it, but I should have. If Jackson should pay, so should Tate. Unless someone had a reason to keep Tate safe.

Like a monetary reason.

Other facts shuffle through me, fast and terrible. The black pens Harrison loves. The look he gave me in the hall the morning I took Jackson down. It all fits.

It could be Harrison's book, Harrison who's texting me.

The door bangs open behind me. I jump, hand at my throat. "Nick?"

"You here to clean up too?"

His smile feels like a setup and my mouth is too dry for words, so I nod. And stare.

He's the last person I expected to find here. But the look in his eyes tells me he was *definitely* expecting me.

CHAPTER TEN

· ·

I follow him up the stairs. He *knows* something. Did he see me with the book in the parking lot? Or did he put it together after he saw me taking pictures of Jackson?

Okay, stop. He doesn't know anything. He doesn't even know there's something *to* know. Unlike me, he's probably just here to help. That's what good guys do, and Nick is obviously a good guy.

Boots Gray, Brown, and Taupe sure seem to think so at least.

The girls titter as he repeats their names. Nick's nodding his head while they wax on *ad nauseam* about their very detailed plan for clearing the rows of trash. Obviously an excuse to stare at him like he just stepped off a Hollister bag. And…well, *yeah*. But it's annoying.

"Well, if you ladies have it covered, we'll get to work on the mess up there," Nick says.

With the girls in agreement, Nick strolls back down the center aisle toward the front row. He plants a palm on the stage and swings his long legs up. I head for the stairs with sweat blooming between my shoulder blades.

I don't like this. He's picking up a random shirt, frowning at a pair of jeans with *LIFTED* written down one thigh. The disappointment in his face stings me, which is stupid. Kristen is neither a saint nor a victim; she's a criminal. Since she didn't end up in jail for stealing all the crap on this stage, she got off pretty easy.

I grab a sweater with *FILCHED* across the front. The handwriting isn't familiar. All block letters, different than the writing in the book but still decent penmanship. Could be the same person. And man…they really pulled off something today.

These clothes are definitely Kristen's. Even the stuff I haven't seen her wear looks like her style. I trace my fingers over a smooth cotton shirt, wishing away the questions in my head. Like, how did Harrison get these? Could he really do this?

But I don't know that it's Harrison. Not for sure. He's just one person who has a reason to steer me away from targeting Tate.

Nick would have a good reason too.

I spot him out of the corner of my eye. Why is he here? Is *he* involved? Is Tate?

That doesn't feel right. I can't imagine either of them doodling in a diary or hiding behind texts. Guys like that would probably opt for the take-them-outside-and-pummel-them flavor of vengeance. But then, could anyone see me doing any of this? Probably not.

I should at least feel him out.

"I'm a little surprised the police didn't take this stuff. It's evidence of a crime, right?" I glance around the stage for effect.

No flinching or sudden tension. If he's behind this, he's playing it cool, that's for sure.

"Kristen's too embarrassed to file a police report," he says.

I decide to try a different angle. "Well, maybe she's nervous because she stole most of these clothes to begin with."

I can't help saying it. This whole school has danced around the truth since she started palming extra fruit snacks in the lunch line in fourth grade. Kristen's a thief. No question.

Nick frowns. "Maybe."

Okay, he's not in on it. No freaking way. He doesn't even see the truth about Kristen. Probably doesn't see the truth about any of his friends.

I scoff. "I know Kristen's in your crowd—"

"What does that even mean? You talk about that a lot—our lunch table, our crowd. We don't have a membership list, you know."

"You don't need one," I say. "It's crystal clear who's with you and who's not."

I turn away, my neck and cheeks flaming. I don't want to talk about this with him. He doesn't feel like one of them anymore. Nick's never personally done a thing to me. Which makes me feel like a jerk. "I'm sorry. I missed my daily dose of manners this morning."

He doesn't quite smile, but I can see the promise of it in his eyes. "Are you always this hostile around fellow volunteers?"

That makes me laugh. "No, really not. Believe it or not, I thought about joining the Peace Corps."

Nick's smile could power small cities. I'm almost grateful when he turns away, heading for the rafters. I follow behind, trying to bite back my own grin.

"I'll go get the sign down," he says, pointing up at the catwalk that spans the stage.

"I could get it," I say, because I want to poke around up there. See if I can find any Harrison-shaped evidence. "I could probably finish this up if you want to go."

"You that eager to get rid of me?" he asks.

"No."

"Because you seem nervous."

I am. And it's not just because he's a tasty boy with a killer grin. Every time I see him, I think of Stella. And I'm pretty sure he does too.

I meet his eyes dead-on. "Yeah. Well, the timing of your sudden attention still seems…convenient."

"For such a talented photographer, you're good at missing the big picture."

No, I'm not. I know an interested boy when I see one, but why me? And more importantly—why *now*? It's too easy. He's suddenly hot for a girl about twelve rungs down the social ladder? I'd be crazy not to think there's reason he's here with me. But Tacey's right. I have to stop holding grudges.

I bring my hands to my burning cheeks and then drop them with a sigh. "I know I'm being weird. I'm sorry. This is hard for me to wrap my head around."

Nick reaches for my hand. "Come up with me to get the sign. Maybe we'll figure out a way to make it easier."

My stomach ties itself into a bow. I look down from his teasing smile to his long fingers. This is a terrible idea. Nick reaching for my hand is a joke, and I'm probably the punch line.

But I let him do it, because it's just a hand. It doesn't change anything. His fingers wrap around mine and my breath catches. Our eyes meet a beat too long.

I was wrong. *So* wrong. This changes everything.

• • •

I try not to fixate on the feel of his palm or the strength of his grip, but I can't help it. It's like my entire brain has been transported into my hand. I probably couldn't tell anyone how to make toast right now, but holding Nick's hand? I could write a book about that.

I huff, frustrated with myself. I'm not here to let Mr. Football lead me across the stage. So why am I still holding on?

We stop in the shadowy space behind the curtain. This isn't the second grade, and I am perfectly capable of scaling the ladder myself. I tug my hand free.

"Do you want to go up first?" he asks.

What's worse? Him staring at my butt all the way up or me looking at his? God, this is ridiculous. I am not this girl. *Please* don't let me be this girl.

I don't even bother to respond. I just start climbing. It's steeper than I would have guessed, but the platform at the top feels sturdy enough. I hold on to the railing all the same, looking out at the narrow metal catwalk that spans the length of the stage. I can see a box at the platform on the other side, the side closer to the podium.

"He must have kept everything close to the podium and then escaped down this side," I say. "The clothes fell over there."

"Gutsy," Nick says. He's still a few rungs down. Giving me enough space to breathe.

I glance at the box and think back to the way my partner slipped down the stairs. He planned this carefully. He knew exactly how to escape. Sounds like Harrison's style if he were going to do something like this. He probably has a to-do list for his morning shower.

I take a few steps onto the walkway, trying to repeat my partner's route in reverse. Nick follows behind me, the weight of his steps shuddering gently through the metal bridge. I dare a glance down and immediately wish I hadn't.

"Damn," he mutters softly.

I swallow hard. "Yeah."

"Okay, let's do this."

My fingers tighten involuntarily on the railing. I'm not exactly afraid of heights, but I'm not comfortable enough to go sashaying across this catwalk either. This feels like a tightrope. A metal tightrope with rails, but still.

"I can get it if you want," he says. "Do you want to just go back down?"

Yes.

"No. I'm already up here. It's fine."

And then there's nothing left to do but walk. I keep one hand on either rail and command my fingers to release their death grip enough to slide with each step. I inch along so slowly it's like pulling teeth. Ten steps out from the platform, the catwalk shudders. Just a little. Totally normal, I'm sure. Still, it takes everything in me to keep moving.

Metal groans and I freeze. A wave of vertigo rushes over me and I strangle the railing, eyes shut tight.

"Whoever was up here was little," Nick says.

I'm almost too breathless to reply. "What?"

"Somebody my size would have made noise. Especially if they had to move fast. It couldn't have been anyone big."

Harrison's small. It's not proof, but it's a whole lot of pieces pointing to the same puzzle. My mouth turns to sand. I'm pretty sure it's him. It still wouldn't hurt to get some proof, though. I focus on the box on the platform, willing some evidence to be in there.

"My offer still stands if you want to go back," Nick says.

I don't want to look like a complete wimp here. "It's not that far."

"No, it's not bad," he says, and damn him, he sounds like he means it. It's probably easy to mean it when you aren't in the lead.

"Then let's get moving. That way we can die together."

He chuckles and I feel the walkway shift with his even, heavy steps. Maybe I should have thought this through. Can two of us even be out here, or will it collapse?

Do not think collapse. Do. Not. Think. Collapse.

Every jostle makes me jump a little, but I force myself onward. Nick stays close behind me now, not commenting on my snaillike pace. Which tells me he's either supremely polite or he values his life, because I'm so tense, I might kill him if he tried to rush me.

Halfway across, he speaks again. "Should we talk about something?"

My jaw hurts and my palms are so clammy I'm probably leaving sweat tracks on the handrails. "As long as it doesn't involve fall-related injuries."

Another laugh. Soft and low. All boy. "No. I thought you might want to talk about why I'm always around."

Talking about that scares me more than falling. I speed up, not seeing the floor below anymore. All that matters is the distance between us. Because I don't trust this.

Soon enough, I step onto the platform, where I can see a box full of extra ropes and a plastic tub of what looks like feathers. Theater department stuff, not vigilante stuff. I search around. Nothing useful.

"Your silence speaks volumes." Nick's teasing tone doesn't hide his disappointment.

"I doubt my silence is saying what you think."

"Yeah?" He sounds hopeful.

I like Nick. Which is why this…isn't a good idea. I can't let him think anything even close to what he's thinking right now. Because as much as I like him, I can't imagine crossing that line. Holding hands with Nick. Sitting with other football fangirls watching the games.

I sigh and he taps his knuckles against the handrail of the catwalk. "Piper, you don't have to talk to me. If you're not into this, it's cool."

I laugh. "Nick, there isn't a *this*. We've barely ever talked and now you're suddenly, what? Interested in me?"

"Why do you think that's so crazy?"

"It's not." I don't know why my skin goes so tight and hot every time he talks about this. But he's not like other guys. There's no beating around the bush. No coy flirting. It's all out there in the open. "I can tell you're interested. But I can't help but think it's…situational."

"Big word. You mean the Stella thing."

"Yeah. I think maybe that started this. Maybe you think it connects us."

"It does connect us." He steps onto the platform then, disarming me with his closeness as much as his words. "We both think about that day. We both probably wish it had gone differently, that it hadn't happened at all."

He reaches down, messing with ropes at our feet while I stand there, unable to reply—equally unable to stop watching his shoulders bunch and flex as he works.

The *Five-Finger Discount Club* sign slips free and flutters down to the stage below. Nick is watching me again. There's nowhere to go to gain personal space. It's like standing in a broom closet with…well, with a football player.

Something in me snaps. I think it was the thing holding my words inside. "Yes, I wish I'd said something. I could have."

"Maybe you could have, but I *should* have." His voice is hard, catching me off guard, but he goes on, not waiting for a response. "You weren't even involved—you barely knew Stella. But I'm friends with everyone who was out there. I could have stopped it, but I didn't because I was staring at you."

The breath I take catches in my lungs, refusing to come out. I feel my cheeks go crimson. Breathe. I need to breathe.

Nick moves for the ladder, and I remember how my lungs work. I pull air in and push it out. In and out.

He stops, ready to descend but still so close. "Just so we're clear, Piper, I'm not suddenly interested. I've *been* interested. The only difference now is that you're noticing."

I force my hands into fists and Nick descends in silence. I let him go, because there is nothing to say. There's nowhere to go.

Next year, I'll be in college. Even if he weren't in a different social universe, this isn't the right time to start dating anyone. Before I know it, he'll be catching touchdowns at State, while I'm hundreds of miles away at NYU.

It's infallible logic. And it still doesn't keep my heart from pounding when Nick looks up at me one last time.

• • •

I need a name by 9. Don't forget.

Harrison's face flashes in my mind as I read the message Friday afternoon.

The message ticks me off. It would be just like Harrison to delve out hard deadlines like this is a group project and not a probably illegal vigilante scheme. So, now what? I could confront him. Tell him I know, and end this whole mess right now. There's a part of me that's sure this is the wise choice. But another part remembers Jackson and Kristen. For years, they got away with everything. They were untouchable and now they aren't.

It's the closest thing to justice our school has seen in years. So how the hell is ending it the right choice?

I sigh, tossing my phone on my dresser. It's going to have to wait for now. Manny made it crystal clear he'd throw a fit of epic proportions if I tried to punk out of the concert tonight.

I don't even know the band—some grunge-metal-meets-electronic indie group that's too obscure to find its way onto *my* iPod. Could be fun. And I just got things right with Manny. If I have any chance of talking him back into college, things have to stay good.

So I'm taking the time to deal with eyeliner. I'm also trading in my standard-issue jeans for a skirt that looks like it survived a war and a shirt that's snug enough to prove I made an effort. The girl in the mirror still looks like me. A hotter, slightly older version of me, but at least Manny can't accuse me of forgetting about our plans.

My phone rings and I pick it up, cringing at Manny's blaring music.

"Are you ready yet or what?" he asks.

"I did offer to drive myself."

"Yeah, but you said you'd love to talk. Which I assume means you'd love to try to remind me of all my potential or condemn me for my attendance record villainy?"

"Nope. No nagging. But I'd be lying if I said I was going to let it go forever. I still think you should consider—"

"Enough with the public service announcements. I'm in your driveway. Let's roll."

I scoff. "Have I told you how annoying you are?"

"Mission accomplished."

That gets me laughing. "Give me two minutes."

My mom is at the kitchen table when I walk in. I grab a water from the fridge and say hello. She's got the cell phone bill laid out in front of her and when she looks up, her eyes are red. Has she been crying?

"Hey," she says, frowning when she catches sight of my makeup and skirt. "Oh, wow. Remind me again I can trust you."

"Skirt notwithstanding, my dignity will remain intact," I say. "You okay? You look upset."

She folds the phone bill and puts on a plastic smile. "All good. Except that my daughter looks like she stole her look from *Cosmo*."

I shake my head. "Way too much black, not enough sequins. We're headed to Dry Dock."

"That place with the awful pizza?"

I shrug. "They bring in bands, so the food's allowed to suck. Be home by midnight?"

"Be safe," she says.

I lean in to kiss her cheek. Yeah, she's definitely been crying. I start to ask, but then Manny honks outside, reminding me this probably isn't the time.

We pay our ten dollars to a kid from my French class last year. The building is already packed. It's also very quickly reminding me why I stopped coming. At least half the people here are from my grade, proving we seriously need more crap to do in Claireville, Indiana.

The place is a dive. There's a stage on the back wall, a dance floor in front of it, and probably fifty tables arranged randomly around the room, all of which appear to be full. I also heard a bunch of voices from the patio when we came in, so God knows how many people are in here.

I check my phone. Forty minutes left before I need to text a name. I don't even know what that means. What's he going to do if I don't? If it's Harrison and I tell him I know, what will he do? Will he deny it?

"Are Connor and Hadley here?" I shout over the music being pumped out of overhead speakers.

Manny nods, looking around. "You order the pizza. I'll find them."

Naturally, the order window is at the back corner of the building, so I'll have to weave my way across the sticky floor and through clusters of shrieking, hair-sprayed girls. It's like a pep rally gone wrong.

I move through the crowd, turning sideways and dodging tables as I go. I try to take advantage of my high heels, but every path that seems to open up closes just before I arrive.

"Pardon me," I say to a girl who's gesturing with her cherry soda.

She turns and I realize who it is—Aimee Johnston.

"Piper!" She smiles widely. "How are you?"

"Not bad."

Candace grabs Aimee's arm and then pauses, looking at me. She's all frosty lips and thin brows, like always. Maybe it's that she looks so sickly next to Aimee's heart-shaped face and dark skin, but I'll never get what Manny sees in that girl.

Still, I know my manners. "Hey, Candace."

"Hey," she says before turning away.

Aimee drops her voice and narrows her eyes. "Rude. Sorry about that. She's been annoying me all night, but I promised the squad I'd take a study break."

"Midterms were awful. How'd you do?"

She brightens. "Good! You know, not good enough to take number one, but whatever."

It's not *whatever*. You'd have to be blind to miss the way her face goes tight when she says that. And who the hell can blame her? She's thrown everything but the kitchen sink into her work, and she's always landed in Harrison's shadow.

Aimee leans in, making sure her words are just for me. "Can you keep something quiet?"

Isn't that the million dollar question these days? "Yeah, sure."

"I heard a crazy rumor that Harrison might be cheating in chemistry, getting answers on his phone."

My heart falters, finds its beat again. The glow under his desk—I wasn't imagining it. "How? Did you see it?"

"No. Shay did. She sits up front by him. I saw him throw his phone in the bottom of his bag right when we walked into class, but Shay says he wasn't using his normal phone, that it was a different phone."

"A different phone?"

"Yeah, so the answers can't be traced to him."

And maybe so he can text somebody anonymously.

124

The blood's draining out of my face so fast, my skin is tingling. Like it's fallen asleep.

Harrison isn't just a cheater. He's selling papers; keeping a big, fat sin log; and orchestrating takedowns like he's some noble, by-the-people justice guy. And I'm going along with it.

It felt better when I didn't think about him being behind it, when I could believe it was someone…better.

"Hey, look, I shouldn't have said anything," Aimee says.

Crap. I can only imagine what my face looks like right now. Probably pretty bad, because she obviously thinks I'm disgusted with her.

"Aimee, no, we're cool." I reach for her arm, but my hand is cold and slick with sweat. So I let it drop. "It's just a complete shock."

For reasons you can't imagine.

"Well, it's never coming out, even if it's true. Shay tried to talk to Mrs. Branson."

"What did she say?" I ask.

"That it was a very serious accusation to bring against the most esteemed student in Claireville High."

"She didn't even listen to Shay?" It's one thing for us to ignore each other, but Mrs. Branson is a teacher.

Aimee shakes her head. "She offered, but Shay said she had a bad feeling that nothing would come of it, except Mrs. Branson hating her more than she already does. That kid is bulletproof."

"I guess," I say, the things I know about Harrison going bitter on the back of my tongue. "But we could all watch him. Turn him in to the principal if it happens again."

"Maybe. We don't even have another serious test for two months though." Candace tugs again and Aimee grins. "I've got to go."

"I'm really sorry."

"Don't stress, okay? Everything works out, yeah?"

No, it really doesn't. Harrison is getting away with everything—he's snowing *everyone*. Everyone except me.

My hand grazes the phone in my pocket. I know things Harrison doesn't want me to know. I just need to figure out how to use them without him turning the tables on me.

If I text him his own name as a target, maybe it'll turn up the heat. Make him squirm until he realizes he has two options: take himself down or confess he's the one texting me. It's a no-brainer—he'll fess up.

And then what?

Then I agree not to turn him in for the cheating—since I don't have evidence anyway—as long as he agrees to let Aimee take the academic lead.

"Are you joining the cheerleading squad?" Manny's voice jolts me out of my thinking. He's standing behind me, arms crossed and brow arched.

"I…no…Aimee just—"

"Yes, smart girl bonding, blah, blah, blah. You do realize you haven't ordered our pizza, right?"

"Oh my God, you had Cheetos in the car twenty minutes ago! I'm going already."

"Don't forget my soda!" he says.

He ventures over to Candace, who plays it coy, her smile tight when he approaches. But he's wearing her down. I grin when her shoulders turn toward him, her pale cheeks just a little bit pinker. Then I see Aimee and my chest goes tight.

She catches me looking, mouths something to me: "It's okay." Does it twice, so she's sure I see her.

I pull out my phone. It's not okay now, but it will be. I'm going to make sure of it.

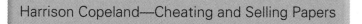

Harrison Copeland—Cheating and Selling Papers

CHAPTER ELEVEN

. . . .

Texting Harrison's name is different than Jackson or Kristen. It's not just about nailing him as a cheater. I'm not his lackey anymore. I know every bit as much as he does, so we're equal. And he knows it. When he doesn't respond, I grin and slide my phone back into my pocket, prepared to wait him out and enjoy my evening.

My luck holds when I find the food line, which is miraculously short for so close to showtime. I walk up to the ordering window, a ten-foot wide hole in the wall that opens into the kitchen. The metal counter is chest high and spattered with cornmeal from the bottom of the pizzas.

Menu options aren't great. Pizza, a sub—which is essentially a pizza on top of a bun—or some rubbery wings that I wouldn't eat if threatened at gunpoint.

I pull out a twenty and lean against the counter, waiting for someone to arrive. Someone who looks a lot like Nick rushes out of the kitchen, a baseball hat backward on his head. Before I can tell my throat to stop going tight, I realize he doesn't look like Nick.

He *is* Nick.

He comes up to the counter and stops short, watching me.

"I swear I'm not a stalker," I finally manage. *Way to put him right at ease, Woods.*

He half smiles, dimples flashing before he's back to business. "I only started this summer."

"Right," I say, and then I just stand there, taking in way too much of what's going on behind that counter. He looks so different—the Ramones T-shirt he's wearing and the thick line of a black tattoo I can see at the edge of his sleeve. "I didn't know you had a tattoo."

Tell me I did not just say that.

He just looks at me, his mouth a little open. Can I blame him? What's he going to say? The last time we talked, he told me he was interested in me, and I basically told him to kiss off. Now I'm making cutesy comments about his tattoo?

Someone nudges me from behind. "Hey, are you going to order or what?"

"Give her a minute." Nick's eyes flash dangerously.

The nudger snorts. "Or what?"

"Or I'll come out there and tell you again." Nick presses closer to the counter. "Now, what can I get you?" That megawatt grin comes out again, and my insides curl up and purr.

This has bad idea written all over it. I have to get out of here. Right now. "I'll have a large pepperoni and two Cokes, please."

"I'll bring it out to you," he says.

I barely mutter a thank you before I bolt, pushing my way through the crowd. I've got no destination in mind—only escape. I'm halfway back to the door when I hear someone call my name.

I follow Manny's wild waving over to the table, where Connor and Hadley are waiting, a couple of drinks between them.

"Hey," I say.

"How was the order window?" Manny asks with a wink.

"You knew he was there?"

"Oh, you like him and you know it," he says, waving it off. "You get me a drink?"

"Your arsenic should arrive shortly."

I check my phone. No message. It almost makes me grin more. For the first time since this mess started, I'm not the one second-guessing. I feel a rush of confidence and tap out another quick message.

> Did you get that message? The one about Harrison?

I press send and have to hide a snicker behind my hand. And then Connor checks his phone, his smile faltering as he opens the message. My stomach falls end over end.

The table laughs, so I join in, but I don't know what we're talking about. The only thing I know is that Connor checked his phone two seconds after I sent my message. He could have been checking my message.

Paranoid.

I'm completely paranoid, right?

But Connor does see everything in this school. People love and trust him, so no one censors. He's exactly the kind of person who could get every bit of the information in that book. But would he write it all down? Keep it in some diary gone bad?

I rub my suddenly cold arms and try to push the idea away. It's ridiculous. I *know* him.

Still, my mind drags up memories of Connor's persuasive argument on elitism last year in speech class. It was a great speech. He drew parallels between the social problems during the Civil Rights movement and the problems in modern-day high school. Afterward, we laughed about how many of the popular kids applauded, totally missing that the entire speech painted their crowd in a very ugly light.

Was that when this started? Was that speech the tip of some social justice plan?

Hadley's hand suddenly covers mine. "Piper? You look pale as a ghost. Are you sick?"

Sick doesn't touch what I'm feeling. I'm way past sick. Could I have been wrong about Harrison?

"I'm just a little hot." I strangle out the lie, forcing myself to breathe.

"Let me check you." Hadley pushes her hands against my forehead and cheeks. "God, you're ice cold."

My stomach rolls and I try to pull away, but she pats my hand. She needs to stop touching me. I can feel Connor's dark eyes on me, but he says nothing. His expression is a blank canvas.

Suddenly Hadley moves away and Manny shoves in. He smells like his dad's Old Spice deodorant for some reason and that feels better. Familiar. I breathe it in, tears welling in my eyes.

He grabs my chin in his hand and pulls my face toward him. "You sick?"

Connor's phone buzzes again and I see Hadley tilt her head toward him. Connor drops his voice to explain, but I can still hear him talking to her. "Jacob's giving Mom trouble. She's been texting me all night."

Jacob's his brother. Just got his license. Connor shows Hadley his phone and they share a wry grin at whatever text messages are firing back and forth. Which means…they aren't my messages. Connor isn't texting me. And I should have known that, because Connor's number is in my phone.

How could I be this stupid? Jumping to every possible conclusion.

Manny pokes my shoulder. "You sure you're up for this? I can run you home."

So I can dream up another ridiculous person behind these texts? It's Harrison. I know that. I know that, and I need to just settle down and wait. Because the ball's in his court now.

I shake my head. "I'm fine. Sorry. I just need to eat."

Manny nods. He's not buying it, but he won't push. Manny never pushes and he's always there, and I completely take that for granted sometimes.

"You're pretty awesome, you know," I say softly, into his sleeve.

"Uh, did the cheerleaders slip something into your soda?"

"No, I just didn't want you to think…you know, with the nagging and everything."

He laughs. "Is that why you're worked up?"

It's not, but I shrug anyway.

"We're all right," he says, giving me a sideways hug. "It's going to be a good night. Candace gave me her number. You've got a footballer getting gooey with y—"

"Manny, I swear to God, if you don't drop that—"

The band takes the stage, effectively cutting me off. Manny thumps my arm and the whole building goes crazy. People cluster tightly on the dance floor in front of the stage while the band does sound checks.

"I'm heading out there," Manny says. "Who's coming?"

"I'll go!" Hadley says, getting up. "I think I see Tacey. Connor?"

"I'll be there in a minute," he says.

"Pi?"

I shake my head at Manny.

"She should wait for the pizza," Hadley says. "Connor, make her eat some food, will ya?"

"Technically, I'm not sure we can classify anything in here as food."

Everyone laughs and Manny jabs a finger in my direction as Hadley tugs him toward the floor. "Half a slice and I want your butt on this floor, Pi. No arguments."

He's giving me crap, but it's good. It's normal. Right now, I'm aching for ordinary.

As they head to the floor, I check my phone, discovering a text message. Apparently, somewhere in the midst of my paranoid delusions about Connor, I missed it.

Got it.

That's it? Got it? What does that even mean? It doesn't confirm or deny or tell me anything. It leaves me right back where I started—holding more questions than answers.

● ● ●

A guy who *isn't* Nick delivers our pizza and drinks, apologizing for the wait. I'm still reeling from the whole Connor situation, and now I'm pissy about Nick not showing up personally. Which is…ridiculous. I've spent pretty much every interaction with him trying to push him away. Now I'm mad that he's not chasing?

I try a slice of pizza. The plastic cheese and a thin layer of tomato paste do nothing to improve my mood, so I drop it on a wad of napkins—do they even have plates here?—and scowl at everything in my general vicinity.

Manny grabs my arm when the band takes the stage for the next set. "C'mon, Clown. Time to turn that frown upside down."

Leave it to Manny to make me laugh when I least want to. I try to shake my head, but then Tacey and Hadley are dragging at my arms. And frankly, I can't sit at that table one more minute. So I go.

I'm not much of a dancer, and I'm even less of a screamer. But for once I follow them right to the front of the stage, hoping the unrelenting press of noise and bodies will override my racing mind.

The band isn't bad. Maybe not something I'd listen to every day, but there's a dark, rhythmic thread that ties the racing guitars and frantic vocals together. It's good—loud and hard and just the thing to make me forget.

Eventually, I feel a little smothered out here, where the air reeks of sweat and hormones. I edge over to the side near the speakers, where every beat shakes me. I don't just hear the music—I feel it. So I close my eyes and let myself go.

A hand brushes my arm and I whirl around, finding Nick behind me. His apron is gone, but otherwise he looks the same. His hat is still twisted backward and there's a flour stain on Joey Ramone's head.

"Hey," he says.

Or I think he says it. I really can't hear crap, but when his lips move, it looks like it could be "Hey." He says something else and I can't make it out at all. I shake my head, pointing to my ears, and he leans in with a smile. I feel his hand at my hip for a moment and I'm aware. Way too aware.

"They're good, right?" His words are against my neck.

I shiver—though it has to be ninety degrees on this dance floor—and nod, because I don't trust myself to speak. He couldn't hear me if I did anyway. But Nick leans in again, and the entire room seems to shrink down to the pinpoint feel of his fingers against the side of my skirt.

My hands clench instinctively, grabbing on to something for leverage. I realize it's Nick's arm when he starts talking again.

"It's loud," he says. "Do you want to go outside?"

Go outside? Like to the patio? I picture it in my mind—me and Nick in that weird half-lit porch where smokers and couples

135

congregate. The place was designed for horny teenagers looking for somewhere to make out and… I nod at him.

Because I've totally lost my mind.

Nick brings me back with a smile, reaching for my hand and pulling me through the crowd. We twist and weave across the dance floor, and I don't care if Manny's looking for me or if Hadley saw Nick come up to me. I just know that our fingers are interlaced and we're holding on tighter than we need to, like if we squeeze hard enough maybe it will explain what in the world is going on between us.

There are two sets of doors leading out to the patio, and we're heading for the ones farthest from the pick-up window. He pushes them open and we step outside, letting them close behind us. My ears ring in the sudden quiet, phantom bass beats tainting the sounds around me.

It's a little darker out here, but I smell the promise of snow and the sting of smoke. Through the steam of my own breath, I spot a couple making out on a picnic table. I look away, grateful for the darkness that hides my red cheeks.

Nick suddenly seems a little sheepish. "Huh. This may have been better in theory than practice."

He heads to the right, and that's when I realize we are still holding hands. I jerk mine free and try to recapture some semblance of my sanity. This is ridiculous. What am I doing out here with him? Standing on the stage catwalk, I laid out a very convincing list of the many reasons I can't be wandering into dark spaces with Nick Patterson. Reasons like social circles and futures that are, literally, a thousand miles apart.

"So, what's up?" I toe the sidewalk underneath me and pretend I can't hear the girl moaning on the table four feet away. "I mean, did you want to talk about something?"

"Well, I hadn't planned an agenda," he says, shoving his hands into his jeans pockets.

"Well, I guess we can chitchat about all the common interests we probably don't have." I'm trying for playful and coming off all wrong. I used to be better at this, I think.

He laughs anyway. "Well, I'm not sure how you could know since you've never asked about my interests."

Point to Nick for rolling with the punches. He smiles and it warms me all over.

"You're right. What are you interested in, Nick?"

"You, for starters." His smirk makes him look like trouble. It also renders me incapable of speech.

He takes a breath. "So, there's you and football and great pizza—"

"Hugely shocking so far," I say, feeling more at ease now that we're back to banter. "And your plans after graduation?"

He gives me a mock-harsh look. "I was trying to get to that before you interrupted. I'm working here so I can take the summer off to travel."

"Let me guess. Cancun? Palm Springs?"

"I was thinking more Nepal, Tibet, maybe Bhutan," he says, shocking me into silence. "If I can't afford Asia, I'll probably head to South America—Peru or Chile…"

He trails off, probably noticing the way I'm staring at him. Like I've never met him. Because suddenly, that's exactly how I feel. I

137

try to picture it—Nick Patterson in Bhutan. Before this moment, I might have doubted Nick knew Bhutan was a country. I don't think I like what that says about me.

He shrugs. "I like mountains."

"You like mountains."

Nick nods. "I also like world history, water-skiing, horror movies, and Ansel Adams."

My voice is barely more than a breath when it comes out of me. "Ansel Adams is a…"

"Photographer?" He looks at my mouth.

"But you don't—"

"Take pictures?" He gives me a look that shouldn't be legal. "I still know talent when I see it."

My heart doesn't race; it *gallops*—so hard and fast that I feel it throbbing in the tips of my fingers. I think of stepping away, because I should. But I don't. Not even when he tilts his head.

Oh hell. I think he's going to kiss me. And I think I'm going to let him.

"Nick!"

I wince and Nick turns over his shoulder, his eyes still heavy-lidded. "What?"

"Come over here! Tate needs help." The girl, one of Marlow's cronies, if I'm not mistaken, looks like she's not sure if she should laugh or cry.

"Can it wait?"

"I think you'd better come now," the girl's voice—I'm pretty sure it's Shelby Keaton, come to think of it—is high and pinched.

Nick heaves a long sigh and touches my wrist. "I'm sorry. I should check him."

I don't know why I follow Nick across the patio, bumping past the table with the couple, and then a group of guys who probably *aren't* passing around a Camel Light. My stomach is still fisted over our almost…*something*.

The girl—definitely Shelby—lets us in the opposite door and we step inside the darkness again. This door is closer to the bathrooms. Not the kind of place I want to linger, but Shelby glances at the men's room door, looking squeamish.

"He's in there."

I get it as soon as I take a breath. A potent blend of vomit and booze clouds the air in the narrow hallway. It always smells sort of rank if memory serves, but it's much worse than normal tonight. Gives me a pretty good idea of what's going on with Tate in the bathroom, even if the music's too loud to let us hear any sound effects.

Nick heads straight in, leaving Shelby and me alone. I'm tempted to leave. I spot Connor and Manny at the stage, hands in the air, having the time of their lives. Which is what I'm supposed to be doing. And who I'm supposed to be with. But something is holding me here in this nasty hallway with a girl I rarely speak to.

That *something* walks back out of the bathroom, glaring daggers at Shelby. "He's wasted, Shel! How'd he get here?"

Valid question. The hardest thing they serve here is Red Bull, so this obviously happened before he arrived.

"I don't know," Shelby says. "I just saw him come in a little while ago."

Nick takes a breath, his patience clearly gone. "You've been trying to get with Tate since last year. Don't sit here and act like you don't know *exactly* how he got here and who with."

She fights giving him an answer for a minute, but then her gaze shifts to the bathroom door and she frowns. "Jackson. Jackson dropped him off, but he left when Tate got sick."

I shift uncomfortably, not wanting to be in the middle of this anymore. It's not like I'm helping. But now Nick's standing in between me and the rest of the bar, and I don't know if I can just push past him. So I wait.

He shoves a hand through his hair. "All right, we've got to get him home, and we're going to need a bucket. If you drive, I'll keep him in the backseat."

Shelby visibly recoils, her pink nails digging into her soft phone cover. "Nick, I can't! I have my dad's car."

"We'll take my car."

Shelby looks around, obviously panicking. "The Jeep? I-I can't drive a stick shift."

Nick shakes his head, looking confused. "Then I'll drive and you can—"

"No, I can't! I just…" She cuts herself off, shaking her head.

Nick narrows his eyes, but it's not going to work. She's checking out. I can see reality dawn in Nick's eyes, his big shoulders slumping.

"I can do it."

They both look at me, so I apparently said that out loud.

Dumb. These are *not* my people, and this is *not* my problem. And if Shelby's thin-lipped look is any indicator, I'm not welcome.

There's something about her look that picks at my temper though. I bat my eyes, feigning innocence in my sugar-sweet voice. "Unless you want to maybe lay down some garbage bags in your car or something, Shelby."

She tenses, turning back to Nick. "I'm sorry. I really am," she says, and it sounds like she means it. But even if she does, she still walks away, leaving us alone.

Nick looks at me with an expression I can't read. "You don't have to do this."

Strangely, I'm pretty sure I do. Even if I don't know why.

I try for a smile that only works halfway. "How about you take bucket duty and I'll go get your car."

He waits for another long moment before he hands over his keys and tells me where it's parked. I wrap my fingers hard around the metal, grateful for something to do. If I'm doing things, I don't have to think.

Nick insists on having one of the bouncers walk me out. I follow a big, quiet guy to an older, white Jeep with cracks in the leather and a couple of sweatshirts flung across the passenger seat. It smells enough like Nick in here to make my fingers tremble, but the bouncer is waiting, so I start it up.

I only stall once backing out of the parking spot, and by the time I pull it around to the staff entrance, I've gotten the hang of the clutch. I text Manny and Hadley while I'm waiting. I hope to God my pathetic *I'm helping out a friend, they'll drop me home,* won't generate a bunch of questions, because I sure as hell don't have any answers.

Nick appears within a couple minutes, one arm slung around his half-conscious friend. Tate looks up at the Jeep. His eyes are bloodshot and the front of his shirt is stained. He looks like a supermodel with a heroin addiction. Pitiful doesn't even cover it.

Nick loads him into the back and I settle behind the wheel, trying not to breathe too deeply.

"I think he's mostly done," Nick says. "But I thought that two minutes ago too."

"I'm done," Tate says.

He's not. One block later, he pukes again. I can't be sure, but I don't think all of it lands in the bucket.

I roll down the window a little and Nick reaches for one of his sweatshirts.

"I'm sorry, I'm sorry," Tate says, sounding so sad that it makes my stomach ache and my eyes water. Or maybe it's the smell. I don't even know, I just know it hurts.

"It's all right, man. Just breathe," Nick says. God, he sounds so genuine. Just soft voiced and not concerned that he's mopping up some guy's vomit with his clothes. My grip on the wheel goes tighter with every word Nick says and I keep wondering if I would be as cool as Nick in the same situation. I want to think so, but am I sure?

"Take a right up here on Main," he says to me. "He's in Glenwood Estates."

"Which street?" I ask.

"Birchview."

"Who the hell is that?" Tate asks, every word slurred.

"It's Piper. She's cool. Just keep breathing, Tate. Get that cold air in you."

He doesn't puke again, but I hear him sniffing every now and then. Nick directs me to the cul-de-sac where Tate's house—a sprawling brick-front monstrosity—is situated.

Nick helps him out, and a streetlight illuminates the side of Tate's face. Tear tracks glisten under the orange-yellow glow. Nick drags the bucket out too, dropping the sweatshirt on top.

Tate looks down at it, face crumpling. "Sorry, man."

"It's cool."

Tate shakes his head. "It's not cool. She's gone." He lets out a low sound that cuts right through me. A sound I know I will never, ever forget. "She's gone, man."

Nick sighs, dropping a hand on his shoulder. "Let's get you inside."

They shuffle up the driveway. I don't ask if Nick wants help. It wouldn't matter if he did, because I feel boneless and hollow.

I swipe at my own completely stupid tears. I have no right to be crying. Shivers crash over me in waves while I wait, so I crank up the heater all the way. It doesn't help. I don't think I'll ever be warm again.

CHAPTER TWELVE

· ·

Nick drives me home with the radio low. We don't talk much. I tell him where to turn and he asks if anyone's home.

"Let me walk you in," he says when he pulls up to the curb.

"No, thanks," I tell him. "It would probably freak out my parents."

Probably not exactly true, but I *am* twenty minutes past curfew and I really don't want any more reasons for them to ask questions about the walking Adidas ad who dropped me home.

Nick turns off the engine. It's weird and quiet, and I don't know what to say or do, so I reach for the door handle and smile. "Well, thanks for the ride."

"Wait," he says, reaching across me to hold the door closed.

He pulls back enough to give me space, a muscle in his jaw tensing. "Piper, what you did tonight—"

A sudden rush of panic forces me to cut him off. "I drove a car, Nick. It's not a big deal. Really."

"Yes, it was. And you know it."

I squirm. What I did tonight, sure. That was nice. But I tried to target Tate for a takedown. And deep down, some part of me still wants it. My gaze drifts to my front door. I want a cup of green tea and my dad's old Led Zeppelin T-shirt, the one that's buttery soft and hangs to my knees. The one that will take me away from all of this.

"Tate wasn't himself," he says out of nowhere. "He doesn't even really drink."

I can feel myself crumbling. The image of Tate, so awful and so broken, is seared into my mind; those weird, nonsense tears burning at my eyes again, so I shift closer to the door. "I'm glad he got home safe. I should go."

He looks a little mad now, shoves himself back into his seat. "Will you stop acting like you lent me a pencil, for God's sake?"

I want to run, but I can hear every breath shaking out of him in the quiet car. Each time he takes another one, I feel it in my chest.

I can't do this. Every second I sit here, he's pulling at things, things I don't want in the open. I want to bury them deep. Forget about them forever.

"Just say something *real*," he says, voice pleading. "Anything."

My resolve crumbles.

"He was *horrible* to her," I whisper, wishing I could pull it back in, but I can't. The truth always finds its way out, I guess.

"Yeah." The word's like a torn stitch. "And it's so messed up because he was *crazy* about her. You don't even know."

I close my eyes tight. "I don't want to know." When I open them, he's watching me. When I look at Nick, I hurt for Tate, and Tate doesn't deserve that. He's one of the reasons Stella's dead, and I can't let that be okay.

Nick's face closes off, like everything is being buttoned down for a storm.

"I still appreciate your help," he says.

Something's tearing on my insides. I want to reach for him. I want to tell him a thousand things about how I'm feeling and how damn confusing all of this is.

Because wrong is supposed to be wrong and right is supposed to be right, and it's all a fat, gray mess and I hate it. I want to tell him all of that, but I don't. I step out of his Jeep and watch him drive away.

• • •

Jackson's pictures arrive in Saturday's mail. I ordered them half out of habit and half because I expected my texting friend to request them. I'm learning quickly that I have no idea what I should expect.

Harrison hasn't said a thing since the *Got it* last night before the Tate disaster. Maybe it means he's done with this. It should be a good thing, but it feels…incomplete. Or something.

Dad taps the brown box of photos on the table in front of me, and I recoil like it's a nest of cockroaches.

"Pure genius inside?" he asks with a wink.

I hide my failure to smile in a spoonful of granola.

"So, why were you late last night?" Mom asks.

I chew. Swallow. Prepare to spit out more lies. "Manny got wrapped up with some girl."

"That boy needs to rein in his hormones. And you need to keep better track of the time."

"Noted. Sorry."

Dad claps his hands together. "Enough discipline." He ignores Mom's frown and jabs the box again. "Want to show us your latest and greatest?"

A punch to the gut would hurt less. "It's duplicates. Homecoming stuff. I'm really behind, actually."

I look toward the stairs. Mom wraps a cranberry muffin in a paper towel and hands it to me. A wholesome snack for their lying, scheming daughter.

I lock my bedroom door and open the box, sliding the pictures out around my desk. They're strong photos. Good angles. Nice lighting. I analyze the pictures like I'm grading them.

The portraits of the crowd are good, but the ones of Jackson are better. I've got a phenomenal shot of him pacing—the TV in the background, his smile too predatory to be kind. And then the best of them all—his hands in his hair and his mouth screwed up in horror. There's only one word for this shot: humiliated.

And he *should* be.

I slide open the bottom drawer, finding the notebook. I tuck Jackson's pictures into the pocket, because where the hell else am I going to keep pictures of a guy watching a tape like—

Wait a minute.

I think back over the tape, and it hits me like something heavy. All those code names I wanted to uncover. I can figure out Jackson, at least.

I grab a notepad and scrawl out a quick list of everything I can remember from that tape. The gross crap with Marlow. Throwing a fit. Mocking Chelsea. Something's going to be in there. *He* saw all of it. He knew what to look for.

I start scanning the pages fast, finding a couple of things that could be Marlow. Nothing jumps out, but then, I guess it's all kind of vague. A lot of this book could be Jackson.

And then I find it. September 20th. Halfway down the list.

Shortstop imitates Chelsea's compromised gait

My skin prickles. Chelsea doesn't have a nickname. I don't know why. Maybe because Harrison feels like it'd be shitty to nickname someone with so many challenges. Or maybe because he doesn't think she's worth one.

But Chelsea's name isn't the one I'm interested in. Jackson's is. And his name is Shortstop.

I can't chew my lip hard enough to keep my smile at bay. I pull out my metallic pens, a gift from some birthday past, and start moving through the book, beginning to end. I hesitate at first, my pen a hair's breadth away from the paper.

This isn't my book, but I doubt it's something Harrison plans on passing around at the dinner table. Besides, he pretty much gave me an author's invitation to add my own touch. I draw a careful metallic green circle around the first reference on page 4, and then again on page 6. Page 9. The Chelsea incident on page 10. And finally one more at the bottom of 11. Five times this jerk made someone suffer. So five times I write his real name above his nickname.

I flip to the back of the book, to a fresh new page. That's where I paste his pictures, one on top of the other. I surround them with crisscrossing borders, the same ink that I used to highlight his deeds.

This book won't fix anything on its own. It's not a weapon unless it's in the wrong person's hands. For me, it's a source of honesty. From Manny to my parents to my own vigilante side gig, my world's sinking in lies. It feels pretty good to have something that's true.

• • •

The yearbook team meets for lunch at Waffle World on Sundays. As usual, I'm early, which gives me time to enjoy my tower of praline pancakes in peace while I mock up an idea for my newly assigned yearbook pages on the back of a napkin.

Manny slides into the booth across from me, sporting a rumpled T-shirt and dark circles under his eyes.

I frown up at him. "You look like crap."

"I was up late," he says. "Though sadly, not because of Candace. So, did you bang the quarterback?"

"He's not a quarterback and you're not funny," I say, pointing at my crude napkin design. "What do you think?"

He shrugs and helps himself to the table coffee. "Tacey will want more pictures crammed in. So fill me in on your sweaty adventures."

"There was no sweating. You're disgusting. And why were you up so late?"

He scratches the back of his head. "If you must know, I'm trying to get that government paper done."

I don't like it. It's not like Manny to do homework in advance, and I know that paper isn't due until next week. Makes me wonder if he's in trouble. Or if he's messing with attendance records again. The thought makes my stomach go sour, but I keep my mouth shut.

"I thought you were done with the nagging."

"I am!"

"Those eyes are nagging eyes."

"Whose eyes are nagging?" Tacey asks, announcing her arrival.

I sigh. "No one's. Let's talk layout. I still have a ton of homework to deal with. Take a look at this idea. For the homecoming court spread."

Tacey pulls out her laptop—scary idea with all the syrup on this table—and we dissect ten pages of the yearbook, which feels a little heavy on the throttle since the full book isn't due for three months, but whatever.

"Okay, one more thing," she says. "I want to add another page to the football layout."

"The section we just finished?" I ask.

Tacey frowns. "I wanted one final page of the stadium. I think I'm going to put coach quotes on there."

"I'll do that," I say, because I'm itching to have a reason to be behind my camera, to feel the heft of it in my hands and the thrill of a shot that I *know* is amazing the second the shutter snaps. Plus, I could definitely deal with a distraction right now.

"I'll come with," she says. "Do you need to stop and get your equipment?"

"It's in the trunk," I say.

Manny heads out, and Tacey and I pay the tab. We take my Subaru to the high school. The day's cold with a flat, pale sky stretching overhead. Not the best light for a shoot. I snap a few from the front of the stadium and pull back to thumb through them. Everything is cast in pale gray, the sky bone white above us. Kind of haunting and gorgeous, but I know Tacey.

"It's going to need to be black and white," I warn her.

"You were born in the wrong decade."

"Since I can't imagine life before Nikon went digital, I doubt it. But you won't like this lighting. Do you want to try another day?"

"No, grayscale will work. If I use red font, it will pop, right?"

I feel a little buzzed that she's game for it. Black-and-white landscapes are my favorite. Maybe I could even leave the brick in color. And the chipped paint on the bleacher seats? Yeah.

"You're going to love it. I'm going to go grab a few from inside."

Tacey's nose deep in her phone. "'Kay. I need to make a couple calls. Can I use your charger?"

"It's in the car."

Tacey disappears, and I close my eyes, savoring the solitude. One deep breath and everything falls away. The notebook, the texts, Nick, Tate—the smell of dry leaves and cold air clears them out. No more test shots. No more light checks. I stretch my fingers around my camera and start for real. It's like seeing the place for the first time.

I take a few more pictures of the outside walls, first the front and then the concession stand. The field is still hidden to me, but I'm saving it, working my way into the stadium frame by frame. I slip into the hallway where I confronted Nick, catching some great shots of the light from the bleachers streaming onto the cement walk.

It gives me an idea for a shot of the field—a shot from *behind* the bleachers. I fold up the tripod and lean it against a wall, feeling the itch of excitement over doing something different.

I step into an alcove. Bleachers stretch overhead, wooden planks that have weathered sixty Indiana winters. I wonder how many first kisses have been shared under these bleachers.

Suddenly, I hear laughter and then a grunt. It's coming from the field, but I can't see anyone out there. I try again at the next set of bleachers, spotting two guys moving back and forth on the green. Tate and Jackson.

Something small and hard lodges in my chest as I watch the football sail back and forth between them. Tate misses a pass and the football thuds to the ground two sets of bleachers over. I start walking that way. I'm not sure why, because my jaw feels tight and hot, and I'd rather walk through fire barefoot than be near either of them. That doesn't stop me from slipping closer and closer.

They're both by the ball when I stop. If I go farther, they might see me. Tate's tossing the ball from one hand to the other while Jackson scuffs the grass with his shoes, a scowl on his face.

"What's with all the power passes?" Tate asks.

"What's with you turning into a girl?"

Tate steps back. He doesn't look good. He's pale and his cheeks are sunken. I try to think about the way he was earlier this year—almost *too* handsome. The kind of guy who people figured might end up on TV or modeling somewhere. He's a million miles from that now. Jackson stretches his thick arms overhead. "You've been moping for *weeks*. You didn't even want to come today. Now you're moaning that I'm throwing too hard."

"I'm not moaning. You're pissed and it's obvious," Tate says. "Your dad's pissed about the eight-game suspension, huh?"

Jackson rockets another throw at Tate's middle. He catches it and flings it back with a smirk. "I'll take that as a yes."

Jackson shrugs. "He left my face out of it, so whatever."

"It's messed up, man. You should tell someone."

"Why? So I can turn into a mopey little shit like you?"

Tate's expression goes hard. "Maybe because if you stop getting punched in the kidneys, you'll throw a better pass."

The tension between them is painfully thick. It presses on me until I feel like *I've* been punched.

Jackson finally relents under Tate's stare down. "I'll make him pay, you know."

"Your dad?"

"No. Whoever put that tape up. The same guy that took down Kristen."

I stop breathing, my face going cold as the blood drains from it.

Tate shrugs one shoulder, looking off into the stands across the field. "It'll blow over."

"I'm not going to let it blow over. I'm going to find him. And make him pay."

Jackson's voice is cold enough to burn. My hands shake, and suddenly, I realize—they could see me. Not that it means anything. I'm a school photographer. I have an excuse to be anywhere.

But I'm also the girl who took pictures of Jackson watching that tape. The same one who took pictures of Kristen. If he starts connecting dots, he's going to find me at the middle.

They don't speak again. Eventually, Tate shuffles down the field, and Jackson throws him the ball. That's about the time I start breathing again.

I back out of the stands carefully, making sure I don't step wrong or bang into something that will give me away. The second I'm clear of the bleachers, I speed up. I just want to be out of here.

Tacey's still on the phone when I get to the car, but she hangs up quickly after catching sight of my face. "What's wrong?"

"Nothing."

Everything.

I start the engine and Tacey twists sideways. "We're leaving? What about the pictures? Did you get enough? Why are you so shaky?"

"I have enough."

I don't have enough. I don't even have one of the actual field from inside, but my hands are slick on the steering wheel and I can't stay here one more minute. I pull out of the lot with the radio up, but it's Jackson's threat that's ringing in my ears.

CHAPTER THIRTEEN

. . . .

t's the worst kind of dream, the kind where you know
you're sleeping and you still can't wake up. Nick's standing at
my locker in his backward baseball hat with his hand stretched
toward me. He says my name, and my whole body blooms when
he smiles.

I touch his fingers, and Tate appears beside us in his stained
shirt. But it's not Tate. Not really. His eyes are white, a milky film
covering the irises. Deep purple bruises shade the hollows of his
cheekbones and his skin is gray blue. Corpse pale.

I try to look back at Nick, but I can't tear my gaze away from
Tate's ruined eyes. Stella is here now too. She watches us with eyes
that are cloudy like Tate's, her skin withered and filthy. Nick says
my name, but I can only see Tate's chalk-white lips and Stella's
hair hanging in matted hunks around her shoulders.

"He's coming for you." Stella blinks her white eyes and I gasp,
breathing in her rot.

Nick's hand tightens around mine. Warm. Safe.

"Who's coming?"

"I'm coming," Nick says. But it isn't Nick.

It's Jackson.

He squeezes my hand until the bones in my wrist grind. I dig in my heels. Try to jerk free. But he has me. Oh God, he's pulling me in.

I wake up with a shout, goose bumps trailing up my arms and legs.

It's okay. I'm okay.

I press a hand to my chest and will my panting to slow. Three days after I saw him at the field, and I'm still on edge.

My bedroom is lit by the desk lamp I forgot to turn off, but it's still dark outside. I check my phone on my nightstand. It's too early to get up, even for a school day, but I'm not risking snoozing my way back into that nightmare.

I slip into the bathroom to take a quick shower, and return to my room, hair pulled into a wet ponytail. My stomach clenches at the brown envelope my mother left on my desk while I was sleeping. Kristen's pictures came. I'm not really sure I want to look at these. But I have to.

I rip it open decisively, sliding the new pictures out one by one. I'm too low in the seats to get quality shots of the stage, but a few aren't bad: Kristen at the podium, a pair of red-stained jeans blurring past her shoulder, one of the sign, one of kids pointing, and the one of her crying.

I push that one under the pile. Part of me wants to turn it facedown, maybe even put it in my drawer. Instead, I pull out the notebook and choose a glittery pink pen. Just like I did with Jackson, I look for her sins.

I'm starting to memorize these pages, but I check them again, entry by entry. Only two stand out, but I'm sure they're her. One bragging about a stolen leather coat back in early October. And another lending a freshman advice on lifting makeup at the mall. Her nickname? *Couture*. I cross it out in both entries and write Kristen's name above it. Then I paste her picture on the page behind Jackson's, listing her sins again in shimmery pink script.

Now what? Harrison hasn't owned up to being the texter yet, but he's obviously not going to take himself down. That means Kristen could be the last. Two takedowns. That's it? I skim my finger down a line of entries. Cruelty and violence spelled out over and over. All these other people? They deserve justice too. I'm going to have to find a way to do this. Maybe without a partner.

I keep working with my glittery pens, crossing out the names I've figured out, writing real names over the top. I hesitate at Manny's name, and I hate it because it makes me a hypocrite. He's guilty like all the rest, but he's Manny. My friend. There's more to him than these three entries.

Which is why this book can't get out. In the wrong hands, this thing could turn into a witch-hunt, and I can't let that happen. Not to Manny. Not to anyone else who ended up in this book for stupid reasons.

I have to choose carefully, and this book is only one piece of that choice. It's a reminder of how bad it can get and why all of this is worth the risks I'm taking.

My phone rings, and I pick it up without checking the number. "Hello?"

"Piper? This is Nick."

A flash of milky irises from my dream sends a chill down my

spine. I pull my feet up on my chair, hugging my knees close to my chest. It was just a nightmare. Not real.

"Are you there?" he asks, and I realize I haven't said anything since hello.

"I'm sorry. Hi. What's up?"

"I was calling to see if I could drive you to school. I have something I want to ask you about."

I think of riding to school in his bumpy Jeep, his voice up close and personal.

"You can't just ask me now?" I ask, sort of squeaking.

"I could. Wouldn't mind the company though."

I smile and sigh at the same time. God, he's making it hard to remember why I'm supposed to not like him.

He chuckles like he reads all that by my sigh alone. "All right, I'll spare you more awkward silence and just ask. Do you think there's any chance Connor Jennings did the stuff to Kristen and Jackson?"

I swallow hard and close my eyes. "No, I don't."

"I know he's your friend, but he's some sort of computer genius, right?"

"There are plenty of people slick enough to do it."

"Maybe, but Connor's the kind of guy to stick up for people, right?"

Right. But totally wrong. "Connor didn't do it. I thought he did too, so I checked into it."

He sighs. "I thought it was a solid idea. After his speech last year, he obviously isn't a fan of the popular kids."

I tilt my head, surprised he understood the speech but more bothered by his assumption. "Why do you think it's about popularity?"

Except I have targeted popular kids, haven't I? I wasn't thinking of their social status when I picked them, though. I wait for him to answer, listening to the silence scream "Liar, liar, liar!" at me.

"C'mon, look at the people who have been taken down. Jackson? Kristen?"

I can't argue that they're unpopular, so I don't. "You think they didn't deserve it?"

"It's not about what they deserve. Humiliating people isn't going to fix anything. It's just going to cause more problems."

"Why? Because your friends are getting what's coming to them?"

"No, because it's going to go bad. The police are trying to get Kristen's mom to press charges. Jackson's on the damn warpath. It's a mess."

"Well, it's not your mess, right? I mean, you didn't do anything, so you should be fine."

What am I doing? Why am I acting like this? Nick's been nothing but decent to me, but God, I can't see him apart from *them*. Jackson's laughter from the hallway trails back to me and I shudder.

I just wanted them to pay. For Stella. I thought that's what this was for, but now?

Nick sighs, bringing me back to the present. "Hey, I'm going to go. I'll see you at school, yeah?"

"Yeah."

I hang up the phone before he can say anything else—or maybe before I can make it worse than I already have.

My fingers shake on the cover of the notebook. *Malum non vide*. See no evil. Except I'm starting to see evil everywhere. Even where it might not exist.

• • •

I look around the chemistry lab, feeling uneasy. I caught Harrison's eye walking in and made a point to say hello and ask how he's feeling since he was absent the first two days this week. And Harrison? Didn't even flinch.

He briefly explained that he'd been on a college tour—the kid is incessantly touring colleges—and then excused himself to his seat.

If he is the texter, then he could win an Oscar for playing it cool. I've been staring at the back of his neck so hard it's a miracle it hasn't lit on fire, but he hasn't looked back at me. Not once. What gives? The pressure should be eating him alive to fess up.

I don't know what it means or what to think. But if Harrison isn't the guy, I'm pretty sure I'm screwed. Because I have no idea who else it could be.

The minutes tick by and Mrs. Branson strolls up and down the aisles, commenting on our measurements and stir speed. Ten minutes before the bell rings, I feel my phone buzz in my backpack. It's against the rules to check it during class, and usually it doesn't go off, because anyone who'd text me is probably *also* in class.

So, who is it? Mom? Dad? If it's them, something's wrong. Like one-of-them-is-in-the-emergency-room wrong.

Way to wax theatrical, Woods.

I need to chill. No one's dead. It's only nine minutes until the end of class, and I don't need my phone confiscated for the rest of the day because I've decided to embrace my neurotic side. But I still reach for the loop of my bag with my toe and drag it closer.

This isn't smart. I can wait eight minutes to check a text message. I think.

Screw it. I've never been big on patience.

Mrs. Branson turns her back and I reach forward, my whole body on high alert as I slowly unzip the side pouch. I have got to get myself together. I'm not sneaking into a Homeland Security database here, I'm checking my phone.

I snag the phone impatiently and cringe at how loud it is. Like opening candy in a quiet theater. In the next seat, Andrew Lane looks at me and then away, clearly not caring a bit.

Mrs. Branson also doesn't care. She's fairly preoccupied showing one of her super-smart-person magazines to Harrison. Of course.

I finally pull up the screen and deflate. It's from the texter. Which means it can't be from Harrison; my eyes have been on him like a second layer of skin.

I pull it up.

> Be in the north parking lot in five minutes.

Five minutes? My head shoots up, panicked. The north parking lot is easily a five minute walk from here, even if I didn't have to stop by my locker for my camera. Plus, I got this text four minutes ago.

I shove my phone in my pocket and launch my hand into the air, not bothering to wait for her to call on me. "Mrs. Branson, may I please use the restroom?"

She looks up from her magazine—and her golden child—with a look of bewilderment. "Miss Woods, there are five minutes left in this period."

"It's an emergency."

At the table up front, Shay snickers, and I shoot her a withering look. Mrs. Branson dismisses me with a wave, telling me it's too close to period end to bother with a pass. Which basically means, she's too busy fawning over Harrison to get up and write me one.

Works for me. I'm way too late to wait. Once the classroom door clicks closed, I sprint down the hallway. I think of cartoon characters sliding around corners as I fly toward my locker, hoping against hope that no one in the office is watching the camera screens right now.

I'm panting hard when I get there, my fingers spinning right then left then right again. The lock opens and I yank my bag over my shoulder. Camera in hand, I run, not even bothering to lock up. They can have my textbooks if they want them that badly.

Because I can't miss Harrison's takedown. I didn't even expect there to be a—

Wait.

My feet slow to an awkward jog. I just left him in advanced chemistry. If this is about a takedown, what am I doing going to the courtyard when he's inside?

Unless this isn't a takedown for Harrison. Maybe they've turned the tables. Maybe this time I'm the target.

Heart hammering, I look around. It's so quiet I can hear the faint buzz of the fluorescent lights. The murmur of teachers talking to their rooms.

Ignore it.

I could just slide my phone back into my pocket and get back to class. It'd be easy.

But if I'm wrong…if I miss it because I'm afraid—no. No, I walked away from that scared girl the second I texted Jackson's name. I can't look back now.

I push open the door to the courtyard, which is neither a court nor a yard. Really it's a cluster of additional tables situated next to the teacher's lot and the baseball fields. Still, the sky is blue and cloudless, and I know pictures out here will be wonderful. Crisp and bright with that kind of supreme clarity that only direct sunlight can offer.

I'm not sure I'll be so excited if I wind up being the subject.

I stumble forward a few feet and spot something in the parking lot—a newer white sedan backed halfway out of its parking spot, almost like someone left it in neutral and it rolled out on its own. But that's not what happened. I'm pretty sure whoever spray-painted the back windshield and the lid of the trunk pushed it here.

I read the messages.

Cheating Your Way
Text for Answers!

Cheating? Need Help?

Dread settles in my stomach like a rock, but I follow my instinct and lift my camera. One, two, three pictures.

And then I freeze in horror as I realize something. Holy crap, there are security cameras on this patio.

I feel like I'm sinking in quicksand. Suffocating. I'm going to be caught.

I lean in to take a ridiculous picture of one of the empty tables, but I know this is stupid. It's too late to cover anything anymore. They'll see me out here. They'll put the pieces together. I've been at every one of these takedowns. *Documenting* them.

I turn, oh-so-casually, and there it is. One of the cameras. I can't be sure, but I think it's more focused on the baseball fields. This lot is for staff only, so it's probably not a place where they expect kids to be. I search the other corner, but that camera is definitely pointed at the tables behind me—the ones I just walked through to get here.

I'm in a dead spot. From the look of it, the whole lot might be a dead spot. Maybe. I might get away with this.

Is that even what I want anymore?

I take a breath. So cold it burns.

A shrill ringing blares out of speakers all around me and I jump, jaw snapping. Just a fire alarm. I bring a hand to my throat and will my pulse to slow down. My heart ignores me and races on because it already knows what I'm only just figuring out. This is no mandatory drill.

Someone set this alarm off. Half of the school is going to be out here in two minutes. And whoever spray-painted this car planned it that way.

The doors open and students pour out, tugging on jackets and clogging up the sidewalk and tables. Kids are laughing and talking as they move to line up. It takes a minute before someone sees the car. A pretty freshman spots it first, pointing with a gasp.

It takes less than a minute for the lines to dissolve into chaos. Students press in closer to the parking lot. Whispers and murmurs ricochet from one group to the next.

"Whose is it?"

"No, you idiot, Mr. Stiers drives a Honda."

"Mrs. Stamper has a minivan, right?"

"Somebody's *fired*!"

My mouth goes bone dry. Someone *is* going to get fired. And I'm pretty sure it's Mrs. Branson.

No. This isn't right. This isn't what I wanted. It was about Harrison. It wasn't even about that—it was about letting Aimee win because she deserves it. And people should know that Harrison doesn't. That's what I wanted to show.

But this is the truth. Just not the truth I wanted.

It's too much. I lift my camera, hiding behind the lens, safe with the metal body firm and true in my hands. I force myself to turn toward the approaching crowd to get a few shots. One of Mr. Goodard, his eyes falling to the car with a grave look. Another shot of teachers whispering just as harshly as the students, the messages on the car blurred behind their bent heads.

A sudden sharp cry takes the breath right out of me. Mrs.

Branson's finally here. Her eyes are wide and she's got a hand at her chest. The expression on her chalk-white face is beyond fear or regret. It's panic, pure and simple.

I snap one image of her. It's the first picture I've ever hated myself for taking.

The answers tumble together in the whispers and images around me. Lots of people knew a little. Put together the bits, and we see the whole picture. Chemistry was Harrison's weakness, but he realized it too late to drop the class. A longtime student in Mrs. Branson's AP science classes, Harrison trusted her. They somehow struck a deal.

Some think it was her phone he used. Others think they're sleeping together. Mrs. Branson's close to sixty, so I doubt that, but it doesn't matter. She's finished. He's finished. It's over for both of them. It hits me like a hammer then: One bad call, that's all it takes. One big mistake shot two futures apart in the most humiliating scene I've ever witnessed.

This will haunt them forever. This will be on the *news*.

A flush of regret creeps up my neck, hot and angry. I shrug my shoulders, trying to shake it off. It's not my fault. They would have been caught anyway. It would have come out.

But not like this.

I'm like a stone dropped in still water. I sink away from the chaos until the only noise I hear is the sound of my guilt.

The police—called for her car, I guess—pull into the parking lot while they're still counting us. Nervous teachers bark at us to be quiet, but no one listens. My heart races and my feet shift, and

I'm grateful Manny and Tacey are in different classes because I can't talk right now.

A police officer is taking pictures of the car when I finally catch sight of Harrison at the back of my line. He's still close to the school, his face gray as ash. He looks like he's about to walk in front of a firing squad and he's probably not far from wrong. I've met his parents. Saw them rip him to pieces for a 93% in social studies in the fourth grade.

The teachers start ushering us in, and I spot Mrs. Branson, who's speaking with the policemen near her car. Mr. Stiers gives her a gentle pat on the shoulder, and Mr. Goodard's expression is cool and professional. The face of a man who knows he's about to lose a teacher.

I feel sick. Guilty. Embarrassment is one thing, but this? It's too much. This changes their lives forever.

Stop it!

They earned this. It was their choice. I'm as sure of it as I've ever been about anything and it shouldn't feel this bad. But it does.

I press a hand to my forehead as we push back into the building, the sunlight giving way to the dim school interior. I breathe deeply. I need to get a grip. I really do.

The conversations inside are at a roar. Teachers bark at students, but it barely dims the noise. Everyone's talking, pushing, texting. Harrison comes in behind me and the hallway falls silent.

His mouth goes thin and hard as he steps away from the wall. For a minute, I think he might say something. To me. I know it's not possible, but some part of me thinks he knows. That he'll tell.

Of course, Harrison's got much bigger problems than me today. And so do I, because if Harrison isn't the texter, then I have no idea who I'm working with.

CHAPTER FOURTEEN

I follow Harrison to the office because I have to be sure. I'll play sick if I have to. It's not really a stretch. In the end, I just can't let this go without talking to him. I know he didn't send that last text, but what if the pressure got to him? What if he orchestrated this whole thing today as a way out?

I know it doesn't track. But Harrison still feels right somehow. Maybe he's not the texter, but he's involved.

I need to talk to him. And if I don't do it now, I might never get the chance. After this mess, who knows what will happen? Suspension? A school transfer? I might not ever see him again.

The secretaries aren't at their desks, so apparently the apocalypse really is nigh. I can hear them back in the counselor's office, no doubt discussing Mrs. Branson's fate or Harrison's.

I sign my name on the office check-in list. Halfway through my *W*, I stop, my eyes drawn to the distinctive black writing above my line.

It's creepy that Harrison signed himself in for a disciplinary conversation. But that's not what what's choking the breath out of me. I owe that to the penmanship—writing I've only seen in one other place.

The notebook.

I wasn't wrong. That's Harrison's notebook. His chronicle.

I hold on to the counter, because if I don't, I might fall down. I'm almost sure my knees won't hold me. Of course, I can't stand here forever. I need to sit down. A sick student would sit down.

"Piper, it'll be just a minute," Mrs. Bluth calls out from the back. "Have a seat in the waiting area."

I propel myself away and find the row of chairs around the corner, two empty, one occupied.

Harrison.

My heartbeat stutters. I could run. Turn and leave right now. I could cross off my name and go. He hasn't looked up, though he probably heard Mrs. Bluth say my name.

I glance at his fingers, imagine him with something sharp, scraping at the eyes on those photographs.

A warning bell rings and I flinch. He looks right at me. Until this moment, I'm not sure I've ever really met Harrison's eyes. Or maybe I did and he didn't have all this anger pouring off of him.

He doesn't speak, but he doesn't stop watching me. His expression practically dares me to ignore him, but I'm not going to do-si-do around this anymore. I came here to talk to him.

"Hello, Harrison."

"Piper."

I swallow the fear lodged like a fist in my throat. "This timing is awful, but I think you should know I have your notebook."

The quiet is palpable. I can hear the soft ring of the phone, the muted conversation in the principal's office between the teachers and the police.

"You found it on the steps," he finally says. He doesn't ask which notebook or play stupid. I give him points for that. He doesn't ask for the book either, which is good. Because I don't have it on me, and I wouldn't hand it over. After this, he has nothing to lose. He could decide to use that book to drag as many people down with him as possible.

He goes on, maybe because I'm not speaking. "It's the only place it could have happened. I was late and it was windy. Once I got inside, I would have heard it hit the floor. All this time, I assumed the janitors had thrown it away."

I nod, wondering how much I should hold back. "Who else knew about the book?"

He laughs. "Do you think I'd show that to fellow students?"

But if there's no one else who knows... No. It makes no sense. This is all connected.

"Harrison, do you know about the texts I'm getting?"

He looks at me like I'm out of my mind. And then something new dawns in his expression—suspicion. Maybe he isn't the chemistry mastermind he wants to be, but he's an irrefutable genius. He was polishing off *Great Expectations* when the rest of us were struggling through easy readers.

I said too much. He's putting clues together faster than I can cover them up. He'll figure out I had something to do with what happened today. It's only a matter of time.

"Piper—"

"Harrison." Mrs. Bluth can't decide what expression to wear. She tries a smile and then a frown and ends up looking like she's got a facial tic. "Your mother should be here shortly. The principal will see you then."

My stomach squirms and Harrison nods. He looks calmer than I am watching Mrs. Bluth walk back to the desk.

"What kind of texts?" he asks, dead calm, giving nothing away. But I don't miss that his hand is fisted at his side.

"Never mind. Just tell me about the book. Why keep a book like that?"

"Because no one else bothered." He waves it off, like an annoying fly. Like it doesn't matter. "Tell me about the texts."

"Someone anonymously texted me about cheating." The lie is lemon sour on my tongue. "I thought maybe—"

"You're lying."

My grip tightens on the arms of my chair. "I guess that makes us even. You invested time in that notebook. Photographs and code names. You didn't do it because no one else *bothered*."

"I did it because I believe society has a responsibility to record events and cultures. Every individual views this school through a social filter. It's all *personal* and *subjective*." He says the words like they've gone rancid. "I wanted something less…variable. I wanted facts."

Because that's the language he understands. Cold as he seems, I can still feel the pain simmering beneath his words. It's hiding in the pinch of his mouth and the hunch of his shoulders.

"I'm listening," I say softly, trying to urge him on. By the way his face changes, I wonder how often this happens, how often anyone actually hears him.

Misery blooms suddenly, etching itself into every line of his face. "I know it shouldn't hurt me. I see these petty social games for exactly what they are, but the pain, the fear? It's all still there."

I've never seen this side of Harrison, all that icy confidence melted away, leaving something raw and broken underneath. Something like all the rest of us.

"You wanted to outthink the pain." It's a guess, but I can see him start to nod.

"On your feet!" The voice that comes from the doorway hits me like a glacier and Harrison like a whip.

He jerks out of his chair, head ducked, chin on chest. There's no pride left. There's nothing left at all that resembles the strange, brilliant boy I was just sitting with. His mother strides into the room with steps that snap, even on the gray rug in front of the chairs. She clamps on to his arm, pressing until his skin squishes up like dough between her fingers.

"You will say nothing, nothing, when we walk in that room unless I ask you a direct question. Are we clear?"

I might as well not exist. I wish I didn't exist. Not here with Harrison's mother looking at him like a stray dog that took a shit on the living room carpet.

"Yes," he says. It's not even his voice.

"Yes, what?"

"Yes, ma'am."

She's wrenching him toward the office hallway now, and his close-set eyes are trained on the ground. All I can think about is what he'll endure later, away from prying eyes. Who is Harrison

173

without his grades? What's left when everything you've ever worked for is taken away?

The office opens, and Harrison and his mother disappear inside. My stomach rolls in all the wrong ways. I know he loaded this gun. But I really didn't think before I pulled the trigger.

"Piper? How can I help you?"

"I need to go home sick." It isn't an excuse anymore.

The crease in Mrs. Bluth's forehead tells me I must look terrible. She bustles into the waiting room smelling like rose water and Sharpie markers. The back of her hand presses against my forehead, just like Hadley's at the club.

God, people are going to think I'm dying.

Feels like it.

"You sit tight. I'm going to call your dad to see if he can come down to sign you out."

My head bobs up and down. A puppet nod for a puppet girl.

Because that's what I am, right? Sure, I'm picking the target, but none of this was my idea. I'm playing along, being fed every line by a person I don't know. I wanted to believe it was someone decent. Someone who wanted to make things better, but now?

This could be anyone. A sicko. A mean girl. A criminal.

It hits me then—this is dangerous. And I'm in way over my head.

I pull up my phone with shaking hands, loading my last message, the one about the courtyard. My fingers tremble at the letters. It takes forever to get the spelling right, but I'm careful because I only want to do this once.

> That was too intense for me. Sorry, but I'm bowing out.

I've barely closed my eyes when the response comes in.

> You're not out. You pick or I will. Next Friday by 9.

CHAPTER FIFTEEN

· ·

I leave my phone in the bottom of my backpack for three days and ignore the fact that he won't let me quit. That he's demanding a name two days before Christmas. I ignore pretty much everything—from the low-battery warning beeps on my phone to the emails from Tacey when her calls start going straight to voicemail.

I can't deal with any of it. Denial is all I have left.

I roll over and look at the alarm clock. 6:15 on Sunday night. Ugh. If I don't get my butt moving, I'm going to spend my entire Christmas break in pajamas. I have to snap out of it. Do something.

But what? If I pick, I continue to play his game. Or her game. Whatever. If I don't—I don't know what happens. He picks someone himself. And if the texter knows anything about Manny's extracurricular activities, he could be a prime target.

Mom and Dad are getting worried though. They were cool at first, bringing me toast, asking basic questions. Now they're checking more often. They even offered a doctor's visit, a rare occurrence in our holistic-happy house. I don't think they make a pill for this problem, but I haven't explained that.

Three times I've tried to tell them, but how? My parents met in the Peace Corps. I don't know if I can look them in the eye and tell them the kind of destruction I'm wrapped up in. I'm not sure any of us could handle it.

I roll over and blink at the ceiling. I can't stay in this bed until I rot. The last time I left my room was to shower and drag a brush through my hair at noon. This is passing pathetic. It's tiptoeing dangerously close to psychologically unstable. I should be wrapping things or decking halls. At the very least, I should try to get some stuff together for the Thursday yearbook holiday gathering. The one I'm probably going to skip.

I hear the doorbell and I flop onto my back, heaving a sigh. Tacey, no doubt. She's probably ready to threaten me with flogging if I bail. I glance around my room, wondering if there's any way for me to convince my parents that I'm too sick to see her. Unlikely, since I told them both I was feeling better earlier.

My mom knocks on my door. I can tell as soon as she opens it—just by her face—that it isn't Tacey.

She takes a breath. "Piper, there's a boy here to see you."

Manny is *Manny* and Connor is out of town, so I already have a pretty good feeling who *boy* refers to. I sit up in a rush of flailing limbs, feeling my hair slide wildly around my shoulders.

"What boy?"

"Nick. Nick Patterson. He insisted he'd wait outside. He's very…" I mentally fill in the blanks while she searches for a word that fits. Tall? Athletic? So not your type? "Polite."

Yeah, that works too.

I give my reflection a passing look in the mirror. It's bad. And it's going to take more than a coat of lip gloss and a spritz of perfume to tidy me up, so I head downstairs. At least I showered. He should have called first anyway. Except that my phone's doornail dead.

I pull open the door and there he is, hands plunged into his coat pockets and cheeks pink from the cold.

His smile is hesitant. "I, uh, tried to call."

"My phone's dead."

"Ah. Gotcha."

"Piper?" Mom says from behind me. She's clearly not down with this super rude keep-your-half-frozen-guest-out-on-the-porch conversation.

I should invite him in. My mom is obviously prompting for that. But I try to imagine it—Nick on the couch next to my dad, talking about what? Jackson Pollock? Or maybe he can chat with Mom about one of her troubled orphans.

"Let me grab a coat," I say.

Mom laughs kind of breathlessly. "Piper, for heaven's sake, invite him in out of the cold."

I relent with a quiet sigh, pushing the door open. Nick shuffles in looking worried and *ridiculously* tall. It's not even normal the way he fills up our entry.

Mom extends her hand. "I'm Diana."

"Nick, huh?" my dad says, appearing just behind my mom's shoulder. He's got paint in his hair and a Pink Floyd T-shirt on. "I'm Tim. Sorry about this. Believe it or not, we trained her not to leave guests shivering on the porch."

I will kill my dad later for that. For now, I watch him shake Nick's hand.

Nick knows to do all the right parent things. He offers to leave his shoes by the door and thanks my mom for taking his coat. He's not kissing up or painfully awkward—he's just like he always is—friendly and courteous and, just…Nick. Even my dad, a man who normally pushes me toward creative types, seems completely enchanted by this lumbering jock creature.

Mom has him follow her into the kitchen. Dad comes too and everyone's talking about the holidays and college, and it's like I'm watching the whole thing in a movie. I know people put on their Sunday best for company, but this? This doesn't even *resemble* my family.

"So, did you need my chemistry notes?" I ask pointedly.

My hope to rattle him fails. Nick looks over at me without flinching at my ridiculous question. He and I both know he's not in my chemistry class. We also know that since we are on winter break, notes aren't a top priority.

"No, but thank you."

I arch a brow. "No? What's up then?"

Dad gives me a hard look over his mug of green tea. I don't dare glance at Mom. She's surely got her gaze switched from stun to kill.

"I have a special project I want to have done before the end of break," Nick says. "I was hoping you could help me with it."

"Is it about photography?"

"Actually, it's about social justice in high school," he says.

There's no change to his smile, but there's something in his eyes that pins me to the floor. Looks like Harrison's not the only one putting pieces together. My parents smile, completely oblivious to the fact that I've turned to stone in the middle of the kitchen.

Nick seems all too happy to wait for me to think it over. Adrenaline races through my veins, sending pins and needles down my spine. How much does he know? What is he going to say? Is he here to *threaten* me? Is that why he's here?

The idea sends a jolt through my middle. I need to get him out of here. Right now.

"I'm *starving*," I say, pushing enthusiasm—and maybe even a smidge of flirty—into my voice. "Nick, would you be willing to talk over a burger? It'll only take me a minute to change."

"That'd be great."

I fly into my room with my heart hammering wildly. I can still fix this. I don't know how, but I'll figure it out. Because I don't have a choice.

• • •

We take Nick's Jeep. It still smells like him, but it smells like something else too—some sort of citrus cleaner that I'm guessing he used for Tate's issues the other night. I figure we'll just launch right into it, but he doesn't. And God knows *I'm* not going there, so we proceed to back out of my driveway with the radio playing and snow drifting around us.

He's completely relaxed, shifting easily through the gears as he works his way out of my neighborhood. I'm perched like a steel beam at the edge of the seat, my hands fisted at my sides.

We pull up to the stop sign at Haywood Road and he looks over at me.

"So, where do you like your burgers? Are we talking Randall's or McDonald's?"

"Are you serious?"

"I thought you said you were hungry."

"I thought you just came into my house and basically accused me of being in on this vigilante crap!"

Which I totally am, so all this righteous indignation is a little misspent. And really, he didn't accuse me of anything, but apparently, I've marinated in crazy sauce for the last three days. I feel like a pressure cooker with a crack in the lid.

"I didn't accuse you. But yeah, I do want to know what's going on."

"Nothing's going on."

Nick sighs. "Look, I know I'm not in all of your AP classes or whatever, but I'm not a complete idiot. You've been there every single time, Piper. *With* a camera. And I hate to say it, but it's right up your alley—pointing out how immature and unaware the popular kids are."

Fire shoots through me. "And *there* it is."

"There *what* is?"

"The real reason you've been so attentive," I say.

"I'm attentive because I like you, but liking you doesn't make me an idiot. Stop treating me like I'm too stupid to put this together. You're involved in these takedowns, so just talk to me. Help me understand."

"I—" My voice cracks. Splits. Just like the rest of me. I hate this. I'm terrified to tell him, terrified of what he already knows. Most of all I'm terrified because I believe the kindness in his voice. And I'm setting myself up for a fall.

"It's complicated," I finally say.

"I'm sure coordinating massive humiliation stunts is complicated," he says, and this time there's a sharp edge to his voice.

God, he thinks I planned the takedowns. The thought tangles my insides, makes me cold all over. But how is what I did so much better? Maybe I didn't choose the sentence, but I enjoyed every last bit of it.

No. Not all of it.

"Fine," he says. "Don't tell me. But, Piper, as smart as you think you are, I'm telling you, someone else is going to figure this out."

I bite my lip, heat crawling under my coat, sweat rising on the back of my neck. He's right. I'm going to get caught. And Nick's going to hate me. A lot of people are going to hate me when they find out about this. God, how did this get so out of control? A memory of Jackson on the football field—coal-black eyes and a promise of vengeance—turns my vision muddy.

"I'm sorry, Nick. I am. You should probably stay as far away from this as you can."

I open the door and slip out of the Jeep, my heart slamming against my ribs and my breath coming in gasps. What am I going to do? Where do I go? Telling someone before seemed crazy, but I still had some control then. I didn't know I couldn't quit. I didn't know my partner would ruin lives.

Nick parks by the curb and jogs my way, hands shoved into his coat pockets.

I hate it. God, I *hate* it, but I'm crying now, so I wipe my cheeks and try to look calm.

"You don't have to run away," he says. "I've known you were involved for a while. I'm not trying to threaten you."

"I know that."

"Then why won't you talk to me?" He reaches for my arm, turning me around so that I can look at him. Our breath is steaming all around us, and it's so, so cold. My tears burn down my face and my heart is turning to ice in my throat.

"I-I can't talk to you," I say. "I can't. I don't want you to hate me."

My words choke on a sob and I can see his face waver, emotions warring in those pretty green eyes. He's afraid of me. Afraid of what I've done.

I can't blame him. But I don't think I can face him either.

I try to move past him and see him close his eyes, his jaw tight. Then, he grabs my sleeve and pulls me closer. It's like pushing a button, and suddenly, I'm grabbing him. It isn't a choice. It just happens. My cheeks flare with heat, and I remember myself, remember that he won't want this. Not now.

But his arms go around me and his chin settles on the top of his head, and everything in me goes quiet. Still.

"You're cold," he says, his voice rumbling under my cheek.

He reaches for my arms, pushing my hands inside his unzipped coat. I don't resist. My palms curl around his sides and I sink into his warmth. All the buzzing in my head is just gone. Silence descends and I hold on tight.

"Let's find a place to talk."

"Why?" I ask. "You know I'm part of this. You can't be okay with that."

"I don't think I am." He squeezes me tighter, like he can't help himself. "But I need to hear it from you. All of it. I need to understand."

I close my eyes and surrender. "I'll tell you."

In the end, he drives me to his house. It's a small, well-kept ranch in a neighborhood not far from mine. When I comment on the dark windows, he explains that his brother's home from college for the holidays but with a girlfriend tonight. His mom's a nurse on third shift because teaching community college art doesn't pay the bills.

I ask about his dad, and he just shakes his head. "Not since I was ten."

Then he pockets his keys and comes around to open my door. He must see the hesitation on my face, because his shoulders tense. "We don't have to go in. We can still get food."

"No, it's fine," I say, though I don't know if it is. I'm in completely new territory here.

Nick fiddles with a key and swears softly when a large brown dog bounds over, floppy ears wagging and bark turned all the way up.

"Cool it, Moose." He turns to me. "He's harmless. But I can put him in the backyard if you want."

"No, he's good." I automatically scratch his satiny ears while I steal a glance at the half-dark house. The living room looks comfortable, with a big TV and end tables crammed with framed pictures. Nick takes my coat as I pull it off.

"C'mon, let's get you something warm to drink," he says. I follow him into a kitchen that smells like cinnamon and coffee. He opens the fridge, revealing cans of soda and plastic tubs of lunchmeat. In my fridge, there's soy yogurt and leftover curry.

"What about hot chocolate?" he offers. "Or coffee? We don't really have much tea, I don't think."

"Cocoa's fine," I say, shuffling a little absently. There's a dinette table at the back of the kitchen, but I feel weird sitting down, so I don't. I just stand there shivering while he puts a kettle on the stove.

Nick frowns at me and then disappears into the living room. He returns seconds later with a sweatshirt that I assume is his and starts tugging it over my head. I work my arms into the sleeves and take a deep breath—soapy boy and something else. Lemons, maybe. Nick, definitely.

My head finds its way out of the neck hole and my hair is all caught on my face. Nick helps me brush it free. In that second, I see something in him that almost makes me cry again. I've assumed *every* bad thing about this guy. I've judged him and pushed him and snapped at him, and he knows I hurt his friend. He knows and he's still here making me cocoa and offering me his sweatshirt.

"I'm not the vigilante," I say without warning. "But I'm helping him."

I can see his questions coming, but I hurry on before he can ask. "It started with texts. I don't know the number and reverse lookup doesn't work on it. I think it's one of those untraceable num—it doesn't matter. I text him the names and he sets up the takedowns. That's how it works. He tells me where to be so I can take the pictures."

His brow furrows. "Why you?"

"Because I see a lot of things that go on around here—injustice stuff. And because I was there the morning that Stella got torn down." I pause. Swallow hard. "He told me this would be a chance to do right by her. And I wanted that. I failed her and I wanted to fix that."

"Piper, that had nothing to do with you."

"Yes it did." I laugh bitterly. "I just stood there, Nick. I stood there and heard them rip her apart. And I didn't say a word."

"Neither did I," he says.

"Actually, you did. You tried to get them to stop." I shake my head. "Eventually you pulled them both off. I didn't. I thought I could make it better, maybe stop it from happening to someone else. But now…it's just not what I thought it would be." My breath hitches, tears strangling me. "I tried to quit. I tried. He-he won't—"

I can't come up with the words, but I don't need to. Nick lets out this shaky sigh and I know he gets it.

"Do you hate me now?" I ask.

"Maybe I should. But no. No, I don't."

Our eyes lock and it scares me. His hands move to cradle my

face like I'm something that matters. I can't handle him like this. When he touches me I don't care about the fact that I'm planning for NYU this fall. I don't care about how different we are. I want him anyway. No logic. No plan. I just want him.

The tags on Moose's collar jangle as he makes his way into the kitchen. A cold dog nose presses into my fingers and Nick's hands slide down to my neck.

He kisses me.

For one millionth of a second, I wish I had my camera. I wish I could catch this image, with his lips slanting over mine and his touch light as feathers—I wish I could hold this moment forever.

The gentleness doesn't last. I reach up, finding his slightly scratchy jaw. I pull him. Push myself. He makes a sound that sends my heart into my throat. My hands move to his hair and his fingers are on my waist. He's bunching up his own sweatshirt around me to tighten his grip. Closer. I need him closer.

It's so awkward, him so crazy tall and me stretched high on my toes, but I want all of it—the strange angles, the click-hiss of Moose's claws against the kitchen floor. I've been underwater too long and every brush of his tongue feels like coming up for air.

A phone buzzes. I cringe and Nick sighs. He pulls back, one hand still locked behind me with an apologetic smile. That's when I realize it's his phone, not mine.

I slump against him, breathing hard against his chest, listening to his heart race under my ear. I see the worry flash over his features when I look up at him.

"It's Jackson."

CHAPTER SIXTEEN

. . . .

He moves to the other room to talk. I stand in the kitchen, trembling because I've just been kissed half to death. The tea kettle whistles and I fumble with the unfamiliar stove to turn it off.

I find mugs in the cupboard and put them down on the counter, but I don't know where the cocoa would be hiding, so I kind of stall out. In our house, we make cocoa from scratch, some crazy organic chocolate concoction. Here they probably have the easy little packets, the ones with the freeze-dried marshmallows that my mother thinks will kill me.

I turn one mug around. A logo blazes across the front. *Proud Cougar Mom—ROAR!* It doesn't end there. Ten, twelve, heck, I can't even count the number of pictures on the fridge—all of Nick or his older brother, Michael, in their uniforms. I think of my own kitchen—the Matisse art calendar on the wall, the Chilean clay bowls in the cupboard.

Stop it. Just stop the comparisons.

I shake my head, reminding myself that my friends live in houses closer to this than to mine. It's not like I check their coffee tables for a modern sculpture book before I agree to come inside, so I need to quit.

I pull my hands inside the sleeves of Nick's sweatshirt and try not to think about kissing him again. It works for almost two entire seconds.

Nick walks in, running a hand through his hair and showing a thin band of skin beneath his Nike sweatshirt. I look away.

He spots the mugs and pulls two packets of hot cocoa out of a box in the cupboard. One point for the packets, but no little marshmallows, so I guess I haven't pegged everything. I watch him pour the water and mix our cocoa.

"Jackson's losing it," he says. "He's even talking about Harrison being a victim. It's all just fuel to the fire now. Jackson was a bad choice."

My temper flares, even though I know it shouldn't. "Why? Because he's your friend?"

"No, he's messed up and it makes him dangerous. That's why he's a bad choice. You've got to get away from this. You do want to get out, right?"

"I do. But I don't know how," I say softly. "I think he's blackmailing me."

"Who, Jackson?"

"No. My…partner, or whatever you want to call him. When I told him I wouldn't do it, he said if I didn't pick, he would. It felt like a threat."

"Have you thought about calling the police? I mean, they're already kind of aware something's going on."

Yeah, I've thought about it. I could hand over my phone and the book and let them sort it out. But that's the whole problem. I did this. *Willingly.*

"Are you afraid of getting in trouble?" Nick asks.

"Yes." I sigh. And then I tell him the rest of it. Finding the notebook, those first texts, figuring out it was Harrison, and then learning I was wrong. All of it. I finish with a frown, slouching back against his counter. "It seemed so simple at first, you know?"

"Honestly, no," he says. "But I believe your intentions were good."

I cringe, because I'm not so sure. "I need to find out who this is. If I can find him, maybe I can talk to him, try to get him to see why this isn't working."

Nick's expression turns dubious. "You think he'll listen to you?"

"I think he picked me for a reason. And I have to try, don't I? I helped him make this mess. I should try to help him make it right."

"All right, then let's figure it out." He talks like it's already decided, like there's no possibility of him *not* being involved now that he knows.

But there is a possibility. A really *big* possibility. If Nick gets involved and ends up in this guy's crosshairs, I could never forgive myself.

"Look, I appreciate you wanting to help, Nick. I do. But I can't get you mixed up in this."

"A little late for that."

"I know you figured it out, but it's still *my* problem. I know I can't stop you from warning your friends—"

"Do you actually think I'd do that?"

"You have to think about yourself, Nick. I know you have goals. Football. A social life."

I look up at him, surprised to see the anger flashing in his features. "Really, Piper?"

"Yes, really. I don't want my screwup to reflect on you with your friends."

"Right, because why would a jock like me do anything that didn't benefit his *social life*?"

Wait. Crap. I raise a hand, horrified. "Nick, I swear I didn't mean—"

"I think you *did* mean it. You don't even realize it, do you? You only see what you're looking for. Jackson's dad is an abusive drunk. Did you know that? Did you know that despite his seriously messed up home life, he hasn't missed a day of school in three years?"

I gape, unable to form a response, but Nick's not done anyway.

"He's no saint. I get that. He earned what he got. But anything remotely redeemable about him didn't make the cut in your little tape. Because you see nothing but his worst. Same with Kristen, and probably with Tate. They're easy targets, but they are *still* people—not popular kids and football players and…shoplifters. Just people."

My breath leaves me in a rush. All my empty spaces are filled with heaviness that runs bone deep.

"Nick," I say, but he recoils from me, jaw tight and eyes dark.

He walks out of the kitchen, closing the conversation. I'm too stunned to follow for a moment, but when I hear him at the door, I join him. He's standing there, holding my coat.

Tears sting my eyes but I don't say a word as I slip it on. I don't try to talk on the drive or when he pulls into my driveway and walks me to the door, because he's obviously been ingrained with the kind of manners that would never allow him to just dump a girl he's kissed off without a proper walk up to the porch.

"I can't do this." He says it on my bottom step, his eyes cast down.

"This?"

"You. Me."

Two words and they tear me into countless pieces. "We don't have to. We can just—" *We can what? Pretend it didn't happen? Pretend we're just buddies?*

Nick laughs, but there's no humor in it. "We both know I'm too far gone to pretend I just want to be friends. So let's just…not."

A burst of panic goes through my middle. I reach, fingers grazing his palm. His breath catches and my stomach goes tight. He doesn't want to go. I can feel it in every inch of him.

"I want to make this right," I say. I didn't know how much until now.

"Then you have to figure out where it went wrong in the first place."

• • •

I take cookies to Stella's mom the Wednesday before Christmas because cookies feel like a good excuse this time of year—and I *need* to see her.

Nick was right. Where it went wrong first was in that hallway with Stella. And I did absolutely nothing to stop it.

It snowed, so I drive slower than usual, checking the address I jotted down from the school directory. I pass her mom's church first, a plain brick building with a single steeple and narrow windows evenly spaced down the sides.

Five houses past the church, I find the van with a Claireville Cougars Swim Team logo on the back windshield. I hit the brakes a little too hard, coming to a dead stop in the middle of the street. Stella's name is scripted above the logo in slanting letters.

This is where she lived. It's a simple, pretty house—a white Cape Cod with shuttered windows and flowerbeds that are probably bright with color in the spring. There's still a fall-themed wreath on the door, but I can see a small nativity set up near the tree in the front yard.

Of course there'd be a nativity. Stella's mom is a pastor. Stella probably spent her holidays singing in choir and attending candlelight services. Not this Christmas though.

Pictures form in my mind, conjured out of nowhere but crisp as snapshots. I can see Stella leaving the house the night she died. Another image of her turning onto the sidewalk, adjusting the volume on her headphones. And then another—the one I wish I couldn't see. A police car in this driveway, an officer at that red front door waiting to deliver horrible news. I don't know if that's how it went down, but it's all I can think of right now.

I swallow the lump rising in my throat and force myself to get out of the car. Stella's driveway seems two miles long and paved with glass. I cross it anyway and ring the doorbell before I can come up with a good enough reason to bolt.

Mrs. DuBois opens the door with a sandwich in her hand and

a curious look on her face. I force my brightest smile. "Hi. Uh, Merry Christmas."

She is a slim woman with a friendly face, but the set of her shoulders tells me she probably wasn't the mom to let Stella get away with much either.

"Hello," she says.

My voice catches, sticks. She sounds *so much* like Stella. I clear my throat and offer the cookies awkwardly. "I'm Piper Woods. I went to school with your daughter."

That was stupid. Maybe I should have said Stella's name. Maybe I should have brought a picture. God, I'm screwing this up already. I should leave. Nick wouldn't go though. More importantly, I don't *want* to go.

She nods and then looks at the plate I'm still holding against my hip.

"Oh." I feel my cheeks grow warm. "I made these for you. I didn't even think to ask if you like cookies."

"Does anyone not like cookies?" She smiles then, obviously trying to put me at ease. I hate that I made that her job somehow.

"Come on in, Piper. It's freezing out there."

I follow her in through a living room with armchairs and a pretty piano. The attached kitchen is bright and airy, and that's where she puts my cookies, in the center of a glass dining room table. She's not eating there though. I see a plate with the other half of her sandwich and a can of diet soda on the counter next to the sink.

I hear the foil crinkle as I look around the living room. There's no Christmas tree, no row of Christmas cards. Nothing. And what did I expect? The woman lost her daughter. My eyes find a row of pictures on the mantle, mostly of Stella, but one of the whole family, Dad, Mom, and a very young Stella in pigtails.

Did her dad leave? Or did he die too? I'm not even sure which feels more unfair.

"These cookies are delicious," Mrs. DuBois says, sounding only a little forced. "Do you bake a lot?"

"Never, actually. I was a little afraid they'd be bricks."

"You didn't try them?"

I realize how odd it is that I didn't and frown. "Weirdly, no."

"Maybe *you* don't like cookies."

I smile, but she's preoccupied wrapping the foil back over my plate. I scan the mantle, which includes a poster-sized group shot of Stella with her school friends. Stella's in the middle and there are lots of in-crowd players around her.

"There's something about the cinnamon," she says. "It's amazing."

"My mom is kind of a health nut, so it's organic. Could be that," I say, stepping closer to the picture. "Though half the time I think organic is just an excuse to charge more."

She laughs then, but the sound is strained. I messed up. I shouldn't have talked about my mom. I don't even know what that word means when your only child dies. Does that mean it doesn't apply to her anymore?

"Stella looks really beautiful here," I say, pointing at the group shot.

"Stella always looks beautiful," she says, and now she's much closer, looking at the picture too.

It's true, she does, but this one captures more than a collection of pretty features. She's wide-eyed and looks like she's on the verge of an unexpected laugh. Nick and Marlow are in the picture, Marlow's hand wrapped around his bicep. Candace is on her left, and Tate and Aimee are on her right. And of course there's Jackson behind her, sort of *looming* with his flinty eyes and too-white smile.

Everyone is looking at the camera except Tate. My heart sinks as I realize he's looking at Stella. Pictures tell a thousand words, but I wish this one didn't. His open body language, the affectionate tilt of his chin—even the depth of his expression are so clear I don't know how I missed it before.

Hearing him say it was one thing, but this is different. Nick was right. Tate loved Stella. Absolutely one thousand percent adored her. I take a step back, feeling breathless.

"It was the last week of junior year," Mrs. DuBois says. I try to find something else in the picture. Like Jackson, who looks more sinister with every passing second. I realize his arm is curved at an awkward angle behind Stella's back. I can't be sure, but it almost seems like he's grabbing her butt. The photographer in me calculates the angles, while the girl in me catalogs the difference in their faces. Jackson's canary-in-my-teeth smile against Tate's open adoration.

"I miss her," Mrs. DuBois says, and her words bring back an eerie echo of Tate with his stained shirt and empty eyes.

I have to say something. I started this for Stella. Because of the things I didn't say. If I don't say them now, I don't think I'll ever breathe right again.

"Mrs. DuBois…"

She looks at me with patient eyes. I feel the pressure of her desperation though. She's hungry for some bit of comfort—some answer about Stella that I know I don't have. I don't think we'll ever know what happened to her on those tracks. Not for sure. The things I do know feel worthless, but they are true, so I say them.

"I didn't know Stella very well," I say softly, looking down at my feet. "My locker is next to hers, and I've taken a lot of pictures of her because I'm on the school yearbook committee. But I don't know that we were friends. Not really."

"Did you take this one?" she asks, covering any disappointment.

"No. But I chose the photo for her locker."

"The picture with her hand in her hair?" Her smile is tremulous and I can feel that mine matches it.

"Yes, that one."

"I loved that. It was so *her*."

I look at my hands, because I still feel this great awkwardness, like I should do something with them, only I'm not sure what. In the end, I put them in my pockets. "I have no idea what I should say right now. I just know that I wish I'd known her better or that I'd reached out to her when she needed somebody. I wish…so many things. Most of all I wish so much this had never happened to you. Or to her."

She sighs and pulls me in for a brief, tight hug. "You did just fine."

"I'm sorry?"

She wipes her eyes but looks a bit more composed. "*No one* has any idea what to say. Half the job is just showing up."

Mrs. DuBois walks me to the door, forcing me to take a couple of cookies. She's right. They did turn out pretty good.

Inside my car, the sunshine is deceptively warm through my windshield. I close my eyes and soak it in, my mind wandering back to the group photograph. To Jackson and Stella and Tate. To all the things I got wrong.

Today I got something right. Maybe if I'm lucky, I can make it a habit.

Mom calls when I'm halfway home.

"Hi, honey, is that your car in the background?"

"I've got you on speaker, don't worry. Where are you?"

"Philadelphia. They're asking me to stay a few more days. They have an approval they're trying to squeeze through before Christmas. Seven-year-old twins."

"You're a modern-day hero." I grin.

"I actually didn't agree to it yet. The storm there is rolling this way, and I'm worried about not getting home until Christmas Eve. I don't want to make any plans without talking to you."

"Mom, I'm not eight. I can handle less time on Christmas Eve. As long as Santa still comes."

She laughs, which makes me smile. "*Santa's* in good shape with your Christmas list, no worries, but, sweetheart, would it be too much trouble for you to pick me up a couple of things at the mall?"

The mall? At Christmas?

"You hate the mall," I say.

"I know, but your grandmother wants perfume. I hate to ask, but—"

"It's totally fine. I need to pick up something for Tacey anyway."

"You're the best kid in the world, you know."

We disconnect before I can tell her she's wrong.

• • •

There's a reason I usually do my Christmas shopping early. Being in the mall two days before Christmas is a special kind of misery. For starters, I'm pretty sure every person who's ever said the word *mall* is in here with me. Fortunately, my grandma's perfume was easy to find, so I'm done with that. I just need something for Tacey.

I dodge a couple of twentysomethings, shopping bags stacked up each arm. Then there's a twitchy guy with a bag from a jewelry store and six or seven girls who are probably in junior high. I still haven't found anything for Tacey and I'm getting beyond sick of being here.

So, decision time. She loves makeup, but one glance at the throng that's descended on Sephora, and I ran like the coward I am. Now, I'm sitting in the atrium, wondering how bad a friend it would make me to get her a gift card and call it a day.

A girl with red hair walks in front of me and I bite my lip, pulled back to the morning with Stella's mom. There's holiday music and everyone's jolly and of course, I think of Nick. For the three millionth time in the last few days.

This is stupid. There is nothing going on between us that can't wait until after the holiday. Hell, that can't wait forever, because no amount of apology is going to make us a perfect fit.

Us together would be messy and awkward. And I still want him so badly my chest hurts.

A kid runs past, squealing about Santa. I step out of his path and pull out my phone. I've dwelled enough. I'll call. I'll call and apologize, and it will be weird, but I'll feel better when it's over. Then I can get on with my holiday without being sucked into a guilt spiral.

Nick picks up on the second ring. "Hello?"

I cringe at the Christmas music blaring in the background. "Hey, it's Piper."

"Yeah, hey," he says. I can hear him moving, shuffling around. The music dies down a bit and he speaks again. "Sorry about that. I'm out shopping."

"You don't happen to be at the mall, do you?"

"Close. I'm at Sports-n-Stuff. Michael wanted new shoulder pads."

I bite my lip, not sure where I should go from here. I know crap-all about sporting equipment and he's busy. I need to find a point, or I need to hang up the phone.

"You were right," I say, clenching my fists. This is harder than it was with Mrs. DuBois. "I saw a picture of Tate with Stella, and it was obvious how he felt about her. I guess it would make anyone crazy to see someone they love with someone else. Especially like that."

I take a breath, but he's still waiting. And I can't hold back. "You were right about me too. I do see what I want to see. I decided that you were all the same. I don't know how to fix that, or how to fix any of this, really. But I wanted you to know I'm trying."

He sighs on the other end of the line, and I close my eyes, wishing I could see his face, that I could see the expression he's wearing. I can hear music in his background, warbling on about Santa coming to town. Here, it's "Jingle Bells." The songs war against each other, grating my nerves and making Nick's silence more painful by the second.

"Nick?"

"I'm here."

Did I say the wrong thing? No. I think I said it right. Just at the wrong time.

"I shouldn't have called so close to Christmas," I say, trying to keep the threat of tears out of my voice.

"Where are you?"

"In the mall atrium. I know it's loud. Look, I'm sorry I bothered y—"

"Can you just stay put for a bit?" he asks. The music's getting loud on his side again, like he's walked back into the heart of the store. "Just wait there. Give me ten minutes, okay?"

"But I—"

He hangs up before I can protest, leaving me completely confused. He wants me to wait here? For him?

I look around, trying to figure the chances of him actually spotting me. There are like fourteen million people crammed into this atrium. They're eating hot pretzels and clustering around the giant maps, checking Christmas lists for last-minute gifts.

Heck with finding me—he'll be lucky to find a parking spot. But then, maybe he just meant he'd call back. Maybe I should just text him. God, maybe I should stop second-guessing everything and go buy something for Tacey. And it better be good, because I skipped the holiday thing and she hasn't texted or called me since.

I check my phone. And then I have this seriously annoying urge to check my face in the mirror in my purse, because apparently I am twelve years old.

I buzz the perimeter of the atrium, thinking of picking up a cinnamon roll until I see that the line is two miles long. I cut back through the middle of the atrium then, determined to stop thinking about the Nick situation and to start thinking that *gift card* is getting more appealing by the second.

I'm digging out my keys to leave when I feel him come up behind me. I stop dead in my tracks. He doesn't touch me and he doesn't speak, but I know. I just know it's him.

"Piper."

I turn around.

He's breathing hard, like he's been running. And I'm not prone to swooning—I'm practically the Antichrist of swooning—but he looks *so* damn good. He's flushed and sort of sweaty, and he's staring at me like I'm the only person here.

"I'm going to kiss you again," he says.

I can't say anything. I don't even remember what language I speak. He steps closer and I swear it is a Christmas miracle that I continue breathing.

"I'm going to kiss you *right here*, Piper. So, if you have any lingering doubts, or any hesitation—"

I pull him down by the collar, because I'm pretty sure he should already be kissing me. His hands touch my face and every crazy, whirlwind feeling rushing through me just stops.

Shoppers are rushing and music is playing, but I am anchored by his stillness, by the soft, warm slide of his lips over mine.

We kiss like we've done it for years, maybe entire lifetimes. I know how to tilt my head and he knows when to pull me closer. I knot my hands in the back of his hair, and, breathless as I am, I feel like I'm coming back to life.

When we part, we're both panting. "How was Sports-n-Stuff?"

"Not as good as the mall."

"Shoulder pads are overrated."

Nick laughs. "Nice try, Woods, but you're still kissing a jock. What will your art friends think?"

"They'll probably urge psychiatric evaluation," I admit.

I love the grin he cracks, like he's *charmed* by my absolute lack of tact. He really is over the moon because that's definitely not one of my endearing qualities.

"That came out totally wrong," I say.

"I know," he says. "And I don't care what anyone thinks. I never even considered it."

"I believe you. And that's one of the many reasons I'm standing here."

"Kissing a football player in the middle of the mall."

"Well, right now I'm not—"

I can't finish the sentence because he kisses me again. And I think, maybe this time, I don't need to have the last word.

• • •

Nick makes it okay to be in the mall at Christmas. We talk and laugh until my sides hurt, and I forget about the crowds and the commercialism. Most of all, I forget all the awful things I'm tangled up in.

It's eight o'clock when the inevitable catches up to me. I eye my phone on the table between us. Because all the kisses in the world don't change the fact that it's Friday night. And I owe my partner a name.

The threat churns in my gut until I push my cinnamon roll away and turn my phone over, pressing the button to bring the screen to life.

"When are you supposed to text him?" Nick asks. He finishes his roll and points at mine with puppy dog eyes.

I push it across the table. "Go for it. I have an hour."

"You could text my name."

I roll my eyes at him. "Sure. And what will this takedown be for? Nick Patterson—stealer of kisses and cinnamon rolls?"

His hair falls over one eye, but he shakes it back and winks. "I'm a rebel."

"Seriously, what is with your boy scout self? Have you ever done *anything* wrong?"

"I don't know. I stood up Hannah Cromley in the ninth grade.

I still feel bad about that. I've lied to my mom. Oh, I puked in Tate's gym bag once and never fessed up."

"Karma got you back on that one," I say, and we share a sad smile over our adventure with Tate.

"You could call his bluff."

"Call his bluff?"

Nick saws off another hunk of gooey goodness. "The way I see it, there aren't that many options. Turn in the book and your phone to the school."

"I can't. I don't even know that everything in that book is legit. I think I've brought down enough people. I don't need to invite more trouble over something Harrison might have misinterpreted."

"You could take your phone in, though."

I sigh. "If I don't find out who's doing this, I don't think I'll have a choice."

He reaches for my hand then, fingers grazing my knuckles. "So, back to calling his bluff. Is it so crazy to just walk away? Ignore him altogether?"

"It scares me." Because I have a best friend with some serious baggage.

"What's the worst-case scenario?"

"He targets someone I love." Someone like Manny. Because Manny has done things that are takedown worthy. Broke or not, changing records is wrong. But I can't stand the idea of seeing him tortured like that.

God, that makes me such a hypocrite.

"Then send my name." He tilts his head, shoulders hunched.

"I don't think I can sit here and watch you target someone else. I'm trying to be open-minded—"

"I don't think I can either."

After Harrison? Just no. I can't even imagine the holiday at his house now. Permafrost glares around the Christmas tree. My throat goes tight at the idea.

"Then my name it is. It'll buy you a week to figure it out, and we'll just have to deal with whatever your jerk partner scrounges up on me."

He's offering to walk into the fire for me. Why? Because he doesn't have anything to hide. I study him across the table. Green eyes. Good heart. Some of my cinnamon roll stuck to his upper lip. No. No way in hell is he going to pay for my mistake.

I shove my phone to the middle of the table.

"You know, I think I'm going to call his bluff. My targeting days are over."

CHAPTER SEVENTEEN

· ·

December 25 starts all wrong. I wake up at eight to a bleak, pounding rain and the sound of my parents fighting. It isn't the silent, sniper-comment affair it's been for the last year either. This is a *real* fight.

My mother's voice is too loud and high. I can't make out the words, but I can tell she's upset. She's talking more than he is, her voice rising and lowering. My dad is on the defense, his few words firing back like bullets, sharp and hard.

I sit up slowly, careful not to let the bed creak as I pull my knees up to my chest. My eyes move to the window, where the rain is sluicing through a sickly sky. The snow that blanketed the world in white is washed away, leaving everything wet and gray.

It doesn't feel like Christmas.

I take my phone from my bedside table and there's no text from my partner. Whatever he's planning is still a mystery, but I'm less worried than I was. The only person in my circle of friends that feels like a potential takedown target is Manny. And that's if the texter knows about the blackmailing stuff, which seems unlikely since he didn't write the book after all. Either way, Manny's in Kentucky with his family for Christmas, so today I can probably relax.

Fat joke with World War III brewing on the first floor.

I text "Merry Christmas" to Tacey, Manny, Hadley, and Connor. I think about Nick, but I decide to wait. God knows I might need the cheering after dealing with my parents.

A couple of messages flurry back.

From Manny:

> Aunt C. made rum balls! Y weren't U at yearbook thing? Shit went down!

And then Hadley:

> Merry Christmas! Connor is wearing a ridiculous sweater. I'm sending you pictures.

And she does. Somehow he manages to look cool and classic at Hadley's family breakfast table, despite the giant reindeer stitched across his chest.

Tacey doesn't answer. Weird. I didn't hear from her after the meeting I missed either, which means she's probably *really* not happy with me. Can't fix that now though.

I put my phone in my pocket and stare at my bedroom ceiling. I can't pretend to sleep forever. I will have to go downstairs and open presents and pretend that I didn't hear them. We'll play this up all day, this little act of being the perfect, happy family. And I don't really get it, why we do this. There isn't one person left who actually believes it.

I stomp out of bed and the voices below go silent. Terrific. I throw on my robe and brush my teeth, staring long and hard at myself in the mirror.

"Let the games begin," I say.

I come downstairs to my parents sitting on either side of the couch. They wish me a merry Christmas and I wish it back, and we all pretend we don't know what's really going on. We eat cinnamon-banana pancakes and drink freshly squeezed orange juice and then we open presents with Irish Christmas music in the background. None of it is bad, but none of it feels right either.

As soon as the last present is opened, my dad disappears to his studio and Mom heads into the kitchen to do the dishes. Back to life as usual, except that I want to cry a little. My phone buzzes with a message. Nick's name appears on the screen and I smile for the first time all day.

> Merry Christmas.

I flop down on my bed to reply.

> Merry Christmas back.

> Did you get everything you want?

For one second, I think of telling him all the things my parents so desperately want me to believe—about my wonderful Christmas and my perfect family. But then I remember the feel of his chin on my head, his throat against my cheek. I can't ruin that trust again. I won't.

> I wouldn't list it among my best holidays this year.

> Would a drive-by guest help?

My heart does obnoxious fluttery things. I ignore it and text him back.

> How soon can you be here?

> Thirty minutes. I have to be quick though.

I slip upstairs to trade in the penguin pants for a pair of jeans and a blue sweater. Since I normally spend the entire holiday in pajamas, this sudden makeup-wearing, hair-fluffed version of me isn't lost on my mom when I head into the kitchen.

"Nick's stopping by," I explain.

Mom's dishrag pauses on a plate. She tries to hide her smile, but I can hear it in her voice. "That sounds lovely."

"What sounds lovely?" Dad asks as he walks in.

"My friend Nick—he's going to stop by for just a minute."

Dad tugs the hem of my shirt. "That explains the sweater."

I heave a sigh. "Dad, please don't make a big deal. Please."

It feels like forever before he nods, but then everything is fine. They clean up wrapping paper, and he warns me that he's not getting out of his flannel pants, incoming boy or no.

When the doorbell rings, Dad acts like he's going to get up, but Mom clears her throat in a way that warns of imminent death, so he sits back down, sulking.

I force myself to take a couple of deep breaths before I walk over and open the door. He's standing on the porch with a plastic tub full of cookies and a sad-looking spruce branch held high above our heads.

I grin. "That's not mistletoe."

He smiles back, pink-cheeked and looking like a Christmas card in his black wool coat and red sweater. "It's the closest thing I could find."

"Well, it works for me." I pull him in before he can say more. His coat is scratchy and the cookies are getting crushed between us, but it's still magic. Warm and sweet, and God, he shouldn't be able to make me forget everything else this fast. But he does.

Until he pulls away, much, much too soon.

"No more texts?" he asks.

"Not yet."

"Good. Maybe that'll be the end of it."

My mother calls from inside, "Piper, stop keeping poor Nick in the cold!"

We grin, still clinging to each other. Then he holds up the cookies. "I'm sorry, I really can't stay. My mom only let me out of the house on delivery duty."

I take the cookies and invite him in. I feel annoyingly warm and soft when he holds my hand and wishes my parents a merry Christmas. He apologizes for being so brief and Mom tells him she knows how busy holidays can be. Dad just looks at our joined hands with an amused smile—probably trying to reconcile this hulking giant with the thin, emo boys I normally date.

And then we're back outside, and he's hugging me good-bye, his lips at my jaw. I feel him slide something into my pocket. A box.

"But I didn't get you anything," I say.

"Yeah you did," he says, and then he kisses me again, letting it linger just long enough to make my head spin.

"I have to go," he says, striding down my walkway.

I pull out the small box he left in my pocket as he makes his way back to his Jeep. There's a keychain inside the box—a silver figure with a funny jester's hat and a stick by his mouth. Kind of cool but not really making much sense until I turn it over to see the detail better. It's not a stick; it's a flute. Because he isn't a jester. He's a *piper*.

I float back inside on a bliss-fueled cloud, feeling lighter than air and warmer than a May afternoon. For a crap Christmas, it might be one of my favorites.

Mom sees me playing with the keychain after dinner. She leans in, pressing her shoulder into mine. "It's beautiful."

"It's just a keychain." My grin makes it obvious it's a lot more than that.

"I really like him, you know."

A denial waits on my lips. An argument about my possible

West Coast future. About how this is the wrong time for me to like anyone. But I push all of that down with a deep breath.

"I really like him too."

I curl myself into bed somewhere near midnight, leaving my alarm off. Tacey still hasn't texted. It's bugging me. I just got over the weirdness with Manny. I don't want things to be wrong between Tacey and me now too. For a second I think of texting again, to apologize for missing the meeting. Maybe to see if I can swing by tomorrow morning with her present. But it's late. And it's Christmas.

If we're going to fight, we can wait until tomorrow.

I fall asleep with my fingers around my piper keychain. I wake to my mother's hand stroking my hair and more winter rain pattering my window. I blink open my eyes, but the sky beyond my window is still charcoal gray. It's too early to wake me on Christmas break.

Something's wrong.

I roll over to see my mom looking down at me. The clock beside her reads 6:56.

"Baby," she starts, but her voice catches before she can say more.

She's pale. And she never calls me baby. I sit up, the rain suddenly chilling me to the bone, drenching me in an icy fear I can't even name.

"What is it?" I ask, my voice still gravelly from sleep.

"It's Tacey."

CHAPTER EIGHTEEN

. . . .

Please let her be all right.

Please.

"You're scaring me, Mom."

She nods, smoothing my hair back from my forehead. "Tacey's fine. She's not…hurt."

"Okay," I say, but it's not okay. Something's obviously really wrong.

"Tacey's mom called just now."

"At six in the morning?"

"She knows I'm an early riser. She asked me if you'd ever mentioned anything about Tacey acting oddly or being involved in any sort of…"

Her look seems to ask me to fill in the blanks, but there's nothing *but* blanks here. I scoot back to my headboard and pull my knees up but keep them under the covers. "Any sort of *what*?"

"Drugs," she says. "Tacey's been using drugs."

I laugh. Because it's laughable. Unthinkable. Tacey on drugs is like me in a cheerleading skirt. Not possible.

"Piper, I know it sounds a bit odd—"

"Odd? No, Mom, it doesn't sound odd. It sounds *ridiculous*. Tacey is on the antidrug committee for God's sake! She did that extra credit video essay reviewing heroin documentaries last year."

"Honey, I know it sounds out of character, but she was caught red-handed. She confessed."

"Confessed to *what*?" I'm practically shouting, but I can't seem to stop myself. "Shooting up in the library? Come on!"

My mother presses her lips together and looks at her lap. "No, Piper. Not those kind of drugs."

I stop then, holding my breath as I wait for her to go on.

"Tacey's little sister, Tara, is on ADHD medicine. They found her pills in Tacey's purse. Someone knocked it over at the coffee shop the other day. The bottle fell out and I guess a bunch of kids saw it."

The yearbook meeting. The meeting I was supposed to go to.

I shudder at the memory of Manny's text about something going down. But there's more than that. Tacey's endless energy. The lost weight. The way she never, ever seems to slow down. Or even sleep.

No. No, don't go there.

A cold, panicky feeling crawls through my middle, and I can barely find my voice. "Maybe she was holding it."

It sounds pretty desperate, even to me. My mom puts a gentle hand on my knee, and it's all I can do to not pull away.

"Honey, I told you. She confessed. She told them what she was doing."

"I want to see her," I say.

"I don't think that's a good idea right now."

"I don't care if it's a good idea. She's one of my best friends, and she's hurting and—"

"I think she needs some time, Piper. Their whole family probably does."

"Why are you telling me all of this? To scare me away?"

"I told you because I didn't want you to hear it some other way. With the way news spreads in your school, you could have found out through some random text message from a stranger!"

Some random text message from a stranger.

Oh God.

My cheeks ache and my stomach rolls. I close my eyes and bring my hand to my cold, clammy forehead. That yearbook holiday thing was on Thursday night. And then on Friday I decided to be smug—to call his bluff.

No. *Please*, no.

"Who told her parents?" I ask, voice shaking.

"I don't know."

"They didn't say?"

Mom's brow puckers. She can barely keep up with me. If I don't ease up, she's probably going to check *my* bag for a bottle of pills.

"They didn't give a name and Tacey's parents didn't recognize the phone number," she finally says. "Piper, who told is not the issue here. You know that, right?"

"Yes," I say, but she's wrong. Who told is the *whole* issue. I eye my phone on my nightstand but look away quickly. I don't want her spotting it, deciding to take it away before I try to call Tacey.

But I don't want to call anyone. I want to check my messages.

"What can I do for you, sweetheart? How can I help?"

I close my eyes and take a shaky breath. "Could I just have a few minutes alone? To process."

I feel the gossamer brush of her lips on my forehead. And

then the mattress shifts as she gets up, crosses my room, and slips outside.

I scramble for my phone the instant the door closes. The screen blooms to life and I see the message. The too-familiar number. I pull it up, holding my breath.

> You should have given me a name.

• • •

Mom was right about Tacey's parents. Her mom wouldn't even let me in to drop off flowers. So I text Manny, hoping he's home from his aunt's place. He is. He answers the door wearing a giant hoodie and seriously dark circles under his eyes.

"Did you drive through the night?" I ask.

"Ten hours straight."

"You probably need sleep."

"Yeah, well my phone's been blowing up with this Tacey stuff."

"What happened?"

Manny heaves a sigh and rubs his eyes. "Come in."

Mr. Raines is snoring softly in his recliner. It smells like oranges and boys in here. The citrus is probably thanks to the fruit basket on the table. I see a red scarf on the back of Manny's chair. It'll probably end up around my neck within a week. The Raines boys are not scarf people.

I follow Manny into his room and kick some of his shoes out of the way so I can sit down on his bed. He moves straight to his computer, pulling things up before I even ask. I have a feeling I'm not going to want to see whatever he's looking up. But it's time for me to do a lot of things I don't want to do.

Like telling Manny about the vigilante stuff?

Maybe. Probably.

"We were all at the coffee shop—everybody but you and Connor. It was a total waste of time. The typical holly-jolly crap we do was a lot less enthusiastic after Ms. Collins used half an hour and a lot of fifty-cent words to tell us the website isn't coming back. And *then* she tried to dig for information about who had access to what and if we knew anyone that might want to put the tape up."

"You think she wants to break this thing open?"

"Makes sense, right? She wants a real teaching job, not the part-time advising crap. Saving the school's morality or whatever seems like a good bet." Manny yawns. "Anyway, Ms. Collins got up to leave and knocked over Tacey's purse. Those stupid pills flew halfway across the room."

"Okay, but not that many people saw, right?"

"Eh, I wouldn't say that. Aimee was the one who picked them up—she tried to be discreet, but Candace was there. It might have been okay if Tacey hadn't freaked out, which made everything *really* obvious."

It probably wouldn't have mattered. Candace is more effective than an emergency broadcast system.

I'm so shocked I can barely find the words, but Manny doesn't look so shocked. He picks his thumbnail and looks at the wall like none of this is unexpected.

"Manny, did you know about this?"

He shrugs. "I figured. She's been antsy, running a hundred miles an hour and outperforming everyone. Plus, Tara hates taking her meds. What, you didn't even suspect?"

"No." Because I wasn't paying attention. I've been so wrapped up in fixing the world that I didn't see. She *needed* me. My friend needed me, and I was too busy playing vigilante games to notice.

"So the whole school knows?" I ask, voice cracking.

"It's a little bigger than that. Check out the website." Manny rolls away from the computer and stretches out on his bed, face-first. "They got it down, but Connor sent me this screenshot. It was already over fifty thousand visits then. It's on the screen if you want to look."

I don't. The three steps to that computer feel like three miles. But I sit down anyway. Adjust the monitor so I can see the image. Wish I could burn it out of my eyes just as fast as I take it in.

It's a social profile page, but it's not Tacey's. It's her name and picture, but the rest of it looks like it's been peeled off of someone else altogether. The background is graffiti-embossed black, with cannabis leaves in the corners. The *Things I Dig* section includes flying and tripping, and there's a life quote about how good and free she feels with the needle deep inside. And the pictures? Heroin, crack, every awful thing you can imagine.

I close my eyes, revolted. "That's…that's not Tacey."

"She'll survive it. It'll be all right," Manny says, his words muffled by his pillow and slurred by his exhaustion.

I shake my head because he's wrong. Nothing will be right now.

It's my fault this happened. This will affect everything. Her position in the antidrug group. Maybe even her spot on the yearbook committee. All the things that matter to her—I stripped them away. Guilty or not, she would have never been a target if picking her wouldn't have hurt me.

And no one would have picked her if I had swallowed my fear and turned myself in. If I had done the right thing.

I'm back to Nick's words. Back to finding the place where it all went wrong. I don't even know if I'll ever find it. Every layer I peel back reveals a new stain.

Like best friends keeping big secrets.

I square my shoulders and close down the screen on Manny's window.

"Manny? I need to tell you something."

He's quiet and still on his bed. I stand up and walk over, nudging the mattress with my knee.

"Manny?"

The mattress makes a rustling noise, but Manny doesn't move. He's dead asleep. I look down to see a wad of papers sticking out from between the mattress and the box spring. It doesn't look like the kind of thing a boy keeps under his mattress. It's graph paper. A thick stack of it folded in half. Curiosity picks at my fingers, whispers in my ears.

I shouldn't.

God, I know I shouldn't. But one more soft nudge of my knee and the papers fall out, unfolding like an invitation.

I look down at the kind of evidence that warrants expulsion.

Maybe worse. Names, payment amounts, student ID numbers. And the worst part of all. Job descriptions. It isn't much. Tardies for Dean Jiminez. English and history for Shawna Welsh. Which means he didn't just mess with attendance. He somehow did grades too.

My stomach sours and I take a breath. I pick the papers up, because it doesn't matter anymore. I already know too much.

There are four sheets—six names I recognize and more I don't. What the hell? How big is this mess? Is he doing this for other schools? He told me he was done. He kept this from me.

You're keeping secrets too.

Guilt pricks at my chest, curls fingers around my ribs. It hurts. Everything hurts.

I flip to the next page with shaking fingers. Not graph paper. A bill. Claireville Orthopedic and a local address is listed at the top. I scan down the bill. Some sort of preauthorization. A surgical preauthorization. Lumbar fusion.

I think back to Mr. Raines struggling under the desk. To the two weeks this summer when he was laid up in bed. Out of work. He's had a bad back for a while, but I didn't know.

My eyes trail to the patient responsibility amount listed after the insurance payment—$3,164. I close my eyes and swallow down the bitter truth. I didn't know anything.

It's like a nail in my coffin. One that feels like it's been driven through the center of my chest.

I put the papers back where I found them and tug a blanket over Manny. I pull an afghan over Mr. Raines too, before I head outside. The door bangs louder than I intended, and I cringe, hoping it doesn't wake them. I start my car and sit there, shivering and sick in their driveway. I don't know where to start.

My phone shows a list of texts that burn my eyes. Where did it go wrong to begin with? This is where it went wrong. Right here.

I was stupid enough to believe that this was about justice, that I could do right by Stella. But this was never about any of those things. It was me pretending I could make up for something I can never change.

Tacey paid the price. I can't let that happen again.

Nick asked me if I was afraid to get caught. I was. Still am. But I'm more afraid of what will happen if I don't end this.

My fingers fly over the keyboard on my phone.

> You went too far. We need to be done.

His reply comes moments later.

> We aren't done. Lots of people left to punish.

> I don't want to punish anyone. I told you, I quit.

> If you quit, I'll keep choosing. Who do you think I'll find next?

Manny. Rage bubbles up from my center, so hot my head spins when I reply.

> You're the next person to get found. I'm about to make sure of it.

I press Send and shove my phone to the bottom of my purse. Because I don't want to hear back from him. I don't want to read another damn thing he has to say.

I steer my Subaru out of Manny's driveway and take a left at the light. I head into town, past all the places I would normally stop. In the business district, I take the left toward our government offices. It's not an area I'm familiar with, but soon enough I see the brass letters on red brick. The ones that spell out *Police Station*.

I park in the lot and pull my purse onto my lap. Then I stare at the brightly lit double doors that lead inside.

I can do this. I picture it in my head, sliding my phone across a high counter. Speaking to a nameless, faceless police officer. Admitting my part in this awful thing.

Shame burns my cheeks, but it's starting to feel familiar. Just another part of me.

I grab my door handle and my purse vibrates on my legs. My body turns to stone.

Do not check it. Do. Not.

In the end, I can't help it. I tug the phone out and jab the button to bring it to life. The message flashes, black on a glowing white background. I read it once and my world shrinks. Narrows into three sentences.

Go ahead. Turn me in. Let's see how fast I can show the world your daddy's big secret.

CHAPTER NINETEEN

· ·

My dad hunches over the table, sketching something crazy elaborate on the inside cover of the phone book. I've been watching him for ten minutes, staring bullets into the back of his head. If mind reading is real, I definitely don't have the gift.

I have no idea what anyone would have on my dad. But then, I would have never dreamed anyone could find something on Tacey.

"You look great. Stop fidgeting," Dad says without looking up.

I look what? Oh. Right.

I glance down at my sweater and skirt. Nick's supposed to pick me up in a few minutes. There's a lot to fill him in on. Poor guy probably thinks it's just a date. I wish it were. I press my lips together, wondering if I should slap on a little lip gloss. Probably.

If I could stop stalking my dad long enough to go get some.

He caps his pen and reclines back, grinning at me. "You're lucky Mom's in Boston. She'd probably give you a curfew."

His words stab like little needles, and I'm sick of being poked. Or maybe I'm too edgy about all the things we're both hiding. "Mom likes Nick. And she's not like that."

"I'm just teasing you, Peanut."

I think back to Mom's red eyes the night I went to the club. The fight on Christmas morning. "No, you're teasing her. And she's not here to defend herself."

His face reflects his hurt, and I get it. I'm working bitchy like it's a full-time job. It isn't fair. I know he loves me and teasing is just who he is, but I can't shake the idea that he's hiding something big.

Headlights in the driveway signal my escape, so I sling my coat on and grab my purse from the counter. "I'll be home a little after midnight, if that's okay."

"Sure," he says, trying to stay bright. "Have a good time."

I can't even force myself to thank him before I bolt. Nick is halfway up the driveway, looking a little surprised.

"Uh…should I say hi to your parents?"

"If you don't mind me waiting in the car." I sigh. "It's just Dad. We're on each other's nerves. Besides I have texter news."

His face falls. "I was really hoping the radio silence would work."

He rushes to open my door and I give him a sad smile. "That makes two of us."

I fill him in on the way, the mess with Tacey, my idea to turn the phone in to the police, his threat against my dad. He parks in front of a little Italian restaurant but doesn't get out.

"I don't like it. I think you should talk to the police."

Tears blur my vision. "I can't. After what he did to Tacey, I have this awful feeling he'll do worse to my dad. He set that up *before* I was supposed to send a name, so that he'd be ready."

"Did you find out who was at the coffee shop? Maybe you could track it that way."

I wave that off. "According to Manny, the place was packed with students."

"Okay, well do you know what he's after? What your dad might have going on?"

"No idea." But I wonder not for the first time if it's the source of my parents' fighting.

"So now what?"

"I have to find out what my dad's hiding before Friday or I'll have to send him a name. Same song."

"For how long?" Nick's grip on the steering wheel turns his knuckles white. "I hate it, Piper. He's totally in control, and you don't know who he is. This won't end. Not ever. And what if Jackson finds out you're involved? I can't even *think* about that."

"Look, I know the end game here. I have to turn him in, turn myself in. I know that. But I'm not ready. I'm okay going down—I made my bed. But I don't think I'm ready to see my *dad's* name smeared all over this very small town!"

"Hey," he says, voice soft and hands reaching for me. He touches my shoulders, my face. He holds me together with those touches. "I know. I know this isn't easy. I'm just freaked, you know?"

"Me too." I sniff, forcing myself to pull it together. "But I can do this. I know I can. I'm just hoping by some miracle I can figure out my dad's mess, you know? But I swear to you, this ends soon, okay?"

"I can handle that. Now would it be totally irresponsible to not think about this for an hour?"

My only answer is a smile.

For all the ways Nick and I are mismatched, it's so easy between us. He pulls out my chair before we sit down and we want to share the same salad. He's got great stories. He's leaned in using a breadstick to enhance the tale of his first mountain climbing adventure—how he hadn't known how to tie his harness and how he'd almost thrown up when he looked down. I'm laughing so hard I'm afraid we might get kicked out.

"Tate was ready to call the damn park ranger to get me down—" He stops so suddenly, I think maybe he's going to sneeze. Or that he's choking, but he's not. His expression drifts, eyes going cloudy.

"Nick? What is it?" I ask.

"Tate. It's, uh…his birthday party tonight."

"And you're not there?" I can't imagine missing one of my crew's birthday parties. And by the way he's wincing, I'd say this is a first for Nick too.

"Well, I'd obviously rather be with the girl I'm dating," he says, trying a smile. When I frown, he tenses, clearly misreading me. "Oh, come on. I didn't use the word *girlfriend*."

"Would you?"

"Would you actually let me?"

I'm too stunned to answer, because yeah, I think I would. And Nick must see it, because he's looking at me like I handed him the key to the city.

And I give him the only thing I have in return. "I think you should go to Tate's party. He's your friend. That's important too."

I can see an idea bloom in his eyes. And I have a bad feeling

I'm not going to be crazy about it. "How would you feel about coming with me?"

• • •

I'm trying to stay positive, but when we pull up to the house, I feel like a cold, wet blanket's been tossed over me. We're parked at the edge of Tate's wide, flat lawn. The last time we were here, he puked in a bucket. Now, it might be my turn.

There are a handful of people on the porch smoking, and even from here I can hear the music pounding. Girls in micro-skirts and guys in collared shirts are wandering in and out of the house. It looks like…everything I hate about high school.

"I feel like this is going to turn into one of those scenes where someone swings on a chandelier," I say. "Or maybe gets pregnant."

Nick laughs. "Claireville football parties are obviously wildly exaggerated."

"It's not like I *never* go to parties, you know."

"Not to our parties," he says.

I arch a brow at him. "And what about you? I don't see you at the theater kid bashes. Which, for the record, are a hell of a lot more inventive than keg stands by the hot tub."

"Touché." We share a smile and then he tips his chin toward the long driveway. "Last chance. If you're not up for it, I can take you home."

Home sounds better. *So* much better. But Nick ran through a shopping mall two days before Christmas to kiss me. I can put on my big girl panties and deal with an hour at his friend's birthday party.

"No. Let's do it."

I open the passenger door and hop out. Nick meets me at the front bumper of the Jeep. He hugs me hard enough to pull me off my feet. I cross my arms behind his neck and butterflies lift off in my stomach. Even though it's dark, I can see the pale green of his eyes.

"If you keep surprising me, then I'm going to be like a bad penny," he says.

"A bad penny?"

"It's something my mom says," he explains. "It means I'll keep turning up."

He kisses me once before he drops me back to my feet and takes my hand as if there's no question about how we'll be arriving at this party. Nick walks up the drive with his shoulders back and his head high. I command myself not to look sullen. Or scared.

I do great until the door opens and a wave of apprehension rolls over me. The living room is teeming with people I barely know and usually avoid. At least half of them look up to see us stepping inside. An invisible hand squeezes my throat just as hard as I'm gripping Nick's hand.

Terror aside, it's not exactly the hedonistic rave I was expecting. The music is loud and the living room is pretty packed, but most of the cans on the coffee table are soda. I can tell where the liquor is, hiding none too stealthily in the red plastic cups. It's a party. A pretty normal looking party, really.

There are two long leather couches lined with people in the main room. Another group is clustered around a giant wall-mounted television playing a video game. I spot a lot of familiar faces—Kristen, Candace, and Shelby, who's apparently gotten over her little Tate crush if her tongue being in Nathan's mouth is any indicator.

The crowd at the television cheers, and someone gives a triumphant howl. A fist pumps into the air and my ribs constrict. Jackson. He slaps some victory high fives. And then his dark eyes lock onto us so fast I feel like I've got a target on my forehead. He lopes toward us, and Nick's fingers tighten around mine.

"Nicky Boy," he says, grabbing Nick's free hand.

"How's it going?"

"Not bad, not bad," Jackson says, but his eyes flick down to the place where our hands are joined with a less than friendly smile. Nick just pulls me closer. I can't read his expression from my angle, but the way he tilts his head looks like a challenge.

"Piper! Hi!"

It's Aimee Johnston, wearing a red skirt that matches her lipstick perfectly. And she's smiling. Really smiling. "Do you want to come get something to drink?"

"Who's that?" someone says behind her. I think it's Ming. My suspicions are confirmed when she pushes up on tiptoe behind Aimee, revealing heavily lined golden eyes and a smile that belongs on TV. "Oh, hey, you're the school photographer, right? Do you want to take a picture?"

I laugh, but Aimee groans. "She doesn't want to take your

picture, freak." Then she turns to me with a wink. "Come on, let's go to the kitchen. I'll introduce you to everybody."

I hesitate for just a moment, feeling my link with Nick grow taut as Aimee pulls my arm. Nick holds my gaze, a silent question in his eyes.

And I know just a shake of my head, and he'll make sure this doesn't happen. It's up to me. With him it's *always* up to me, isn't it?

Ming makes a knowing sound. "Oh, I wouldn't let Nick go either."

Aimee sweeps me away. She's chattering a mile a minute, introducing me to people I already know and shoving a lukewarm can of soda into my hand when I decline a beer. It's…not terrible. I'm not tempted to pick up a pair of pom-poms or start a more thorough collection of pop music, but everyone's polite. Almost pleasant.

Still, when Nick steps into the kitchen twenty minutes later, I feel my shoulders sag with relief. He walks up to me, ignoring the way Ming coos at our closeness.

I take a breath, surprised at how familiar he smells already. How right.

"Hey."

"Hey back," I say.

"You ready to get out of here?" I try not to nod too hard. And fail. He smiles at me anyway. "Want to come with me to find Tate? I still haven't wished him happy birthday."

"He wasn't out there with you guys?"

"No."

He doesn't need to tell me he's worried. I can see it in his eyes. And it wasn't so long ago that I saw the guy standing beside his own mailbox looking like lukewarm death, so I get it.

"Let's look around," I say.

We don't bother with the back porch, but we check out front where a few kids are still smoking. Then we head upstairs, passing by one room with enough moaning to keep us from knocking. Nick points at a closed door across the hallway, and since he pushes it right open, I'm assuming it's Tate's bedroom.

I hold my breath, half-terrified of what we're going to find in here. After my last experience with Tate, I'm imagining a tabloid overdose scene, him slumped over next to a coke-dusted mirror and a pile of empty liquor bottles. At the very least, I figure he'll be sobbing facedown on one of Stella's pictures.

I'm wrong. He's lying on his back in the middle of his neatly made bed, throwing a baseball into the air. The ball lands with a smack on his palm and he throws it again. The normalcy of it is weirder than any of my imaginings.

"Hey," Nick says, and I hesitate behind him, thinking I should have waited in the hall. Or maybe in the next town.

"Hey," Tate says. His eyes move right past Nick to me. "You can come in, Piper. I don't bite."

I'd really rather light my own hair on fire than hang out in Tate Donovan's bedroom, but I smile tightly and push the door closed behind me.

Tate rolls forward to sit up, scrubbing a hand over his pale hair. He looks better. Like he's at least slept.

Nick shuffles forward, kicking the edge of Tate's bed. "Figured you'd be downstairs enjoying your party. Happy birthday, by the way."

"Yeah, thanks," Tate says. "I should get down there."

"Pretty much everybody showed up." He starts listing names, but Tate doesn't seem interested. Eventually, Nick heaves a sigh. "You know, you could just come with us. If you don't feel like being around all these people. We could grab pizza or something."

Tate looks at me and I force myself to look back, to face this, like I've needed to since that day in the hallway. He's still the same guy he's always been. Too pretty for his own good and spoiled within an inch of his life. He's also the guy who said things to Stella DuBois that will haunt me until the day I die. But I've got ugliness in me too. Things I've done that will trail behind me like a shadow.

Is that why he looks different?

It'd be a nice lie to believe, but I know this isn't about some self-actualization for me. It's about the way he looked at Stella in that picture at Mrs. DuBois's house. He *loved* her. He loved her, and that tape, what she did with…whoever that was. It destroyed him.

It doesn't change anything for Stella.

But it changes everything for me.

"We could sneak you out the window," I say.

Tate smiles. It's strained but real, and the look Nick gives me makes me feel like there's still something good left in me.

"Thanks," Tate says, standing up. "But I'm being a douche, hiding out up here. I'll go be social. Or something."

Nick nods. "If you change your mind—"

"Yeah." Tate slaps Nick on the shoulder. "Thanks, man."

He moves to walk past us, pausing to look at me. I think he's going to say something but he doesn't. He just nods. Maybe we've already said enough.

His bedroom door slams open without warning, banging into the wall hard enough to make us all jump. Jackson stands in the opening. He's obviously started drinking, and he's *way* too interested in the three of us standing in such close proximity.

"Looks like I interrupted," he says with a leer.

My stomach wads up like a piece of trash.

"Jackson, I swear to God." Nick's voice is as menacing as I've ever heard it.

"Relax, Nicky. I'll play nice." Jackson waves his hands, but he's still blocking the door. My feet are itching to run.

Tate tries to shoulder past him, but Jackson bumps into him with a bark of a laugh.

Tate's jaw goes tight. "Move, man."

Jackson pushes him back. "What's the rush? You've *got* to fill me in on all of this. You having a little birthday action?"

"Get out of my room, Jackson."

"Make me."

Nick's hands curl into fists and the air changes. For a second, we're all suspended in the tension. And then Jackson dials his smile up to filthy.

"No need to get pissy, Donovan. If you need a threesome to get you up—"

Nick's fist slams into Jackson's jaw once. Just once. It's so fast I don't have time to breathe. I didn't even see him move.

Drunk as he is, Jackson stumbles wildly in the open doorway. When he finds his feet, his face contorts like someone's hit a switch. "What's your problem, you little shit?"

I snag Nick's shirt, his arm. I pull him hard, but God he's strong.

Tate pushes Jackson toward the door. "You're the problem. Go home."

Nick's struggling in my grasp. He won't turn around, but he's breathing so hard. Like he's about to come out of his own skin.

Jackson catches sight of Nick. Or maybe me. I don't know which of us really, but he launches forward. Tate holds him back. "What is *wrong* with you?"

"Me? What's wrong with me? You're the one who's still too hung up on Stell—"

Tate slams him into the door frame. "You don't talk about her!"

Tate and Jackson are inches apart and the music has cut off downstairs. Now all I can hear is Nick panting and my heart thundering behind my ears. I press myself into his back and he reaches an arm around me. I find his fingers. We're both shaking.

Jackson and Tate are still inches apart when footsteps arrive on the landing. I see three or four shadows in the hallway. Some guy asks what's happening. Another asks if everything's okay.

Not okay. Not even close.

But Jackson's face tames, his features smoothing back into something cool and detached. It looks like a mask to me. The blotchy boy with sharp teeth and feral eyes—that's the real Jackson now.

"Someone is pitting us against each other, Tate," Jackson says, his tactics changed now that he has an audience. "And we all know who it is. Someone's attacking us and we're letting them do it."

A flash of heat rushes through me. My hands go slick, my fingers slippery against Nick's. He holds me steady.

Jackson leans against the door frame. "First me, then Kristen. Hell, even that little smart kid Harrison got a taste of it. Now look at us! *Someone* started this. But I'm going to finish it."

It's the kind of speech that should end a party, but it doesn't. The music turns back up and Jackson finds his way outside. Everyone moves on.

Nick and I slip out the back. After a quiet drive home, he lingers on my porch, his shoulders curved around me and forehead pressed against mine.

"I think I'm starting to hate him," he says.

I don't need to ask who he's talking about.

"It's almost over," I say, stroking his sides, trying to soothe him the way he always does me.

"Thank you for tonight."

I laugh softly. "Uh, tonight kind of sucked."

"Not what you did with Tate. That meant something."

I bite my lip and step back far enough to let my eyes focus. "Nick, I need to tell you something about Tate. I sent his name too. Right after Jackson."

He sighs, and I hate the disappointment in his eyes. But there's no shock. Deep down, he's probably not that surprised.

"But he was never…nothing ever happened to him," Nick says.

I shrug. "My partner said no, that it needed to be bigger than Stella. So I picked Kristen."

"Would you still pick him now?" he asks.

I think of the picture. The night he was so sick. The anguish in his eyes. No one could punish Tate more than he's already punishing himself. "No. No, I wouldn't."

A shadow passes over Nick's face. He swallows hard. "Does it make me a terrible person that I'm glad it was Kristen instead?"

My laugh is weak. "I don't think you've got a terrible person in you."

"I think we all do. If you scratch the surface."

CHAPTER TWENTY

· ·

Manny sits down across from me with a tray full of deep-fried foulness that I can barely stand to look at. He opens his bottle of Mountain Dew, and it's like every lunch since eighth grade. He's still Manny, and he thinks I'm still Piper—his no-drama, no-secrets friend. I feel an ache in my middle, a hollow place where that girl used to live.

I have to tell him about what I found in his room. And about all the things I'm hiding too. The texts. And Tacey.

He clears his throat, waggling his brows at me. "So, if the Mr. Football rumors are true, can I get you to start wearing cheerleading skirts?"

I shove my yogurt away and ignore the comments. "Look, I think we should talk about Tacey. Have you seen her yet today?"

"Nope, but she'll show. Tacey's tough."

I look down, folding under the weight of my worry for Tacey. "Tough or not, what happened to her is serious, Manny. She didn't deserve that."

His jaw goes tight. "I didn't say she did. We all get crap we don't deserve, don't we?" I think of the bill under his mattress. The surgery they can't afford. And the list of names and services he's been selling.

Manny goes on before I can respond. "It'll blow over. Nobody's going to buy any of that heroin crap from the video. This isn't the same thing."

I bristle, hating his glib attitude. "Her parents bought it. They have her in rehab."

Something dark flickers across his features before he speaks. "For what?"

"They think she has a problem."

"For having some peppy pills in her purse?" He seems to recognize his volume, or maybe he just catches the I-will-kill-you expression on my face, because he leans in before he whispers, "Rehab is a total overreaction."

"Well, they're parents. They're freaking out. And it's going to hurt her here too."

His brows knit together over his nose. "You don't think she'll get kicked off the yearbook do you?"

"No, she won't." Tacey's voice comes from behind us.

We both look up, faces falling. I expect her to be pissed, but she's not. She's so calm it gives me the creeps. If there was any time in my life I would have thought maybe Tacey was on drugs, it would be right now.

"Hey, you," I say, and I hate how high-pitched it comes out.

Yes, Piper. That creepy baby doll voice will set her right at ease.

"How goes it?" Manny asks, sounding totally normal. Damn him.

"I've been better," she says. She looks at her coffee cup hard, like she's not sure whether to set it down or take another drink.

"Chin up," Manny says. "One tough week isn't going to take down the legendary Tacey Winters, is it?"

She gives him a tight smile but doesn't answer. I scoot over to give her room to sit down. "Tacey, I'm so sorry. And I really want to talk to you about…about everything."

"No. No talking yet," she says, waving her free hand. "I'm not ready and my empowerment-happy rehab counselor encouraged me to embrace that feeling. So pick another subject. This one is officially closed."

I open my mouth but nothing comes out.

"I wanted to talk about Piper's sudden fixation with a football player," Manny volunteers.

"Nick?" She flips her hair over her shoulder. She's starting to look a little like Tacey again when she smirks. "Ancient news. I've known for ages."

Manny grins. "You really are a newshound, aren't you?"

"Well, I might not always be anchor material, but today I think the title applies. I have something seriously juicy—I'm not the only one in rehab. Kristen Green's mom is too. Booze, not meds."

"Who doesn't have a booze problem?" Manny asks. His dad's been sober for twenty years. Anybody who's stepped into the Raines house has probably seen the plaque of the Serenity Prayer on the wall.

"Wait, friends, that's not the good part." I can't see any good part to any of this, but Tacey leans in with hungry eyes. "Have either of you ever actually seen Kristen's mom? I mean, ever?"

"I wouldn't remember unless she had a nice rack," Manny says.

"I saw her dad a few times," I say. "Tall, balding guy. He seemed normal."

"Well, that must be where she gets her normal from, because her mom is an express train to Alcoholic Whoreland."

"What do you mean?" Manny asks. I wish he hadn't.

Tacey's grin curdles my stomach. "She's a *disaster*. Bleached hair, tanned like a good handbag—she was wearing tiger-striped stiletto heels with *pink* jeans. I'm not even exaggerating." She sits back with a smirk. "Well? Not exactly Best Foot Forward material, right?"

"Fascinating," Manny says. "I'm going to go get a cookie."

Tacey throws up her hands. "I pop a few pills and the social media universe explodes. I uncover *this*, and I get *nada*?"

"What are you *hoping* to get?" I ask, unable to mask the disgust in my voice.

But I don't really have a right to be disgusted, do I? I probably looked just like this when I took pictures of Jackson. Smug and self-satisfied—so *thrilled* to see the golden boy go down.

I really don't want to be this person.

Out of nowhere, Jackson appears. I only half suppress my jumpy reaction, my knees knocking hard into the table while he looks down on us. I force a neutral expression onto my face, but adrenaline pours through me like liquid fire.

He found me out. It's over.

Jackson meets my eyes and…nods. I blink a few times, sure it's still coming. Except he isn't even looking at me. He's turned toward Tacey.

"Jackson," she says, pulling up the end of his name like a question. Warranted, since there are lots of questions that need asking. Like, why are you at our table? And what on earth could you possibly want from Tacey?

"I heard about what happened to you," he says.

"You and everybody else."

"No need to be nasty," he says.

"No need for you to walk down here to state the obvious. What do you want?"

"I wanted to tell you that I think you were set up. I thought a newsgirl like you would have figured that out by now though."

Tacey gives him a look. "I did take the pills, Jackson. It's not exactly a conspiracy."

"Yeah, but who would care enough to air your dirty laundry? No one, that's who. But someone did, didn't they? Just like someone made that tape of me. And someone dropped clothes all over Kristen—"

Tacey waves her fingers, looking bored. "Yeah, not interested."

Jackson tenses, the tips of his fingers going white on the table. "You should be, Lois Lane. It's your rep—"

"She said she's not interested," I say, knowing it's stupid. So stupid. I'm the last person on earth that should be looking for Jackson's attention.

He pivots to face me, his black eyes boring into mine. A gold chain dangles from his neck, the crucifix on it swinging six inches from my nose.

"Let's get this straight right now, Woods. Just because my boy Nicky wants to—"

243

"Piper, there you are!"

We all turn around to see Aimee wearing a white sweater and a fake smile. She reaches out her hand and gives me a chastising look. "I knew you'd lose track of time. So, you are coming, right?"

I'm not sure my voice won't fail me. But when she grabs my hand, I don't hesitate to get up. I'd probably let the devil himself drag me away from this table.

• • •

In the quiet of the bathroom, Aimee puts on lip gloss and I pretend to care about my hair. Mostly we wait for the girls to clear out. And when they do, she turns to look at me, her back pressed against the sink.

"I think you should be careful around Jackson," she says softly.

She's right. Even the sound of his name raises the hair on the back of my neck. But I'm just so *done* with him. "He loves this, you know. People being afraid of him."

"I don't think you understand. Jackson's just…" Aimee trails off, shrugging her shoulders as if that explains it. "He's Jackson. He's used to getting his way. He can't handle it when he doesn't. Do you get what I mean?"

"That maybe I should play nice?"

"No, I don't want you to play nice. I'm hoping you won't play at all. I'm hoping you'll stay as far away from him as possible."

She looks at me like she's waiting for me to get it. But I *don't* get it. Because she can't think I actually want him. Unless…could she actually want him herself?

Nauseating thought. But I force the scowl off my face and try hard to soften my shoulders. "I'm not interested in Jackson, Aimee. Like, *at all*."

"I know that. But it doesn't mean Jackson's not interested in you."

My laugh is short and loud. "No. Definitely no. I couldn't be farther from his type."

She pops one hand on her hip, squaring her shoulders. "See, that's where you're wrong. You're *exactly* his type."

"Uh, how? I'm not busty or popular or prone to wearing dresses on weekdays."

"Maybe not. But you're a girl who *isn't* interested. One who also happens to be dating one of his friends."

Her eyes narrow, and it's only then that I realize it isn't jealousy spurning this. Or even fear. It's anger.

She knew about Tate and Stella. More importantly, she knew about Jackson and Stella. Aimee knows details on the things that are still fuzzy and dark in my mind.

"What do you mean?" I ask, trying to play dumb. "Has he done that kind of thing before?"

"I'm not going to give any details. I'm not trying to gossip."

"I know. I know that."

"But you have to understand that Jackson likes a challenge. And he likes to get what he wants, so if he wants something from you… Let's just say he doesn't handle the word *no* very well."

My stomach clenches, and her eyes glitter. The things she won't say take shape between us. No specifics really—no names or faces. But there's a dark stain that feels like violence. And Jackson.

I take a step forward, but I am so bad at this. Just absolutely bad at it.

"Did Jackson ever—"

She glances at the door, adjusting her bag on her shoulder. "Not me. Don't worry about me. Just watch your back."

Manny's waiting for me outside the bathroom. "Hey, what the hell was up with Jackson? Why was he over with you guys?"

"Being his typical repulsive self. What did I miss while I was in here?"

"Mostly Tacey frothing at the mouth. She's threatened me with bodily harm if I don't take some good shots at the basketball game this Friday."

"Do you want me to come with?" I ask.

"Nah, it's cool. I'll do it. I'm just tired of Tacey's stress being everybody else's problem."

"Maybe we could grab dinner tonight."

He looks down. "I've actually got a couple of things to do."

Like records to clean up?

I narrow my eyes. He's dodging me. It's not good, because I know what he's hiding from me now. But I'm hiding things too. There are things we need to talk about. Vigilante things. And injured dad things.

"Will you get mad if I mention that you seem a little reluctant to look at me right now?"

He grins. "Should I gaze deeply into your eyes like Nick?"

"Manny, I know about your dad." I look at the ground, feeling my face flame. "I know about the surgery. And I know what you're doing to make money."

"How?"

The lie is sitting on my lips, sweet as honey. But I can't. Not anymore. "The other night when I came over. The papers in your mattress." I cringe and shake my head. "I looked at them. I could have put them back."

"No, you *did* put them back. But not until you took a good peek, right?"

I flinch. His voice is cold. So cold. "I shouldn't have looked."

"Is that what you're here for? Is that what you've been wanting to talk about? You want to judge me because you saw my little side business is still up and running?"

"No, no that's not it."

"That's sure what it looks like, Pi. You want to know why I'm selling grades and fixing tardies? You really want to know?"

"I thought… the surgery for your dad."

"You thought you had it all figured out, right? Did you figure out that he'll lose his job if he doesn't get that surgery? *Early retirement* is what they're calling it. This isn't about a couple thousand dollars. It's about us surviving, period."

I feel punched. Breathless.

"Manny." His name breaks on my lips. I want to fix it. I want to tell him everything else, but I can't. The rest of it feels small and stupid. If his dad loses his job…"I want to help. Let me do something."

"You can start by trusting me to handle my own life."

"Trusting you won't fix this."

"Trust fixes lots of things, Pi. I don't count on this world for anything anymore," Manny says. "I can't afford to. But I've always trusted you. For once, I'm asking for your trust."

I can't find anything to say, so Manny leaves. I just stand there, watching him walk away, feeling like I'm knee-deep in quicksand.

The warning bell rings and my phone buzzes with a message that I know after a glance I don't want to open. It's from him. There's an image attached.

> 9 tonight. Or I Send This.

The photograph loads. And my heart dissolves.

CHAPTER TWENTY-ONE

. . . .

I roll over in bed and close my eyes, but it doesn't matter. The image is burned into the backs of my eyes like it has been all day. I'm pretty sure it's there to stay. It's not a particularly good photograph, but it conveys the intended message with three simple facts.

Fact 1: My father is leaning into an unfamiliar car window.

Fact 2: He is smiling, hand cupped on the driver's face.

Fact 3: The driver is not my mother.

I can't tell much more than that. Long, blond hair. A slim arm. Not my mom. Definitely not my mom.

That's pretty much as far as I can get before I have to look away.

A knock at my door jars me from my thinking. It cracks open before my answer, revealing my mother's face. I shove the phone under my leg, feeling like everything is folding and bunching together.

"Oh, you are awake. I was worried you were getting sick again."

"No. Just tired."

She smiles, slipping in the room and sitting down on my bed.

I flush and sweat like I've been hiding the picture for ages, like I've known all along that my father's been stroking nameless not-my-mom women through open car windows.

I feel like I've swallowed fistfuls of mulch. But I force some words out anyway. "How was your flight home?"

"Fine. Honey, you look pale."

"I'm okay."

"Do you want me to call you out of school tomorrow?"

"No, no. I'm good."

She ignores that, which is probably because she can tell it's a lie. I feel the press of her hand to my forehead, cool and assessing.

Does she know about the woman? Is that what all the silent fighting is about? Is this even the first time? My limbs go heavy and numb with the questions.

The answers might be more than I can take. They might tell me how my family will end. Suddenly I feel very young and small. I don't want my mom and dad to not live together.

"How do you really feel?" she asks.

I feel like my universe is being grated. Like cheese. I don't say that. I close my eyes and will myself not to cry. "Gritty. The Tacey thing…lots of things are hard right now."

"We could go out to dinner if you want. You could tell me all the things that are new."

What's new is that I'm a liar. And a crappy person. And that I know things that would break your heart.

I have to talk to her. I can't not tell her what I know.

"Mom?"

Her phone rings and she glances down at the screen, her brows knitting together. "Shoot. This is one of my families. I probably need to grab this. Can we talk in a bit?"

I wave at her, more grateful than I should be for the reprieve. I close my eyes again and will the image away. It's hard forcing sleep to come, but eventually I win. Maybe because I know, when I wake up, my world will be different. I want to hold on to what I know a little longer.

* * *

I have to find Nick because I'm too paranoid to text this and he didn't pick up this morning. It's that ungodly rush before first period, twelve billion people in the halls, shoving and laughing, shouting over one another as if the whole of their future depends on being heard in this craziness. I see a group of guys that might be Nick's friends standing at the end of the hallway. Tall boys in athletic gear, the ones who know their place is secure in the social stratosphere.

Someone steps on my foot, but I ignore it, dragging my way through the hall. The clock on the wall sends a panicked flutter through me. Three minutes. I have three minutes or I won't see him for four periods, and I don't want to text this, because it feels like a big deal.

Today everything feels like a big deal.

I speed up, dodging around someone with a trombone case and then skirting to the right to avoid a couple holding hands.

"Excuse you!" the girl gripes as I bump her.

I throw an apology over my shoulder, but I don't stop, because Nick is in that group at the corner flanked by Tate and a couple other guys I recognize from the baseball team.

There are lots of people around—Aimee and Ming and, God, Marlow could be in here for all I know, but I can't let that matter. What matters is telling Nick about tonight.

He turns just before I get to him. I snag his sleeve to pull him back. I'm panting when he spots me, and I don't want to look out of breath and frantic, but I know I do. I need to find something to say, and there's so much that I don't know where to start.

"Will you come with me to the basketball game tonight?" I practically sputter it.

He laughs, stroking his hands through my hair. "Yes. But you didn't need to—wait, I can't. I work. I'm off at seven though. I can get there a little after halftime?"

"Perfect." I kiss him, right there in the hallway. It's just a brief mashing of lips, but he practically glows he's so pleased. "I'll need a ride to a certain place tonight."

His smile falters, which is why I didn't want to text. I don't have to say police station in person. He can tell just by looking at me.

"Are you sure?"

I reach up, feigning a hug, but mostly so I can drop my voice to a whisper. "I know the secret. My dad's having an affair. He sent me a picture."

Nick's arms move around me. I feel the side of his face pressed against my neck. "I'm so sorry."

"It's okay. I'm talking to my mom today and then Manny at the game. We can go straight to the station from there."

I lay it out like a list of errands, as if I might as well be picking up pizza and a movie on the way home. In truth, I'm terrified out of my mind. I'm a million things, really, in that fraction of a second before he touches me. And then his palm is against my face, warm and true. Nothing in my world is better, but I feel anchored.

The bell rings and my world snaps back into orbit. I blink in the brightness and noise of the hallway, like I'm seeing it for the first time. Nick steps back, nods.

"I'll be there. I'll do whatever you need."

I leave school at lunch to get everything done. It's the first time I've skipped school like this in my life, but I need the time. All of my ducks need to be lined up before I pull this trigger. I order the picture of my dad and that woman at the drugstore. While I wait for it to print, I buy a blank card and write Tacey a letter.

Telling her in person would be better, but there isn't time and Tacey might like the control a letter will give her. After tonight, it's all going to come out and spin into wildness. I want her to know beforehand, even if the information will rip us apart. I leave the letter at her house and head home to wait for my mom.

It feels like preparing for last rites. I slide the notebook out, my fingers drifting over the title. My pictures are tucked in the pocket with Harrison's now, my glittery script over his spidery black print.

This is the last thing I can't figure out. Part of me wants to burn it, but is that because I'm a coward? Would a stronger person turn it in? Or maybe show it to any person who'll look? I don't know. I just don't.

Giving it to the police feels like what I deserve. Because they're allowed to make the hard judgments about what's dangerous and what's not. They're trained, authorized, and paid to do it. And I'm not.

I flip to the back, past my pictures of Kristen. I add in a couple from Harrison, but my pen pauses underneath. Listing out his crimes feels redundant. The spray-painted car sums up everything that needs to be said.

Well, maybe not *everything*.

I press my pen to the page and write one quick sentence.

This is when it stopped feeling right.

I hesitate then, feeling like the work is unfinished. It needs one more thing. Just one more. I rummage through my desk to find a picture that will work.

Dark hair, dark eyes, a hand-beaded bracelet on a suntanned wrist. It's a picture from last summer. A picture of me.

I don't write anything below that picture. I close the book and tuck it into my bag. In a few hours, it will be in someone else's hands.

CHAPTER TWENTY-TWO

My mom comes in when I'm sitting at my vanity, her hair limp and her attaché stuffed with paperwork.

"Piper, I'm so sorry. This day has been crazy."

"It's okay." And it's about to get crazier.

"You look lovely," she says, slipping out of her heels and coming over to me. She runs a hand over my hair and smiles at me in the mirror. "Dinner with Nick?"

"Basketball game, actually."

Technically, it's true. Most of what I tell her is true. I just leave out some really big pieces. Like my creepy vigilante side job. And the woman my father might be sleeping with.

I'm giving Mom the yearbook version of her daughter's life. I'm sitting here in my gauzy shirt and cute boots, pretending that the biggest thing going on in my world is the wonder of a Friday night basketball game with Nick Patterson.

I look away from the mirror. I can't stand to look at myself for another second. And there she is at my shoulder. Mom. Her smile—the one that tells me exactly what mine will look like in twenty-five years—beams down at me.

"I don't think I have to tell you how pretty you are."

"It's not exactly prom," I say, trying to a force a light tone that won't quite come.

"Let me gush. You never let me gush." She touches my face, grins at me in the mirror.

I try to return it, but all I can think about is my dad's hand in that car window. On that strange woman's face. I finally plaster a smile on my lips. I'm not quick enough. Mom's dark eyes shift. She frowns and moves forward, worry shadowing her features.

"Piper?"

"I'm fine. Sorry, I was spacing out."

"You've been spacing out a lot. You're starting to worry me."

She presses the back of her hand to my forehead and cheeks again, and I think of the times I had croup when I was little. She sat with me all night in the bathroom, the shower steaming hot and thick until it was like sitting in a cloud. Sticky as it was, she never complained. She just rocked me and rocked me, telling me everything would be okay.

"Not sick." I barely get the words out—they are a strangled mess on my tongue.

"Look at me, sweetheart," she says, and I turn around to face her. Same no-fuss hair. Same warm eyes. The same hands that have brought me a postcard from every trip since forever. "Do you need to talk to me about something?"

I can't see this happen to her. I can't watch her look at that picture. And I can't *not* watch her either. I'm paralyzed by all of it.

Mom misreads it, of course. "Hey, if you don't want to do this, you call him and it's done. It doesn't matter if *we* like this boy—"

"It's not Nick. Nick's great. Better than great."

"But it's something."

The fact that I don't deny it is answer enough.

"Tell me?" she asks, always so careful about these things. I can see how badly she wants to know, wants to help.

I let her pull me in and hug me, and then I reach for my vanity, taking the plain white envelope. The one I sealed the picture inside. I offer it over, feeling my eyes swim with tears.

"I have to give you this. It's a picture."

"Like our postcards?"

The words cut hard and deep. I shake my head and steady my voice. "No. Not like that. This picture will be really hard for you to see."

Her cheeks go pale, the lines around her eyes drawing deeper with her frown. "Piper? You're scaring me."

"It's not about me. I'm going to be all right. I promise I am. I'll explain everything with me soon enough, but this—" I cut myself off, choked by the ugliness of this truth. My voice emerges small and dry. "This is about Dad."

Her face freezes like a snapshot, eyes not quite narrowed, mouth not quite agape. It's some awful mix of shock and resignation. Some part of her already suspects what's hiding in this envelope. She knows. Maybe not everything, maybe not details—but enough.

All the things that hold me together snap at once. The tears come fast and hard, hiccoughing out of me in ugly sobs. I can't stop them from coming. I can't even slow them down.

My mom shifts into action like she's been injected with

adrenaline. I see her push her own pain to some deep recess of her heart. Her face goes soft and her hands move to my hair.

"Piper. Piper, look at me." She strokes my face just like she did those nights so long ago when I coughed and coughed until I could barely breathe. "It's okay," she says. "It'll all be okay."

I look up at her, feeling seventeen years of steamy bathrooms and postcards and things that make her wonderful and annoying and *Mom*. I can't speak. There's no chance of that, so I try to put it all into my eyes, all of the apologies that I'll soon have to say.

"Whatever this is, I am ready for it," she says, looking at the envelope she dropped reaching for me. "I don't want this to upset you. I need you to trust that I can handle this."

"Aren't you going to look at it?"

A sigh. "No. I'll look at it later. You need to understand this is not the great surprise you think it is, okay?"

She knows. It's written all over her face that some part of her isn't even a little afraid of that envelope. How on earth did I miss that too?

I nod even though there's lots more to say. Things I can't say yet, but I will.

At the police station, probably. It's not fair, but even saying this much has taken everything I have. If I confess to her, she might try to smooth this over. She'll want to protect me because she's my mother. And I can't be protected anymore.

I pull myself together through sheer force of will. Mom helps me brush my hair and touch up my eye makeup. We patch me together until I've been glossed within an inch of my life, and more importantly, Mom is confident that I'm settled down.

At six o'clock, my dad strolls in and if my mom tenses, she hides it fast. He grins at me. "I filled your tank so you wouldn't have to get stinky in your girly clothes."

My heart sinks like lead. I still can't combine my goofy, gas-tank-filling dad with a guy who cheats. Maybe I should hate him. I don't like him very much right now, but he's still my dad. I kiss my mom's cheek, then cross the room to hug my dad. I pick up my camera bag and backpack and make my way toward the front door with both of them following. I check my phone, shifting my bags on my shoulders.

The next time I see them, they'll have talked. Maybe fought. And then there will be facing everything with me—the lies, the vigilante stuff. It's ugly.

The world I've lived in for seventeen years is going to end tonight, and I don't know what comes after. I turn around, looking back at them. They're watching me go. Certainly not arms linked and murmuring sweet parental nothings. But they are side by side and they are smiling. Proud of me.

"Let's get a picture," I say, the need sudden and consuming.

I sling my bag on the floor, the notebook thunking when it hits, and set my camera up on the third plank in our living room bookshelf. It's not our first rodeo with the home self-portrait, but my parents look awkward and shifty-eyed as I shoo them toward the staircase.

"Piper, I've barely dragged a brush through my hair today," Mom says, obviously reluctant.

"But I'm all dressed up. I want proof."

"We can get pictures of you," Dad offers.

"Just smile," I say, the command brittle on my tongue.

The camera beeps faster and we slide into our traditional Woods Family Photo pose—Dad on my left, Mom on my right, heads all tilted together just so. My mom's arm is stiff and cool, but my dad leans against me, all easy warmth.

I squeeze them both as the flash fires, freezing us this one last time as the family we already aren't.

• • •

The basketball game is partway through the second quarter when I arrive, and sadly, if Nick's running-late text is accurate, he'll get here after halftime. Not fun. I've never been to a varsity basketball game, and I really would've been happy to keep it that way. Especially since Manny's already here, and I have no idea how to say any of this to him.

If I tried a letter, he'd call me a coward. If I look him in the eyes, I'm afraid of the words he'll use. But I'm here to do this, so I have to try.

I make my way around the cheerleaders to the edge of the visitor stands. Manny's leaning against them, wearing his camera and a bored expression. He offers me the uneaten half of a giant pretzel and I take it, nibbling mindlessly.

"Tacey sent you to check on me?" he asks.

"No. I was meeting Nick. I just wanted to say hello."

I don't miss the way he rolls his shoulders back, obviously pleased. He gives me a sly smile and bumps into my hip. "So— you and Nick. It's serious?"

"Yeah. I think it might be. Weird, right?"

"It's not weird for me," he says, laughing. "But you can't seriously think I won't give you crap after your lifelong no-jocks vow."

No, I really can't. And he's not lying. I actually had a little pledge after the freshman party fiasco, swearing off athletes and cheerleaders and the rest of their ilk. I did it because it made Manny laugh. And because deep down inside, I believed they were somehow less—less smart, less interesting…less than me.

My appetite vanishes. I pull the pretzel away from my mouth and feel a truth settle into my bones. My partner didn't do this to me. This—the judging and the arrogance—it was in me all along. Since forever.

I wasn't planning on texting a name. I was just killing time to go to the police with Nick there to keep me from falling to pieces. I've stumbled around all day like a martyr, with my letters and my sobbing, but now I get it.

This isn't about me being a good person. This is about me being every single thing I claimed to hate.

The texting? The takedowns? The sin book? None of that is what's evil here—I am what's evil here.

You have to start with where it went wrong.

My throat burns and my chest aches.

I know now, Nick. I know where the wrong started. The wrong started on a sidewalk in the ninth grade when your friends hurt my feelings, and I let the hurt fester into hate.

The crowd cheers at a basket and I startle. I hand the pretzel back and Manny huffs.

"I didn't mean to upset you. Nick's a decent guy. I'm happy for you."

"Yeah," I say. I'm breathless. Unfocused. I think I should feel more. Sick or dizzy or hot. But I don't. I feel numb through and through. Dead.

"You all right?"

No. No, I'm not.

My phone rings. Nick. I take a couple of steps away.

"Hey."

"Hey, I'm on my way. Fifteen minutes out if I hit the lights right. Are you okay?"

"Yes."

"You're not okay. I can hear it in your voice. What can I do?"

Our team scores and the crowd erupts in a cheer. "I'm okay. Just promise me you won't get upset with me."

"Piper—"

"I know it's a lot to ask, but trust me, I thought this through. I know what I'm doing will seem crazy, but I have to. I'll explain on the way to the station."

"I trust you," he says.

I smile, bite the inside of my lip, glance over at Manny, who's making kissy faces at me. I still have to tell him. That'll be the end of the silly faces for a while. Maybe forever.

"Wish me luck, Nick."

"Nothing but. I'll see you soon."

I hang up, holding on to the warmth in his voice. Clinging to the good he still sees in me. I walk back toward Manny, stopping a few feet away to pull up my messages.

The crowd is chanting, stomping feet, and clapping hands in one of those rhythmic stadium mantras. I feel like the death bells are chiming. But it's okay. This time, I *know* I've got it right.

Piper Woods—Liar, elitist, bully.

My ears burn and I look up, startled by the sudden silence. The crowd is at an absolute hush. I see the players arranged near the hoop for some sort of extra shot. The quiet is so intense, I almost lose my nerve.

I hit Send as the player in front of the net dribbles the ball.

The whole gymnasium seems to hold its breath as he shoots.

The ball is soaring toward the net when I hear the phone in Manny's pocket buzz. For one fraction of a second, I'm sure I'm imagining it. Or that it's coincidence. But then I see his real phone in his hand—and then I see his face. The way he looks at me, mouth tight and shoulders hunching. And I *know*. It's him.

The ball whooshes through the net and the crowd explodes. Just like my world.

CHAPTER TWENTY-THREE

. . . .

The halftime buzzer rings while the crowd's still cheering, the sound rattling my teeth and hammering into my bones. I push myself forward on numb, trembling legs.

Manny doesn't try to break my gaze. Neither of us says a word as I move closer. I don't ask. I drop my bag, freeing my other hand to reach into his jacket pocket with a look that dares him to stop me.

He doesn't. He doesn't even look away. I rummage through his pocket like it's my own, and he stands there, jaw ticking as I catalog the contents. Keys. Wallet. And then the thing I'm looking for. A second phone.

My cheeks ache the same way they do when I'm about to be sick. I pull it out anyway.

It's small and cheap-looking. I've seen phones like this hanging under bright No-Contract-No-Problem and Buy-Minutes-Here signage. I stab at the buttons until the screen blooms to life. It isn't hard to find the message inbox. But it's hard to see the string of messages. Most of them from me.

Something in my chest cracks. I think it's something I need.

"Piper—"

"Don't!" I hold up a hand to stop him, his phone still clutched in my grip.

I shake my head because I will not let him try to make this something else. I will not sit here, weak and desperate for my best friend to prove how this isn't him lying to me. Using me. *Blackmailing* me.

The halftime show is swinging into gear, and we can't do this here. No chance of that. I grab Manny's sleeve, and half pull, half drag him behind me. I don't know why I think he'll follow, but he does.

We cross the gymnasium floor behind the bleachers and step into the narrow hallway, the one that leads to the locker rooms. My sweaty fingers stay locked on Manny's hoodie as we slip further down the hallway, past an equipment closet and one of several access points to the basketball court. It smells like sweat and perfume and the popcorn that's fallen through the bleachers. I crunch over a few pieces, hearing Manny right behind me.

Where now? I move right past the boys' locker room, heading for the only quiet place I can think of. The one place no one would be during a boys' basketball game: the girls' locker room.

"We're going to do this in the girls' locker room?" Manny asks.

I spin on him, feeling heat and color flare through my face. "I don't think we have a Betrayal and Confrontation room."

He tries to laugh, but even he can't make this funny. It's tragic. And there's no stopping the tears now. I smear them off my cheeks with angry swipes.

"How could you?" I ask. "You used me. You hurt Tacey! *Tacey*, Manny! And my dad…" I trail off, so angry I can't find the right words fast enough. "They used to babysit you! You got off the bus at my house for an entire year when your dad was training in Chicago."

I can see him closing off, arms crossing. "I didn't *do* anything! If you're going to get pissed about your dad's extracurricular activities, get pissed with him. I didn't mean to bump into that scene in town. But I did take a picture, because I thought you'd want to know."

"Yes, that's exactly how I'd hope a good friend would reveal something like that. A big dose of reality delivered with blackmail and threats."

He scrubs a hand over his head, his cheeks pink. "It's complicated. Jackson was onto me. I got him off my trail for a while when I got you off of Tate and onto Kristen, but in the end, he wouldn't let it go."

The dark circles under his eyes. The exhaustion. I thought it was just the side job. "So, he figured you out, and you what? Decided to keep it going?"

"I figured if I took down Tacey while I was out of town, he'd believe it wasn't me. It would put him off the scent or whatever since she's a friend."

Put him off the scent. My mind hones in on a couple of memories—texts that came in when Manny was with me. "It's not possible. You texted me when I was standing right there *with you.*"

His shoulders hunch. "That wasn't an accident. I set up the texts and then sent them from my pocket so you didn't see it."

"Why? Why did you do this? Why would you hide it from me? Connect some dots for me here, Manny, because none of this makes any sense."

We're both yelling now, but it doesn't matter worth a crap. There's a halftime show banging and thumping so loud the cheerleaders might as well be in here with us.

"Tell me why," I say again, my voice soft this time, almost pleading.

"I didn't tell you because I didn't want you to ask questions."

My rage shrinks into cold fear. I take a breath. Hold it in because I know there's more. And I'm not sure I'm ready for it.

Manny closes his eyes. "I'm the one who put Stella's tape up on the website."

It hits me like a punch. I'm breathless, barely on my feet.

"Jackson paid me," he says. "He'd heard about my side business changing records, thought maybe I could hack into a website too. That's why he suspected me."

"But you liked Stella!"

"I did, but he paid a pretty penny. God knows where he came up with that cash, but I couldn't afford to say no. At the time I thought the tape was her idea anyway, so why would she care?"

"Manny..." My voice sounds like it belongs somewhere else. Maybe to someone else.

Stella *died* because of that damn tape. I know that and he knows that. And if he put that tape up, then he paved her path up to those train tracks. He's so pale, his freckles stark on his nose and cheeks.

"I know I was wrong. I know how Stella's story ends," he says, voice trembling. "I live with that every day. *Every damn day.* I always will. I thought if I did this, if I did this with you—I thought maybe we could avenge her. That tape...what happened to her on those tracks…no one was going to do anything. I had to do something! Something to protect people like her. Something to make the assholes pay."

I am hollow. All the important bits that fill me up have gone. "You didn't need me. You could have done this alone."

"Yeah, but you were broken up about Stella too. Remember the funeral? I knew if you were choosing, you'd do it right. We'd do good things. And we have."

My insides ice over. "Manny, that wasn't right. None of this was right. Doing what we did brought out every bad thing in us!"

"Don't say that! Maybe I pushed it too far, but they *deserved* it. They all had it coming."

"Are you even listening to yourself? You think we have the right to play judge and jury? You took down Tacey! *Tacey*, Manny!"

I close my eyes as the music outside stops. An announcer says something about giving someone a round of applause, and everyone does. My head feels so heavy—like a thousand pounds of something bad wants to climb out through my eyes.

"Tacey was a mistake." Manny edges closer to me. He's trying to reason with me, calm me down. "I screwed that up. I wanted to hurt you and shake off Jackson. I didn't think it would get that big. I just didn't want you to quit."

"So you scared me into sticking with it?"

He throws up his hands. "You were punking out! Freaking. I admit, maybe I made some bad choices in motivating you, but I was looking at the bigger picture. We were settling the score, Piper, leveling the playing field for once in the history of this damn school!"

My skin crawls. Every word he says proves just how far he'll go—how far gone he is.

"You need to turn yourself in," I say, schooling my face to blankness.

His face twists. "For *what*? Spray-painting a teacher's car? It's not like she was innocent!"

"How'd you get Kristen's clothes?" I counter.

He rolls his eyes. "I broke a window. It's not like I held them at gunpoint."

"Well, then I guess it's all fine, Manny. Break a window. Vandalize a car. *Threaten* my family? The ends justify the means, right? Or did it just feel too good to quit?"

I can see the rage slam back into him. His eyes shutter and his face turns cold. Whatever we once were is over. Gone.

He heads for the door and I can hear the crowd roaring. Manny stops, looking back at me. "You want to turn me in, that's fine. Do whatever the hell you want. You know best, right?"

I close my eyes and he leaves. Through the locker room and outside. There's nothing but my shaky breathing and the soft stomp of what I assume is the band moving into formation in the center of the court.

The phone in my hand makes my chest ache. I shove it into my jeans pocket, remembering that I left my bag outside in the gym. I need to get it so I can turn everything in. The notebook, the pictures. Both phones. I have everything with me, so it's all over but the singing. I just need to take it in to the police so I can finish it.

I try to force myself to move, but my legs feel like bags of sand suspended from my hips. I'm heavy all over. Heavy and broken. With a strangled sound, I bury my face in my hands and let myself shake as the team song begins.

Sneakers squeak at the entrance of the locker room and continue moving toward me. I look up, expecting Nick. Hoping for him.

But it's not Nick.

The music rises into the chorus and my body goes cold with dread.

"Jackson."

• • •

"Did you really think I wouldn't figure it out?" he asks by way of greeting.

"Figure what out?" I ask, noticing something.

He's holding a bag. My bag. *Oh God.*

"All this time I thought it was your little BFF, but this makes sense. You've always thought you were better than the rest of us."

My blood turns stone-cold as I watch the rage descend over his features, turning his skin mottled and purple. I take a breath that tastes like a warning.

It's the last thing before he lunges. He barrels into me like a bull. My body flies back under the impact, slamming against the cement wall. My head cracks on one of the painted blocks. Stars swim through my vision. I gasp, tasting blood.

Jackson's words are hot and wet against my ear. "You took me down, you little bitch. And you're going to pay for it so hard."

Outside, the school song reaches its crescendo along with my scream. Jackson drags me up, wrapping a sweaty, thick hand around my neck. I buck and squirm, but he pushes a warning knee against my stomach and squeezes his hand until I can barely breathe.

"You recognize this?" he asks. I blink against the spittle that sprays my cheeks, and then blearily see the notebook he's holding up, the page with his pictures open. "You should because I found it in *your* backpack."

He found the notebook in my bag. That's how he figured it out.

"I should've known. Always there with your camera. Always looking down your nose at the rest of us. You aren't looking down your nose, now, are you, little girl?"

He'll kill me. I can see it in his eyes. Adrenaline sears through me. I slam my knee up as hard as I can.

Jackson dodges, but his hands come loose, and I squirm free, dropping to the floor. I crawl away, low and fast. Someone has to hear me. They have to. I shout for help as loud as I can.

"Whatcha going to do now, Piper?" His hand fists suddenly in the back of my hair. He drags me to my feet, and I howl against the pain. "No cameras to catch me this time."

His arm clamps around my face, mashing into my mouth. I still taste my blood and now his skin—a potent mix of sweat and salt and fear. I yell again but it's muffled.

His laugh oozes over me and then his arm slips down around my neck. He has me in a headlock. Squeezing. Crushing. I fight until dark spots cloud my vision and my lungs burn. It hurts— hurts so bad, and I'm clawing. Screaming on the inside.

Air. I need to breathe. I can't breathe. The song is almost over. I'm almost over.

"Get the hell off of her!"

I feel the bliss of Jackson's grip loosening and then falling away. I open my mouth wide and drag in one ragged breath after another. I test my fingers and my mouth, opening and closing them, making sure I am still here.

I'm here.

I'm still alive.

A horrible smacking and groaning pulls my attention away from my own agony. I stumble to my feet looking for Jackson, looking for my rescuer. Someone tall and blond throws Jackson into the lockers across from me.

Nick?

No. Not Nick. Paler. More angular.

Tate.

Jackson launches at him and they are back and forth, flipping each other over. It's so loud—loud and terrifying and I am scrabbling out of their path.

They knock over one of the equipment stands, field hockey sticks falling in a clatter. Then Jackson's perched over Tate's chest, his eyes feral.

"What the hell is your problem, Tate?"

"Were you ever going to tell me?" Tate screams back, trying and failing to gain the upper hand. "You were with her in that tape. You! Did she even know?"

"One sick little slut is not worth this!" Jackson snarls.

Tate lands an uppercut. But then Jackson drags him to his feet and I can see that the next two punches knock Tate loopy. He lifts his hands to block his face, but Jackson's nothing but fire and violence now. He punches him everywhere. His hands. His sides. His head. Tate isn't coming back from this.

We need help.

Help.

"Help! We need help!"

My voice finds its way out of the chaos. I shout over and over, still too dizzy to run for the door, but I'm back on my feet. Groping the wall, dragging myself toward the door.

The music's done and I can hear the squeak of the players' shoes—why can't they hear us? Why is no one coming?

Tate's hands drop, giving Jackson free reign at his face. And he doesn't let up. Not for a minute. Not even when Tate slumps down.

Jackson isn't stopping. He'll never stop.

I pull the first thing I find off the floor, one of those sticks. I don't even know how to hold it, but there isn't time. No time. I pull back all the way and swing at Jackson's head.

The impact jars my shoulder, sends me down first. Jackson's head is still whipped back from the impact. His chin dips forward. Heavy-lidded eyes look down. Blood dribbles over his chin and drips onto my shirt. My stomach curdles. Jackson sways. And I watch him fall.

CHAPTER TWENTY-FOUR

· ·

Two basketball players and Coach Carr screech to a halt in the doorway. Mr. Stiers is right behind him.

"Out! Both of you!" Coach Carr says to the players. "Go call nine-one-one."

I look back at Tate and Jackson. Tate is groaning softly, rolling onto his side. Jackson isn't moving. I don't even know if he's breathing. I look down at the stick still gripped in my hands. At the blood on my chest. Jackson's blood.

Oh God.

"Miss Woods? Miss Woods!"

A hand touches my shoulder and I shriek. Mr. Stiers pulls back, hands raised and a wary look in his eyes.

"It's all right," he says. "Everything's all right." It's like he's talking to an injured animal.

I have to move. Do something. I force my fingers to uncurl from the stick. It clatters to the ground and I jump.

I cover my mouth and look at the coach. He's watching me like he doesn't know what to do. Like he isn't entirely sure what *I* did.

"What happened here?" Coach Carr asks. "Did you attack them?"

Mr. Stiers shakes his head. "No. We need medical attention. You check on Mr. Pierce."

I look down at Jackson, at the shallow rise and dip of his chest. Alive. Thank God. But he's not okay. And that's my fault.

"He was on Tate." I'm so breathless, every word is an effort. And no one's asking, but I still feel like I should. I still feel like the truth needs to come out. "Wouldn't stop. He wouldn't—I hit him."

The coach calls for help and several adults file into the locker room, some gasping and covering their mouths. One guy in a white shirt marches straight over to Jackson, lifting his eyelids right away and then checks his pulse. Doctor, maybe? Close enough.

Jackson groans and rolls to his side. Everyone relaxes. Except me. I feel like I might throw up. My throat suddenly burns from where his hands were wrapped. I can still feel his fingers squeezing.

Someone's helping Tate sit up and Mr. Stiers is coming closer to me, looking at my neck. The tenderness in his eyes is more than I can take.

"Do you want me to take you to another room?" he asks, voice low and careful.

I know what he's thinking. A roughed-up girl and two boys in a fight. It looks like rape. Or something close.

I shake my head adamantly. "I'm okay. It wasn't—I'm okay. Just…take care of them."

His relief is palpable. Mine probably is too when he turns away. I slump back against the lockers and breathe deep. A commotion outside the locker room ends any peace I might have found. I can hear people arguing. Someone swearing. I hear, "My girlfriend's in there!" and suddenly I feel everything.

Because that's Nick's voice.

And he's fighting to get to me.

Nick bursts into the doorway. A couple basketball players are holding his arms, but he shrugs them off and none of the coaches seem to be too worried. No one would worry about Nick. He's a good guy. I realize in this moment just how good.

Nick takes in the scene. Jackson, answering questions in a stiff but clear voice. Tate, dabbing a wad of paper towels to his beyond-battered face. And me.

The look Nick gives me makes me desperately want to smile for him. I try, but somehow end up bursting into tears instead. I haul myself to my feet and he's already crossed the room. I push my face into his chest, and his arms are around me, and God, I can breathe. I can finally breathe.

Ugly sobs hiccup out of me, but I focus on the feel of his lips against my temple. I try to focus on Nick and tune out Jackson's voice, counting fingers someone is holding up. I try not to hear Tate's crystal-clear account of Jackson's hands on my throat. And that, yes, I did hit Jackson with the stick, but I was only trying to help.

Nick grows so tense then his body turns to steel. But when my hands start to shake on his sides and he feels it, he softens. For me.

"You want me to call your parents?" he asks.

I shake my head, hearing sirens in the distance. There's a low murmur in the crowd outside. What's happening out there? Is the game on hold? Probably. So all those people out there are waiting. Wondering what the hell is going on. Spreading rumors about the big fight.

My eyes fly open. They're going to think that's all this is. A fight. A blowup over a girl. No one will know what I did. They'll think I'm a victim. An innocent bystander, and after this the police probably won't tell them otherwise.

But there hasn't been anything innocent in me for a long time.

I lean into Nick, putting my mouth close to his ear so my words are for him alone. "Get the book. The one under this bench."

I nod discreetly at the ground near my feet. I can hear the crowd in the gym murmuring louder. The police. They're here. I nudge him toward the bench where I see it. "Pick it up and go outside. Show them. The students. Show as many of them as you can what I did."

He rubs my back slowly, instinctively protecting my secret as he toes the book closer, picks it up. It looks so different in his big hands, with his long fingers flipping through the pages. He reaches the two at the back. Reads my sentence about Harrison. Sees my picture.

He closes the book and his face together, tucking the first inside his jacket.

"What are you doing?" I ask.

Anguish pinches his eyes and mouth. "I'm destroying this. It's time to end it. This book only shows parts of the truth. This isn't evidence. It's history. History we need to move past."

I'm desperate. Angry. Officers come inside and my hands ball to fists as I lean in closer to him. "I can't get away with this."

"You'll confess," he says, lips at my temple. "I hate it, but it's your choice and I'll live with it. But I'm begging you to draw the line here. Nothing good will come of this. Please trust me on that."

I don't know if I believe him. I don't know what to believe. But I nod. The officials are here. Police officers. Paramedics. They pull me away, insisting on checking my throat.

"I'll be right outside," Nick says. I can see the book tucked under his arm inside his coat.

The officer stops him, a hand on his arm. I feel my whole body tense, my heart tripping over itself, slamming wildly in my chest. "I think all the parties should stay here."

"I actually wasn't here when it happened," Nick says, looking down at his feet, playing the respect card to perfection—because for him it isn't a card. It's just who he is. "I thought maybe I shouldn't be here."

When the teachers in the room nod in agreement, the officer releases him. My eyes follow him out of the door. The book is with him. All that truth is going away. But maybe he's right. Partial truths can be dangerous things. They leave a lot of room for lies.

"Miss Woods, is that right?" I look up, surprised to see the officer standing near me. A brass rectangle on his shirt reads *G. Denton*. I force myself to look at his eyes. They're brown and a little bloodshot, but kind enough.

"I'm sorry," I say, shaking my head.

"I think we ought to get you checked out," he says.

"No, I'm fine," I say. The paramedics come closer anyway, and

I let them check over my neck while I give my version of what happened. Telling them about the texting and the vigilante stuff is easier than I thought it would be. Recalling Jackson's fingers around my neck stings. And confessing Manny's name as the vigilante cuts me in half. But I do it anyway, tears staining my cheeks and my chest caving in.

The paramedics test my eyes and check my neck. They are all gentle fingers and soft questions. They treat me like something small and broken, and I should be. But I don't feel broken anymore.

"Is there anything else?" the officer asks me.

Anything else? How is this not enough?

"It's what I told you."

Paramedics offer a stretcher, but I shake my head hard. "Please, no. I'm fine."

Denton regards me with a firm look. "Miss Woods, you should go to the hospital. Get checked out."

"I want to see my parents first. I won't go without them. But I will come with you to the station."

He frowns. "You were nearly strangled here tonight. You've been through hell."

I almost laugh. He thinks I'm a victim, but he doesn't get it. All he sees is a little girl with big, brown eyes and bruises on her neck. He doesn't see the calculating seventeen-year-old who painstakingly picked every target, feeding names to Manny week after week.

Denton pats my shoulder, searches his little pad of paper for my first name. "Now, Mr. Donovan already told us you weren't aiming for Mr. Pierce's head. He thinks you were just trying to clip his shoulder, just to stop him."

All I need to do is nod. It will get me out of here. No one would know any different. I was attacked. Terrified out of my mind. It would make sense that I would swing wild, that I would just be desperate to get him away. It might even be true.

But it's not enough. I can't let him believe I'm innocent.

"I didn't aim at all. But I'm every bit as guilty as Jackson."

• • •

I hold my breath as we pass out of the locker room and into the gym. I try to imagine what they'll see. The bruises on my neck? The blood on my shirt? The police officer with a hand on my upper arm?

The bleachers are crowded with faces I've passed in the hall all year. These people know me, so their shock isn't a surprise. I'm not a criminal. I'm Piper Woods, the nice girl with the camera. Or at least I was. Now, I'm something else.

Nick is gone, somewhere else with that book. Burying it. Burning it, maybe. I can't think about it anymore.

The officer pauses at the door, worry in his eyes. "Are you sure you won't let me take you to the hospital first?"

"No, thank you," I say.

He pushes the door open and I look back at the crowd. They're still watching, snapping pictures with their phones. My chest aches as I watch them, wishing I could go back, but you can't ever go back. There's only forward.

The next two hours are not what I thought they'd be. They sit me beside a desk in the station. My parents arrive, clearly rattled but quietly supportive. I can see Tate and his dad too, a few desks away. He's holding ice on his lip and there's a butterfly bandage on a cut on his brow.

Detective Findley introduces himself and sits down at the desk beside me. He's young with reddish hair and blue eyes that crinkle up in the corners when he smiles. Which he does a lot more often than you'd think a detective would.

He tells me right away that Jackson's been arrested for the attack but that he's still being treated. They don't give details on his injuries, of course. But I don't need details. I'm the one that whacked him on the head with a field hockey stick.

"If you're up for it, Piper, I'd like to get all the basics down again while they're fresh in your mind," Detective Findley says.

My mom looks at me with uncertainty in her eyes. She's been through so much today. I squeeze her hand, an apology in my eyes. My dad lays a light hand on my shoulder. I think of shrugging it off, but it's not time for that. That fight can wait.

"Sure," I say.

It's not what I expected. I thought I'd be in a small room with an ominous light hanging overhead. I expected interrogation, but he lets me tell him what happened instead, sometimes interrupting to clarify what room I was in or how long I think something lasted.

I answer without feeling the words. My focus roams the open room where a dispatcher is eating a ham sandwich and a deputy is offering cookies to some of the staff. He even offers one to me.

No one yells. No one interrogates. The same dispatcher brings me a Sprite and then Detective Findley himself steps away to bring me a blanket. I didn't even know I'd been shivering. And I still don't understand why he's treating me like a victim.

Detective Findley saves his report and leans back in his office chair.

"Well, I think that's enough for tonight," he says, smiling again.

"No, it's not," I say. "I've hurt people. I've done awful things and I want to know what happens now."

He tips his head. "Are you thinking I might arrest you?"

I flush, thinking of my walk out of the school. "I guess I thought I *was* arrested."

"When someone confesses to assault, our department's standard policy is to question them properly." He leans in, eyes twinkling. "Even if we really don't want to because we know darn well it was self-defense."

"I was defending Tate, actually," I say, fiddling with my fingers.

He stretches back in his rolling chair, the hinges squeaking as he rocks back and forth. "Regardless, Mr. Pierce and his parents aren't pressing any charges, so no one's getting arrested at this desk."

My mom leans in, her hand a little tighter on my wrist. "But my daughter—"

He levels her with a look that shows me that he's more than a smiling face with a badge on his chest. "Your daughter is a minor who was assaulted by an eighteen-year-old man. I said no one *here* was getting arrested."

"But I'm *not* innocent," I say. "I had a hand in this."

"Did you break into anyone's house, Miss Woods? Did you attack another student without provocation? Or maybe steal confidential security tapes from your high school?"

My mouth opens and closes. It's not that simple. But it's clear that it's very black and white to him.

He bends until he's close enough that I can smell his cinnamon gum. "Miss Woods, what I'm about to say is off the record, because I'm not allowed to pass judgment. But what you did isn't a crime. It's a bad choice. A regret. We'll look through your phone and if we change our minds, we'll call. But until then, go home. Learn from your mistakes."

I nod, swallowing thickly. And then he holds up my phone, bringing my attention back to his eyes. "And bringing this to us? Turning in your best friend? That was hard. It proves all this changed you for the better."

"Not better," I say. But I can't argue with the changed part. There's nothing in me that will be the same.

The detectives leave us in the main room while they talk to our parents in glass-walled conference rooms, probably running down what happens from here. How they'll talk to the school. I run a finger down the side of my untouched soda. The dispatch phone rings and a water fountain gurgles. I look up at Tate, who's sitting four chairs over, staring at his bloody knuckles.

"I couldn't stop watching it," he says out of nowhere.

I look up, not sure what he's talking about or if he's even talking to me. I don't know if he wants me to say anything, so I stay quiet. But I move two chairs closer. Just in case. He looks at me, and I know it was the right thing to do.

"The tape with Stella," he explains through swollen lips. "I don't know why I did it at first. It was like poking a bruise. But I kept doing it and doing it. Sometimes five, six times in one sitting. That's how I figured it out."

"Figured out it was Jackson," I say. My chest squeezes. I can't imagine what he's feeling.

He nods. "The footboard gave it away finally. There's a notch out of the left corner." Tate pulls his hair back from his forehead and I can see a thin white scar right at his hairline. "I made that notch the day he got the bed. His thirteenth birthday party. We were being idiots, jumping off like we were doing skateboarding tricks…"

He goes quiet, obviously lost in a memory.

I suck in a breath. "Do you think she knew?"

"About the tape?" He shrugs. "I don't know. She didn't ever… I don't know."

"My gut tells me she didn't," I say.

"Yeah," he says, sounding strangled. And then he clears his throat, throwing back his shoulders. "You should have targeted me."

My cheeks burn, which is ridiculous. I need to get used to it. "I tried."

"Good," he says.

"It's not good. I regret it. A lot."

"Don't," he says. And then he clears his throat, lightens his voice. "So, Manny was the mastermind?"

"Yeah."

He nods, though he still looks confused. "Manny's your friend, right?"

The word punches through me.

"Used to be."

"Yeah," he says, and I know he's thinking of Jackson now. A boy he tossed footballs with and jumped on beds with—a boy who was his friend once too.

My mom emerges from the conference room, pulling me into a tight hug as soon as she's close enough. I breathe in her hair and touch her hand, noticing her wedding ring still there.

"Mom?"

She pulls back, but shakes her head. "Not now. But I told you, this will be okay. All right? For now, we go home. You rest."

I nod, knowing there won't be any more answers tonight. And maybe that's okay. I think I've had enough answers for a lifetime.

• • •

Four weeks later and all that's left of the madness are three empty lockers. Stella DuBois, Locker 268. Empty because she took a walk on the train tracks and never came home. Jackson Pierce, Locker 221. Empty because Jackson was shipped off to specialized correctional school as part of a plea bargain last week.

And Manny Raines, Locker 164. Empty because he's been expelled. Sentenced to two years of probation. Kristen's parents decided not to press charges, but the Internet libel on Tacey proved to be a big deal. Like two-years-of-electronically-monitored-probation big deal.

True to Detective Findley's word, I was never arrested. But I'm on a disciplinary action plan with an unbelievable number of mandatory school service hours for the rest of my senior year. I think I got off too easy.

I slide my books into my locker and glance at Stella's locker door. It's been covered in stickers since the truth came out. Stickers of rainbows and cartoon characters. Stickers that belong on the back of skateboards and—my favorite—a scratch-and-sniff *You Are Berry Good* that reminds me of the first grade.

I don't really know who started it, but everyone keeps it going. It's stupid, maybe, but it's how we remember. It's a way to keep her with us.

"Hey, you," Nick says.

I smile even before I feel his hand touch the small of my back. Then he takes my books and we make our way down the hall.

"Burgers tonight?" I ask. "That rubbery crap at the Dock is one step away from plastic."

He shakes his head but pulls me closer. "Maybe I like my plastic pizza."

Tacey jogs past. She offers me a quick nod. I smile back, holding my wince. Nick presses a kiss to my head. "She's coming around."

"It's okay." Even if it hurts like hell, it is okay. She needs time. I owe her that. I owe her a lot of things.

"Sadly, that's not the only tough thing you have to deal with today," Nick says. I can tell he doesn't want to say the rest, but he does. "Manny's here."

"What do you mean? He's expelled."

"He is. He's in the office with his dad. Waiting for files or something."

I stop in the middle of the hallway, staring at my shoes, trying to imagine it. I haven't seen him since the night in the locker room. I keep my eyes on the ground. My black shoes. Nick's sneakers.

Another pair of feet comes into view. Just as big as Nick's.

"Hi, Tate," I say without looking.

"I take it she's heard," Connor says from behind me. I smell Hadley's perfume, so she must be there.

"We can just take off," Nick says. "The, uh, five of us. Cut class."

I give him an incredulous look. Talk about a motley crew of misfits.

"Yeah, except Piper and I have service in half an hour," Tate says. He's got his share of school trouble too. It's cool. Gives me somebody to talk to while we're dismantling bulletin boards.

He's right, though. We can't go anywhere. Still, it's nice that they'd try. That they're working hard to be my friends despite this mess. I try to smile at them, but my mind is fixed on Manny.

He's sitting in that office alone.

"I'm going to talk to him," I say.

They want to argue. All of them. I can see it in their faces. But Nick squeezes my hand. "You sure?"

"Yeah, I am. The last time I walked away, we know what happened. I have to live with that."

"Which is easier said than done," Tate says. "I get it."

He probably does. Better than anyone.

"I'll be here," Nick says. "I'll wait."

The rest of the crowd disperses, promising texts or calls, or, in Tate's case, promising nothing.

The office is quiet. Mrs. Bluth is in the back making copies and Manny's dad is filling out forms. Manny is slouched in the chair in the corner, staring so hard at the wall at the back of the office that I'm surprised it doesn't crack under the strain.

I step inside, feet shuffling on the multicolored carpet. Manny's dad sees me first. His face tightens and my stomach clenches, and I can tell right away that he doesn't know what to do.

I hurt him. I hurt them both by turning Manny in. I doubt either one of them want me here.

But he's still a good man. We exchange halfhearted smiles, and I long for the times of burned sandwiches and nicknames.

Somewhere in the office a vacuum cleaner hums to life. I think Manny has seen me now. I hear him shift on the wooden chair, and I force myself to look at him in a vague way that doesn't let me *see* anything.

Ten feet stretch between me and Manny's chair. It feels like ten miles. Maybe ten galaxies.

Enough. Get on with it.

I span the distance and eye the chair next to him. I aim for carefree but end up throwing myself down a little violently. Overthinking it as usual.

"Hey," I say, and that's pretty much all I've got.

"Sure you want to be this close to the criminal of Claireville High?"

There's no friendly teasing in his tone. It's cold and clipped.

"Why are you here?" he asks.

"I wanted to say hello."

"Why? We're not friends."

"We were once."

"Well, if you're expecting me to apologize and get all flowery and shit, it's not going to happen," he says. "I…"

He doesn't finish, but his voice goes soft and I already know. He can't say it. Good and bad, I still *know* him. So I know what it means when his words come out fast and clipped like this. Just like I know what it means when he grips the armrests of his chair so tight I can see his knuckles going white.

He's hurt.

Hurt and scared and probably a few other things. All of them bad.

"I get it," I tell him, dropping my voice to something soft and private. "I don't agree with what you did. I never will. But I think I understand."

He looks at me, eyes flinty. "Stop dressing it up. I went bad. It's that simple."

"It's never that simple."

I don't realize how much I mean the words until they're out of my mouth. There is no room for simple anymore. I'm not sure there ever was.

The secretary is stapling the copies, and I know this little bubble we're in is about to pop. I turn to him, touching his arm.

"There's still good in you, Manny. I won't forget that. I hope you don't either."

"Hey. What did you ever do with that weird book?"

"I burned it." Not technically true. We burned it. Me and Nick. Three days after the mess in the gymnasium. Despite his vow to destroy it, he still let me choose in the end.

He clucks his tongue. "That was a mistake. There was a lot of truth in that book."

"Only parts of it. You can't pick through the pieces. You have to look at the whole picture to see anything."

He doesn't respond, but when he looks back at the ground, I see his face go a little softer. He's thinking it over. It isn't a miracle. It isn't much of anything, but I'll take it.

Nick is waiting outside on the steps. The sun is warm and the air smells like a promise. I move close to him, shielding my eyes with my hand. He leans in and kisses me, and we take off across the parking lot.

I hear a train whistle in the distance, low and long. I smile and think of Stella. This time it doesn't feel like good-bye; it feels like a reminder. I hold it tight and walk on.

ACKNOWLEDGMENTS

Writing Piper's journey was tough stuff, and I couldn't have done it without a lot of support. First and foremost, thank you God for giving me so many wonderful people to help me along the way.

Gone Too Far wouldn't have been possible without an amazing publishing team at Sourcebooks. To Kate Prosswimmer, Rachel Gilmer, Adrienne Krogh, Kelly Lawler, Will Riley, Gretchen Stelter, and all the other geniuses that have touched my book and made it better—my sincerest thanks. Most of all to my editor, Aubrey, I'm so grateful for your insight and enthusiasm for my work—you are the coolest beans ever. Thanks so much for helping me find the heart of this book.

I'm blessed with an agent who's as sweet and funny as she is wise—Cori, thank you for the late nights and holiday weekends. Your friendship and guidance mean the world to me.

I also want to thank Leah, who found a critical missing piece of this story early on. Unlike a Lannister, I have no idea how I'll repay this debt.

I'm so grateful for my wonderful friends Robin and Sheri for always being available to brainstorm and talk me off a thousand ledges at every odd hour. Thanks for making me laugh and keeping me sane.

To my darling Doomsdaisies Meg, Pintip, Cecily, and Steph, and to my lovely friends in OHYA, Erin McCahan, Julia Devillers, Lisa Klein, Margaret Haddix, Edith Patou, Linda Gerber, and my writing soul sister, Jody Casella, you guys are all wonderful.

Gone Too Far wouldn't have gone anywhere without my fifth Doomsdaisy, Romily Bernard. Rom, I'd still be editing this book if you hadn't scraped me off the floor and pried it from my hands. I owe you a bedazzled monocle, my friend. Can we go to the island compound yet?

I'd also like to thank Shaina, who taught me about cheerleading and kept me sane on countless oh-dark-thirty shifts. Also to Angela for her photography expertise, abundance of awesome, and lemon chicken soup. And of course to the real Dr. Stiers, who probably does speak five languages!

A hug and a thank you to Dad, Karen, and Leigh Anne. You read it first and said it was special. I adore you for that. And to Tiffany, who's close to the heart of this story for many reasons.

There are lots of great people in my life, more than I have space to name, but I'm thankful for you all. Some of the newest folks I have to thank include the ones I've met on my publication journey. So a special thanks to the readers, bloggers, librarians, booksellers, and teachers who embraced my first book and are back for more. I feel so incredibly lucky. Truly.

As always, thank you, David. You know the often ugly reality of living with a writer on deadline and I'm so grateful for your support. And to our three children, Ian, Adrienne, and Lydia—you teach me *so much* about goodness. I love you guys.

ABOUT THE AUTHOR

Natalie D. Richards spent years writing factual, necessary things for financial and legal companies before deciding she's much better suited to making things up. She traded in her cubicle for a preferred corner of the couch, where she writes fiction for teens. Natalie lives in Central Ohio with her husband, three children, and a giant fur ball named Yeti.

For more information, visit her at www.nataliedrichards.com or follow her on Twitter @NatDRichards. *Gone Too Far* is her second book.

Forgetting changed her. Remembering might destroy her.

Don't miss

SIX MONTHS LATER

NATALIE D. RICHARDS

CHAPTER ONE

· ·

I'm sitting next to the fire alarm, and my best friend is going down in flames. Irony or divine intervention? I can practically feel the metal handle under my fingers. It might as well be whispering my name.

Tempting. One strategic arm stretch and I could send this whole school into an evacuation frenzy.

I could end Maggie's nightmare *right* now.

At the front of the classroom, she swallows hard. She is as pale and shaky as the paper in her hands.

"The social p-pressures and isolation encountered b-by male n-n—"

I can't let her suffer like this.

Maggie shakes her head and tries to shrug it off with a sheepish grin. "S-sorry."

"It's all right," Mrs. Corwin says, playing with the cat pendant around her neck. "There's no reason to be scared."

She thinks stuttering is a fear problem? Aren't teachers supposed to know about speech issues and all that crap? Then again, what can I expect from a woman who has professionally framed pictures of her beloved Siamese, Mr. Whiskers, on her desk?

Maggie takes a breath. "The p-pressures and isolation

encountered by male n-nurses in a predominantly f-female occupation is a compelling argument f-f-f—" She trails off, going crimson.

Someone snickers from the front.

"Go on, Maggie," Mrs. Corwin says. Again.

I'm going to do it.

Beside me, Blake Tanner shifts in his chair. I know this partly because I have good peripheral vision, but mostly because I have freakishly sensitive Blake radar. I hesitate, breathing in the clean hint of his cologne, watching him softly drum a thumb on his desktop.

My face goes hot. I can't do this with him sitting here. I'm completely invisible to this guy. And now I'm finally going to get his attention by, what? By pulling a fire alarm? Yes, I'm sure that will send a great message. To the guy who's been on the student council since the eighth grade.

Maggie tosses her hair back, forging on. "It's a compelling argument f-for s-s-sexism against men. In most modern contexts, concerns about s-s-s-s—"

Maggie goes pink and then red. Tyler and Shannon laugh in the back, and my eyes start to well up. Screw it. I can't sit here for one more second of one more minute.

I sink down as far as I can in my chair and start sliding my arm back along the wall. I reach up, but I'm grasping blind. It kind of hurts. I touch something cool and metal. Bingo. Two seconds and this misery is over.

Blake clears his throat and I bite my lip. Is he watching me?

What's wrong with me? Of course he's not watching me. I'm invisible.

I turn my head because I'm sure I feel someone's eyes on me. I do.

Adam Reed. He's slouched low in his seat, his dark hair in desperate need of the business end of a pair of scissors.

Adam arches one of his brows at me. The half smile on his lips asks me what I'm waiting for. I don't really have an answer, so I curl my fingers over the alarm handle and pull hard. And then I kiss my detention-free junior year good-bye.

• • •

Maggie is waiting outside the principal's office. She's got a couple of notebooks clutched in her arms and a pencil securing her strawberry blond waves into a bun.

The office door is barely closed when she starts in on me. "What were you thinking? You c-could have been expelled."

I sling my backpack over my shoulder and offer our school secretary, Mrs. Love, a wave. Maggie takes the cue and follows me briskly back into the hallway. Students are slamming locker doors and texting madly in the few minutes between periods.

Someone whistles, and across the hall, Connor holds two thumbs up. "Let's hear it for fire safety!"

The hallway bursts into a smattering of applause and wolf calls. I blush but give a little bow with a flourish of my hand.

We make our way to the stairs, climbing them two at a time.

"So what happened, Chloe? How b-bad is it?"

"I got a week of detention and a lecture about applying my interest in psychology to evaluating my episodes of acting out."

Maggie looks away, and I can tell she's biting her tongue.

I know that look. It means she's working hard to say something in a way that won't offend the hell out of me.

"Spit it out. You're obviously dying to insert commentary."

She sighs. "Look, I know you w-wanted to help me, but you've got to start thinking about yourself, Chloe. Sometimes it's like you're running away from everything you want."

I try not to look as hurt as I feel. "It's not like I'm afraid of being good, Mags."

She just laughs and takes my arm. "You jumped off the Third Street Bridge on a *dare*, which proves you're not afraid of anything. It also proves you're insane."

"Watch it."

I take a breath as we pass the drinking fountains, heading close to the last stretch of lockers in the hall. An otherwise unremarkable place in this building except for the fact that it's the Blake Zone.

As if on cue, he closes his locker door and appears, the tall, popular king of this lonely hallway. He laughs at a joke I don't hear. It's a perfect laugh that matches his perfect teeth and his perfect everything else.

I sigh. "Did Blake seem…disappointed?"

She blows out an impatient breath and rolls her eyes at me. "I didn't really think to dissect Blake's expression in the chaos and p-panic of the fire evacuation."

Blake laughs again, and I turn away, my cheeks burning. "Right. Sorry."

She gives me a sly grin. "Want me to go ask him?"

I slump back against the wall with a sigh. "How is it that I'm not the one who talks to boys? I'm the bridge jumper, the alarm puller—"

"The streaker," Maggie adds.

"That was one time! And technically, I was in my undies, but yes. How is it that you, High Queen of the Honor Roll, are better at this than me?"

"The stutter makes me a wild card," she says, winking. "No one ever sees me coming. And you talk t-to plenty of guys."

My gaze lingers on the stretch of Blake's polo across his shoulders, the ends of his hair curling over his collar. "Yeah, well. Not that one."

"I've got to g-get to class," Maggie says. "Speaking of which, did you remember to pick up your GPA at the office this morning?"

I feign a big, carefree smile. "Gosh, I must have completely forgotten. But I totally signed up for the SAT study group you told me about."

"And somehow forgot t-to ask for your GPA?" she asks, clearly unconvinced.

"Oh, who cares about a GPA anyway?"

She blinks at me, arms crossed. "Uh, every college you'll be applying to."

"Right. Well, finals aren't until next week. I can fix it."

Her eyes go dark. "Fix it? How bad is it?"

"Um, I—" The warning bell rings, saving me from another lie. "Gotta dash. Study hall and all. Yep, that's me. Study, study, study."

I slip inside the door and hear her calling after me. "You're running out of time, Chloe!"

She's got a point. I have exactly six days left of my junior year to turn my GPA into something that won't doom me to serving bad eggs at Trixie's Diner for the rest of my life. The urgency should inspire me to use every minute of my study hall period. It *really* should.

I pick up my biology notes, but it's all *cellular* this and *genetic* that, and my eyelids feel heavy after two lines. Why can't I get my act together?

Everyone around me is in full-force cram mode. Of course they are. Even Alexis, who spent the whole year reading *Vogue* behind her textbooks, is flipping through a stack of note cards. I'm officially the last slacker standing.

Maybe I could make a waitressing gig awesome. Except I don't want a waitressing gig. I only want one gig, and it doesn't involve rushing baskets of fries to hungry truckers.

It involves a doctorate degree in psychology.

How am I going to get through twelve years of college if I can't even stay awake in study hall?

Too bad I can't make a career out of sleeping in class undetected. I could tutor people in *that*. It's all about the posture. Chin in palm says bored. Chin on knuckles says deeply in thought.

And that sunbeam drifting through the window next to my desk? It says, *Go to sleep, Chloe.*

I tilt my head, watching the late May sunshine stroke my arms with soft, golden fingers. I do have all weekend to study. And I've got that stupid study group tonight, so I'm taking steps in the right direction. How much harm could one *teeny* little catnap do?

I give into the warmth and let my eyes slip closed. I'll worry about my lack of self-discipline after the bell rings.

But the bell doesn't ring.

There's no sound at all to wake me, just a cold sinking feeling in my middle. The hair on the back of my neck prickles, and my heart changes rhythm. Skips one beat. Then another.

And I know something is horribly wrong.

CHAPTER TWO

. . . .

I'm afraid to open my eyes, but I do.

Darkness closes around me like a fist. Even still half-asleep, I know this isn't right. I blink blearily, but everything feels off. The room, the air…me.

Dreaming. I must still be dreaming.

Outside the window, everything is dark. Wait, that can't be right. It can't be that late.

Can it?

A slate-gray sky stretches beyond the glass. I see bits of white trailing through it, drifting down like glitter against velvet.

What is that? Flowers? Dust? No, it's just snow.

Snow?

I bolt out of my seat, the scrape of my chair legs shattering the silence. I'm alone. Goose bumps rise on my arms as I stare at the emptiness.

The clock above the whiteboards reads 9:34 p.m. Mr. Brindell, who I've never seen anywhere but behind his desk, is gone. I look around, realizing that it's not just the teacher. *Everyone* is gone. Every*thing* too. Books, papers, backpacks dangling from the corners of chairs. I'm in the belly of a skeleton, the remains of a class long over.

Panic shoots through me like a shock from a bad plug, white hot and jangling every nerve.

No.

No, this can't be happening. It's a scary dream. A mistake.

I lean closer to the window, but the snow refuses to be anything other than what it is. It falls thickly on the brown grass, clinging to the spindly branches of barren trees.

Where are the leaves? For that matter, where is the freaking sun?

Please let me wake up. I *need* to wake up.

But I won't. I feel it in my bones. My heart screams, *Nightmare!* but my mind says otherwise. This is happening.

I press my hand to the glass then snatch it back in shock. My nails—they're filthy. I examine the black half-moons of dirt wedged under each nail, black streaks caked into the creases of my fingers.

Okay, this is too creepy. Like horror-movie creepy and I need to get out of here. Right now.

I reach for my backpack, but it's not there. Gone too is the strappy sundress I zipped myself into today. I'm wearing a black sweater and jeans now. The feel of the soft knit beneath my fingers makes my stomach roll. This isn't right. Nothing is right.

I find the comforting bulge of my car keys in one pocket and my cell phone in the other. Thank God. I pull it out with shaking fingers and turn it on.

Light blooms on the screen, and I deflate in relief. Outside the world is still screaming all its wrongness at me, but this little glowing rectangle is my anchor. I hold it tight.

I inch farther away from the dark window with its impossible snow, my fingers hovering over the keypad on my phone.

Now what? My parents flash through my mind, but they still think I'm crazy after last fall. I might as well just call the psychiatric ward at Mercy Hospital and save the extra step. No, I can't call my parents.

Maggie.

My speed dial for her doesn't work. Too impatient to figure out why, I scan through my recent calls. But she's not on here.

Impossible. I haven't gone ten minutes without calling or texting Maggie since we both got phones in the ninth grade. I texted her on my way to the principal's office like two *hours* ago.

One glance at the window reminds me that wasn't two hours ago.

I keep paging, stopping only to make sure this isn't someone else's phone. Because the list of names in my recent calls cannot belong to me. Finally, on the sixth or seventh page, I find my mom's cell phone and a couple of calls to my house, but no Maggie.

I pull up the detail on one of my calls, and fear slithers through me like a living thing. 11/10—6:32 p.m.

As in *November* 10? No. I read it once and then again. A bunch of other calls are all from November too. I glance up, panicked, finding a calendar on the wall and a flyer for a winter dance that should still be eight months away.

The evidence hits me like icy darts, needling me toward the impossible truth. I've been asleep for six months. A coma or something. Somehow, I've missed *six months* of my life.

But that can't be right either. They wouldn't leave me unconscious in a classroom. I'd be in a hospital, hooked up to machines and watched by nurses. But if I wasn't asleep…

Amnesia?

Maybe I've also got a terrible case of consumption too. Or malaria. I need to get serious here—no one gets amnesia! But what else could this be? The longest lasting roofie of all time? Alien abduction?

A sinister possibility whispers to me. One word, two syllables, and an endless river of humiliation.

Crazy. I could be going crazy.

I heard it enough last year, whispered behind my back. I saw it on their faces too, expressions that ranged from pity to contempt as they looked at the "troubled girl." But troubled is way better than insane, and *what else could this be*?

Sane people forget what they ate for breakfast. Or maybe the names of their new neighbors. They don't wake up in a dark classroom without a damned clue where they've been or what they've done for six months.

Adrenaline flares through my middle, making my joints tickle and my stomach cramp. I feel my body poising for flight, my lips going numb, my heart pumping faster with each beat.

It won't stop there. Not with me. Familiar bands squeeze around my chest in warning, and I clench my fists. I have to calm down before this turns into a full-blown panic attack.

I close my eyes and do all the things my therapist told me to do. I remind myself that I am okay. That I am not sick or dying.

My body is giving me extra energy to figure this out, and it's good energy. It's okay. I don't need to be afraid.

"Chloe?"

My head snaps up at the sound of my name and at the person standing in the open doorway of the classroom. Adam Reed. Six feet and a couple of inches of something that scares me half to death.

I feel the blood drain from my face as he makes his way into the room. The light from the windows seems all too happy to highlight his model-worthy cheekbones and broad shoulders. Adam's so pretty he looks like he could sprout wings and a halo. But angels don't usually come with criminal records.

Is he here because of the fire alarm? He's looking at me like that again, with a little bit of a smile on his face. And Adam never smiles, so what gives?

"What do you want?" I ask, my voice small and frightened.

He chuckles. "You called me, remember?"

The idea of me calling him is so ridiculous I can't even respond. We don't even nod at each other in the halls. Why would I call him?

Despite my little fire alarm adventure, it's not like we run in the same circles. I get along with almost everyone. Adam can't seem to move through the hallways without starting a fight. I sometimes walk dogs at the animal shelter. He sometimes gets pulled out of class by the *police*. We aren't just in different social groups; we're in different solar systems.

He tilts his head, and I take a breath, feeling my shoulders relax. Which is maybe crazier than anything else happening right now. I shouldn't feel safer with him here. I should feel completely freaked out.

So why don't I?

"What are you doing here?" he asks, and though everything about his heavy black boots and ratty cargo jacket screams don't-give-a-crap, he *sounds* interested. Maybe even concerned.

"I'm…" I search for something that sounds better than *I'm losing my mind* or *I'm stuck in some* Twilight Zone *time warp*, but nothing comes. And I don't need to explain myself to him. I don't even know him.

"Why are *you* here?" I ask instead.

"Because you called me," he says, laughing again. Then he nods down at my hands, smirking. "Have you been making mud pies while you waited for me to get here?"

I flush and hide my hands, but I still take an instinctive step toward him. And then I remember that he is a juvenile delinquent and, for all I know, a psychopath. I should be running *away* from him. He doesn't look like a psychopath though. He just looks like Adam.

He crosses his arms and smirks at me. "You *do* remember calling me, right?"

Fear snakes its way up my spine, making my tongue thick and my throat dry.

No. I don't. I've never had a conversation with him, or hell, even stood this close to him until tonight.

Maybe he's wasted. He's got to be, right? But he looks absolutely sober. No red eyes or twitchy fingers. Kind of odd, now that I think of it, because I would have figured him for the type.

He smirks at me then, his blue eyes glittering. "I'm impressed you jimmied the cafeteria door without my help. I was beginning to think you'd never figure that out."

What? I did what to the what?

This is nuts. Completely nuts. I've never *jimmied* anything in my life. And if I did, it wouldn't be the door to my high school cafeteria.

He braces his hands on the back of a chair and tilts his head. A rush of déjà vu washes over me. I take a breath and hold it in, watching him drag his thumb along the back of the chair. I've *seen* this. I've seen him here, looking at me like this. I'm sure of it.

I stare at his hand, feeling my cheeks go white and cold. Apparently he senses the change because his smile disappears, his eyes narrowing.

"You all right, Chlo?"

My nickname sounds right on his lips. Natural. He shouldn't even know I have a nickname, let alone feel right using it. But he obviously does.

"You look scared to death," he adds, frowning down at me.

I'm not sure *scared* is the right word. I'm not sure there *is* a right word for all the things I'm feeling.

"I'm fine. Just tired," I lie.

He walks right up to me, and I swear to God, I can't remember how to breathe. My heart is pounding and my fingers are shaking, but somehow the world feels steady anyway. I'm not afraid. I should be, but I'm just not.

"Do you need to talk? Is that why you called?" he asks. "You know you can talk to me."

"I know that," I say automatically, the words coming from a place I can't find, a great empty space in me where I'm sure a memory should be.

I feel inexplicably sad at this yawning hole, this absence.

What's happening to me? What happened to make me forget?

I bite my lip and feel my eyes burn with the threat of tears. Adam's expression softens, twisting into something pained. Not once have I dreamed him possible of this kind of look. Hell, of anything in the same zip code as this look.

He opens his mouth to say something, and my whole body goes tense, my belly a knot of fluttering things. What is going on with me?

He reaches across the desk between us, almost but not quite touching my fingers. Every centimeter between our hands feels charged. Electric.

"We can't keep doing this, Chloe," he says softly.

The words sting and I don't know why. I don't even know what he means, but I desperately want to argue with him. I want to shake my head and grab his hands and—this is crazy.

Way beyond crazy.

My whole world is sliding into a flat spin. I can't have this guy, this total freaking *stranger*, at the center of it.

If I don't get away from him, I'm going to do something stupid. Something I won't be able to come back from.

"I have to go," I say, retracting my hands into fists and starting toward the door.

"Chloe," he says, touching my bare wrist as I pass.

Something warm rushes through me, making my ears buzz and my face heat up. I hear Adam laughing in the back of my mind, like the sound track to a movie I can't see. I whirl to face him, ready to snap his head off for making fun.

But he's not laughing. Not now. The memory of his laughter fades away even as Adam's hand drops from my shoulder, a hurt look crossing his face.

He lets me pass without another word. My footsteps are even and steady as they carry me into the hall. I wish my heart would follow the example.

THE FORGETTING

Nicole Maggi

WITH EVERY HEARTBEAT, HER TIME IS RUNNING OUT.

When Georgie Kendrick wakes up after a heart transplant she feels…different. The organ beating in her chest isn't in tune with the rest of her body. Like it still belongs to someone else. Someone with terrible memories…memories that are slowly replacing her own. Georgie discovers her heart belonged to a teenage girl who lived a rough life on the streets. Everyone thinks she committed suicide, but Georgie knows the truth. Her donor was murdered, and Georgie has to catch a killer—before she loses herself completely.